DAUGHTER

of

SHADOW

&

BLOOD

—∞—

Book II: Elena

J. Matthew Saunders

Saint George's Press

DAUGHTERS OF SHADOW & BLOOD
BOOK II: ELENA

Copyright © 2016 by J. Matthew Saunders

All rights reserved. This book or any portion thereof may not be reproduced or used in any manner whatsoever without the express written permission of the publisher except for the use of brief quotations in a book review.

This is a work of fiction. Names, characters, businesses, places, events and incidents are either the products of the author's imagination or used in a fictitious manner.

Cover photography copyright © milosk50 (monastery) and Maksim Toome (woman),
courtesy of Shutterstock

Printed in the United States of America

First Printing, 2016

e-book ISBN 978-0-9863331-2-5
paperback ISBN 978-0-9863331-3-2

Saint George's Press
York, S.C.
www.saintgeorgespress.com

For my parents

He who hath bent him o'er the dead
Ere the first day of death is fled,
The first dark day of nothingness,
The last of danger and distress,
Before decay's effacing fingers
Have swept the lines where beauty lingers.
—*Lord Byron,* The Giaour

DAUGHTERS
of
SHADOW
&
BLOOD

—ɯɯ—

Book II: Elena

PROLOGUE

Sarajevo, Bosnia and Herzegovina
15 March 1994

THE BOMB DIDN'T KILL HIM. It had dismembered him certainly, but it did not kill him. The man's torso and head—as well as his right arm—were found in a pile of debris on the side of Radićeva Street opposite the bombed-out cinema. His feet and legs had come to rest a few hundred feet away. The rest of him was never found.

As Police Inspector Nikola Gavrilović stood over the mostly reassembled body in the overcrowded city morgue, a question nagged at him.

Where was the blood?

There was none to be found. Not one drop. Impossible, unless the man was dead before the shell hit the cinema, killed in such a way that he bled out completely. It was the third such body found that year—not that anyone paid attention. Not with death raining from above every day. The Yugoslav army had laid siege to the city for almost two years, and from their positions in the hills outside Sarajevo, they pelted the city with shells almost daily. Nikola had already lost friends and family. Everyone had. As perverted an idea as it seemed, it was difficult to find the motivation to investigate murder on such a small scale when the mere act of venturing out of one's house to buy bread could mean death.

It didn't help matters that of the other two apparent victims, the first was a homeless man and the second an abusive drunk whose own wife refused to claim his body. Nikola's superiors would close this case, insisting the man had died in the blast, and he wasn't in a position to challenge them. He was only half-Serbian, through his mother, but because the Serbs were the ones trying to strangle the city, no one would completely trust anything he said. It didn't matter that he wanted what almost everyone else in Sarajevo wanted—a free Bosnia.

Besides, he couldn't exactly tell the truth. All the signs were there, if one knew how to see them. An old threat had returned to the city, and just as certainly as the Yugoslav army brought death from above, this threat brought death from below. Placing the sheet back over the man's body and then turning to leave the morgue, Nikola resolved to do whatever he had to do to stop it, even if he had to stand alone.

After all, the Serbs invented the word *vampire*.

ONE

Thessaloniki, Greece
6 October 1999

CLARA BARELY DODGED THE BICYCLE as she turned the corner. She didn't understand the stream of Greek the rider yelled as he pedaled past her, but based on his expressive hand gestures, she guessed his general meaning. She gritted her teeth and kept going, pushing her way through the crowded market.

Sounds, colors, aromas swirled around her, everything as incomprehensible as ... well, Greek. Laughter and shouting reverberated off the buildings over the noise of the traffic on the nearby streets. A musician had attracted a small crowd with the frantic strains of his violin. Grey business suits mingled with traditional costumes of bright blue, red, and green amid stalls set up by vendors selling everything Clara could imagine—and a few things she couldn't.

Car exhaust mixed with the smell of concentrated humanity tickled her nose, but as she walked, one scent called to her like a Pied Piper. The sweet and spicy aroma led her to a stall where a young boy was roasting lamb. Her stomach rumbled, and it occurred to her she hadn't eaten anything since the thin cup of coffee and the small pastry at her hotel that morning.

The boy looked up at her and smiled. She reached into her bag, and a wave of nausea pushed the thought of lunch out of her mind—her wallet wasn't there. Panic rose as she probed every corner of the bag. Her gaze darted around the market, thinking maybe she'd see someone acting suspiciously or she'd spot a policeman, and when that failed, maybe she'd see someone—anyone—who looked like they might speak English. All her money, her credit cards, her ID—all of it was gone, but what brought her to the verge of tears was the thought of losing the creased and tattered photo that had been lodged in her wallet for the better part of five years.

She needed that picture.

A hand on her shoulder made her jump. She turned around to find a man smiling at her. Maybe a few years older than she was, he had short black hair and a goatee and blue eyes so pale they were almost grey.

He held up her wallet. "Madame, I believe this is yours."

He spoke English with an accent Clara couldn't quite place, though she didn't think it was Greek.

Stunned, she took back the wallet. "How did …? Was it …? I guess it must have fallen out of my purse."

The man chuckled. "Not exactly." He motioned over his shoulder, back toward where the bicyclist had nearly hit her. The rider sat on the ground with his back to the wall of a building, a package of ice held to his forehead. His bicycle lay next to him, and a surly-looking policeman, nowhere to be found moments before, stood over him.

"I watched him slip your wallet out of your purse as he passed by you," the man continued. "I chased him down."

Clara raised an eyebrow. "You chased down a bicycle? On foot?"

The man shrugged. "The market is crowded. He could only go so fast."

She smiled. "Thank you, Mr. ..."

He shook his head. "No need for thanks. I'm just a Good Samaritan. Please, have a pleasant stay in Thessaloniki."

With a nod, he walked away and melted into the crowd.

She turned back to the boy roasting the lamb. He smiled and held up a piece of freshly shaved meat, rich and hearty smelling. She glanced down at her watch and realized, regrettably, that she didn't have time for lunch. She shook her head and continued on her way through the market.

When Clara came to the end of the stalls, an old stucco building loomed in front of her, its arched windows dark, even with the afternoon sun shining. The road forked to either side, confronting her with a choice. She knew the address where she was going and had traced the route on a map that morning, but now she wasn't so confident she could remember the way. She wished she had thought to bring a guidebook. Having one certainly would have helped in the market. She was lucky the man who had retrieved her wallet spoke English, though it didn't occur to her until that moment to question how he knew she did. Maybe he had opened her wallet and seen her driver's license.

In truth, that she had managed to make it to Greece

with anything more than her toothbrush was a small miracle. Only a week earlier she had come home from work to discover the blinking red light on her answering machine. The message was terse. A man's voice stated that Adam was seen in Thessaloniki in August. He left no name and no contact information, but after two frustrating months of fruitless phone calls, unanswered letters, and pleas to State Department employees in a half-dozen countries, the message was the first news of Adam since he disappeared.

A hastily booked plane ticket later, Clara was walking amid the ancient city's sun-bleached buildings set against the electric-blue Aegean Sea. Yet for three days door after door shut in Clara's face. Smiles vanished and mouths closed every time she mentioned Adam's name, so she was shocked when Arion Tsakalidis, a Romanian language professor from Aristotle University, had contacted her and asked to meet.

Clara chose the road to the left. As she passed by the old building, she glanced up at the once-white façade, grey now from years of dirt and city grime. The building seemed abandoned, but something about it sent a chill up her spine. She wondered what it had been used for.

A flicker caught her eye from one of the shadow-draped windows on the second floor, and a whispered voice drifted down, saying words too low to understand. Her heart all but stopped. Clara gazed at the window, expecting to find some dark figure standing there, only to watch a pigeon emerge to strut along the sill. She looked around, embarrassed for letting her imagination get the best of her. Still, she doubled her pace.

When Clara finally reached the campus of the university, a wave of relief washed over her. Gone were the narrow, clogged streets and noise of the city; she stared now at the open, manicured lawns and broad walkways of a modern university.

Thanks to Adam she knew a lot about universities. Memories came to her of bringing him dinner in his office when he stayed late grading exams, of walking through the fall leaves holding hands, of picnics on the lawn. The corners of her mouth turned up in a faint smile. She thought she had found someone she could spend the rest of her life with.

Professor Tsakalidis' office was on the second floor of a nondescript building that housed the Department of Romance Languages. She almost missed it. Adam always made a big deal about how his office was in the only building that predated the university. That would be difficult to do in a country like Greece.

A lanky man with round glasses perched on the end of his nose answered the door when she knocked.

"Professor Tsakalidis?" she asked.

He smiled. "You must be Clara MacIntosh."

"It's good to meet you face-to-face." She held out her hand, which he took.

"And you as well. Please, come in. Pardon the mess."

Stacks of books took up most of the space on the floor of his office. A computer screen provided the only light in the room apart from the narrow slits of sunlight seeping through the blinds. A coffee cup occupied the only spot on the desk clear of papers.

It could have been Adam's office.

Clara sat in the chair Professor Tsakalidis gestured toward. "Thank you for agreeing to meet with me."

He walked behind his desk and opened the blinds to allow the sun into the room. "It is the least I could do, given the circumstances."

Clara brushed a lock of hair behind her ear and cleared her throat. "That's what I'm hoping you can help me with, Professor Tsakalidis."

"Please, call me Arion."

"Arion then. The problem is that I don't know what circumstances you mean, and I haven't been able to find anyone who will talk to me. Adam was supposed to be on sabbatical in Budapest. He was scheduled to come back to the States in July, but he never did. I only just learned he was in Thessaloniki in August, but I can't imagine what he was doing here. I haven't had any contact with him in months. No one has."

"His family must be worried sick."

"He doesn't have any family. Just me."

"You've been together a while?"

She blushed. "We're not together, not anymore, but we've stayed friends. It just didn't … We weren't …"

It was Arion's turn to blush. "I'm sorry. I didn't mean to overstep."

"No. It's okay. I just want to find him."

Arion sighed. "I'm afraid that may be difficult."

"Why?" Clara asked.

He drew his mouth into a grim line. "Because Dr. Mire may have been involved in a murder."

If there had been anything in Clara's stomach, she would have had to reach for the nearest trash can. "Murder?"

"A colleague in the history department, Marina Dimitriou, was stabbed to death in her office. Dr. Mire was the last person seen with her. He ran from the police when they tried to question him."

Clara frowned. "He would never do something like

that."

Arion shrugged. "I wasn't there, but multiple eyewitnesses have all told the same story."

"I still don't understand. Where is he? Was he arrested? Is he rotting in some jail somewhere waiting for trial?"

"Not exactly."

"What do you mean?"

"The details are little hazy. I can tell you that Dr. Mire was arrested by the local authorities, but then the Hellenic Police took him into their custody."

"The Hellenic Police?"

"Like your FBI."

"So do they have him?"

Arion shook his head. "The car he was in was ambushed. The two Hellenic Police with him were shot and killed."

"But Adam?"

"Nowhere to be found. He simply vanished."

Clara was silent for a moment, struggling to retain her composure. "Do you know why he was here?"

The professor pursed his lips. "The reason others have been reluctant to talk to you is that they are afraid of the consequences. I myself am taking a risk by meeting with you."

"So why are you meeting with me?"

"After having come all this way, you deserve to know the truth, or at least as much as we can piece together."

"What is the truth?"

He leaned closer. "I think Dr. Mire stumbled upon something dangerous."

"Something people were willing to kill over?"

Arion nodded.

"You don't believe he murdered your colleague."

"Never."

"But whoever killed her is trying to kill Adam, too."

"If they have not already succeeded."

Clara bit her lip.

He placed a hand on top of hers. "I'm sorry. I know it's hard to hear, but I don't want to give you false hope."

"Do you have any idea what this 'something dangerous' might be?" she asked.

Arion opened a drawer in his desk and pulled out a stack of loose papers. He handed them to Clara. "A few weeks before Dr. Mire's visit, Marina showed me something, a handwritten journal. She said a friend had sent it to her, but it was all in Romanian. She asked me to translate part of it."

Clara glanced through the pages of neat, precise handwriting. Arion had translated it into English. "What does it have to do with Adam?"

"Marina told me the day before she was killed that she wanted a colleague who was visiting from the States to look at it as well. I can only assume she meant Dr. Mire."

"That still doesn't explain why he was here to begin with."

"Maybe Marina contacted him about the journal, wanting him to see it."

"Who did the journal belong to?"

"A Romanian army officer during World War II."

"Wasn't Romania—"

"Allied with the Nazis? Yes, it was, but the entries that filled this journal, they weren't about the war. They were about monsters."

"Monsters? Like from the movies?"

"From what I could understand."

Clara placed a hand on her temple. "Couldn't he have

been talking about the war, though? After all, there were a lot of people who acted like monsters."

Arion shook his head. "That's the curious part. I didn't get the sense it was meant to be metaphorical. 'Monster' is my translation, but the Romanian word he chose to use was *bală*." He pointed to a line on one of the pages spread out in front of Clara. "The word has several other meanings, though, ones steeped in the folklore of this part of the world."

"And these other meanings? What are they?"

He didn't answer. His gaze went to a small red dot dancing across the papers strewn over his desk. It reminded Clara of the inane laser pointer that Adam had used at one time in his lectures until she laughed at him and told him his students weren't cats. But then an alarm went off inside her brain.

The little red dot wasn't a pointer.

It was a target.

"Don't—"

Arion turned toward the window as Clara shouted for him to stop. The glass exploded, and he lurched backward onto the desk, sending a flurry of papers into the air. A bright red flower of blood bloomed across his chest. His head lolled to one side, his unseeing gaze falling on her, his eyes already beginning to glaze over.

TWO

—∞—

Prague, Czech Republic
6 October 1999

ADAM'S EARS PERKED AT THE sound of footfalls on the concrete floor. No one else should have been there. The special collections room of the library was restricted, access granted by appointment only, and he didn't recall seeing any appointments for that day on the ledger. It occurred to him that one of the other staff could be looking for him. Or perhaps a student had gotten lost in the labyrinthine stacks. There were any number of innocent explanations.

Adam didn't believe in innocent explanations anymore.

The room itself was long and narrow, the shelves arranged in rows perpendicular to its length, leaving only slender aisles around the edges. The one door was situated in a corner, but Adam had been reshelving books and couldn't see it from where he stood. He peered through the metal stacks, trying to catch a glimpse of the unannounced visitor, but in the dim light he could see only shadows.

The footfalls stopped, still several rows away. In the silence Adam's hand went to the crucifix around his neck. Moments later the footsteps resumed, slower and more deliberate, like a fox trying to flush out a hare. Adam glanced over his shoulder. If he could reach the end of the row, he could possibly sneak up the opposite aisle to the door, but his chances of making it all the way without being noticed were slim. He'd have a better chance confronting the intruder. He had other means at his disposal besides the crucifix, but experience had taught him even it would do in a pinch.

As the footsteps drew closer, Adam struggled to control his breathing and slow his heartbeat. His left hand still clutched his crucifix. His right hand hovered over the folding knife he kept in his pants pocket. The footsteps grew louder until eventually a young man stepped into the open space at the end of the row. He was dressed like a typical student—cargo pants, sweatshirt, oversized military-style jacket. His dirty-blond hair fell in front of his face. Their eyes met. He didn't say anything.

"May I help you?" Adam asked in Czech.

"It's possible," the man replied in Serbian. "Are you Edvard Novak?"

"I'm sorry," Adam said. "I don't understand."

He did understand, of course. "Edvard Novak" was the name on his university ID, a quiet, completely unremarkable assistant librarian no one ever had a reason to notice. Adam had played the role since coming to Prague a few months earlier, even going so far as to dye his hair blond and cover his brown eyes with blue contact lenses. He liked Prague. He wanted to stay.

But, he thought ruefully, we don't always get what we

want.

The man laughed. "You and I both know you're lying, but then again it doesn't really matter. I already know who you are."

Adam slipped the knife out of his pocket, concealing it still folded in his fist. "Who? Tell me," he said, switching to Serbian.

The man stepped forward. "Please, Dr. Mire, it will be easier if you don't fight."

Adam seized the book cart in front of him and charged down the row. The cart collided with the man's midsection and slammed him back into the wall before toppling over. Adam vaulted over the upturned buggy and sprinted for the door, but the man shoved the cart away and lunged after him, tackling Adam within a few steps. Adam twisted himself around, open knife in hand, but the man gripped his arm with alarming strength—*supernatural* strength.

He should have been more careful.

"*Crux sacra sit mihi lux,*" he began to chant.

The man laughed again. "Latin chants won't work on me. I'm just as alive as you are."

Their faces were inches apart as they struggled for the knife. Adam studied the man's eyes for any clue, any hint of what he might want. All he saw was determination. Adam could understand that. He let go of the knife. The man's weight shifted as he grabbed for it, and Adam bucked, throwing him off. He jabbed his elbow into the man's stomach and scooped the knife back up off the floor.

"That just mean's you're easier to hurt." Adam held the knife before him. "I take it you're a Chetnik. I was wondering when you guys would give it another try."

The man glared at Adam as he rose to his feet, and despite the silvery glint in Adam's hand, he advanced. Adam took another swing, but the man blocked him with little effort, seizing his arm and wrenching him around. The sharp pain forced Adam to drop the knife, and it clattered on the concrete floor. The man shoved him face-first into the wall and held him there.

"For the record, I'm not a Chetnik," he growled in Adam's ear.

A cloth covered Adam's mouth, and a sickly sweet smell entered his nostrils. His head swam. His knees buckled, and his vision faded. Then the darkness overtook him.

THREE

Thessaloniki, Greece
6 October 1999

CLARA LEAPT OUT OF THE chair and backed away from the desk where Arion's bleeding form lay. She frantically scanned the office for the deadly red dot but failed to find it. She gathered up as many of the loose papers as she could and stuffed them into her bag. The professor continued to stare sightlessly at her, his mouth open, his last words still hanging on his lips, while the red stain spread across his shirt.

She yanked the door open and ran out into the hallway, directly into a man's arms. She pushed herself away, but the man, dressed in riot gear with words in Greek written across the front of his jacket as well as POLICE in large white letters, seized her wrist. Clara looked up into cold, blue eyes set in a bulldog face.

He pulled her back toward him. "Please, miss, don't fight," he said in thickly accented English. "I am trying to get you away from here."

People emerged from the other offices. The man yelled something in Greek, and they all ran toward the stairwell, panic on their faces. The bulldog dashed down the hall after them, dragging Clara behind.

Outside the building, police pushed back the gathering crowd underneath Arion's window. The bulldog, however, took Clara in the opposite direction, around the corner to the other side of the building. He stopped in the shade of a sycamore tree.

"Thank you," Clara said, struggling to catch her breath.

But the bulldog didn't let go of her wrist.

Clara tried to fight until he squeezed. She winced and started to cry out, but he jerked her arm, bringing her close enough to feel his hot breath. He held up a pistol and touched the muzzle to his lips.

Clara glared. "You wouldn't shoot me, not here, not in broad daylight."

The bulldog's mouth twisted into a smile. He eyed the rooftop of a nearby building. "Who said anything about *me* shooting *you*? Now if you don't want someone *else* to get hurt, you'll keep your mouth shut. Don't worry. We're not going far."

He led her a short distance to a circular building lined with Ionic columns, obviously much older than the one where Arion had his office. Instead of the main entrance, he pushed her toward a small door on the opposite side. It opened onto a set of stairs that led down into the dark. At the bottom a short hallway ended in another door. The bulldog pushed it open and forced Clara into a dim room. The only light came from a small lantern resting on a low table. Another man already waited there.

The bulldog slung Clara toward the man. "Here, Filip. Why don't you do something useful and tie her hands. I can tell she's not going to be an easy one to deal with." His smile told Clara he was speaking English for her benefit.

The man he called Filip didn't reply.

The bulldog began stripping out of his police clothes. "Sometime today, Filip. We need to get moving soon."

Still Filip didn't reply.

The bulldog paused and snapped his fingers. "Filip, did you hear me?"

Filip stepped toward him, into the lantern's pool of light. When Clara saw his face, she gasped. It was the man who had recovered her wallet in the market.

"I heard you the first time," her Good Samaritan said.

The bulldog's eyes grew wide. He went for his gun, but before he could get to it, the man from the market fired a shot from his own. With a lurch, Clara's captor collapsed to the floor.

The man turned toward Clara. "Are you all right?"

"No," she replied. "No I'm not."

"What happened? How did they grab you?"

"Hell if I know. I don't even know who *they* are. One minute I'm talking to a professor in his office. The next he's dead on his desk from a sniper's bullet."

The man swore in a language Clara didn't know. If she had to guess, she would have said it was Russian. He reached for her. "We need to get you someplace safe."

Clara jerked away. "That's what he told me. Why should I trust you?"

"Because I very probably just saved your life. And I also did catch the pickpocket who stole your wallet, which is fortunate because you're going to need your ID."

"What do you mean?"

"I mean we have to leave now. You can't stay in Thessaloniki."

Clara shook her head. "Oh, no. No. I'm not going anywhere with you. I'm going back, and I'm going to talk to the police—the *real* police—and I'm going to tell them what happened, and then I'm going to book the first ticket back to the U.S."

"I'd advise against that."

"Why?"

"Because like it or not, you're in danger. And because then you'll never know what happened to Adam."

Clara's heart skipped a beat. "How do you know about Adam?"

"I have an interest in finding him too."

Clara tried to study his face in the low light. "Your name's not Filip, is it? Who are you?"

He motioned with his head in the direction of a heap behind him. "Filip is indisposed at the moment. My name is Arkady Danilovich Markov."

"Why are you looking for Adam? Does that mean he's still alive? Is he in danger, too?"

Arkady held up a hand. "Questions later. Now we need to be going."

Clara hesitated. "How do I know this isn't another trick?"

Arkady sighed. "You don't. I'm not forcing you to stay. You can go back, go talk to the police if you want, but just know that I'm your best chance to find Adam." He paused. "As well as to live to see another sunrise."

Clara struggled to calm her thoughts. A large part of her wanted to leave, to go back to her hotel, book a flight back to the States, and continue with her life. But something else tugged at her. She loved Adam, and he didn't have anyone else.

She stepped back and motioned to the door. "Okay.

Lead the way."

Arkady shook his head. "No. We're going the way your friend here was planning to take you."

"And what way is that?" Clara asked.

Arkady picked up the lantern and opened a door behind him that Clara hadn't noticed. "We're taking the tunnels."

THEY COULD HAVE BEEN WALKING for twenty minutes or two hours. Not long after Arkady led her through the door in the cellar room, the cramped tunnel opened enough that the weak lantern light left the walls in shadow. Occasionally Arkady gave her a curt warning to watch her step as they navigated around fallen stonework and other debris. Somewhere in the distance, water trickled.

"Where is this tunnel taking us?" Clara asked.

"Away from the university," Arkady answered.

"How do we know there aren't more of them waiting for us at the other end?"

"Because these tunnels run underneath most of the city. There are countless ways in and out. There's no way for them to know where we're going to end up."

A lump formed in the pit of Clara's stomach as she envisioned getting lost in miles and miles of pitch-black, maze-like tunnels. "How do we know where we're going?"

"I know the way," Arkady said. "Don't worry."

"If it's all the same to you, I'll worry until we're back on the surface."

Arkady laughed, but there wasn't any humor in his voice.

At the first juncture they came to, he took a tunnel that branched to the right of the main tunnel. Almost immediately, the ground began to slope upward, and it wasn't long before the light seeped back in. The walls of the tunnel were different here, made of brick rather than stone. Soon they came upon another door. Pushing it open, Arkady led her into another cellar. This one was filled with crates, most of them emblazoned with some sort of crest.

"Wine?" Clara asked.

"Olive oil," Arkady corrected. "This house used to belong to a wealthy merchant family. They traded olive oil all over the Eastern Mediterranean."

"Who does it belong to now?"

"It's abandoned."

Clara followed Arkady across the cellar to a set of stairs. With each step she took, Clara's sense of dread grew. Once they emerged on the floor above, Clara knew something was terribly wrong.

She forced down a wave of panic as she and Arkady made their way through rooms full of abandoned, crumbling furniture. Shadows moved, and voices whispered. Like a fog, tendrils of darkness writhed everywhere the light could not reach. Clara glanced at Arkady for any sign that he saw what she did. He didn't look back at her, though his steps took on a new urgency. Once or twice, Clara caught glimpses of figures out of the corner of her eye—black, vaguely human shapes standing in otherwise vacant rooms. When they reached the front hallway of the house, Arkady practically sprinted for the door, dragging Clara with him. They emerged onto the street to find themselves at the market, just as the afternoon sun dipped behind the buildings.

Clara looked back at the house, only to discover the same looming façade she had passed earlier. Arkady glanced back as well, his face solemn. He muttered something under his breath Clara wasn't able to catch before he offered his hand to her again.

"Come this way," he said. "We have a long drive ahead of us."

FOUR

Sarajevo, Bosnia and Herzegovina
7 October 1999

A CRACK BEGAN AT THE floor and ran all the way up the white plaster wall to the ceiling, the first thing Adam saw when he opened his eyes. Like a swimmer coming up for air, he fought through the grogginess and the pounding in his head. The smell of musty fabric hung in the air and mingled with the odor of stale cigarette smoke. He struggled to sit up, but froze when he locked eyes with the man from the Special Collections room. Seated in a threadbare chair, he glared at Adam from beneath a mop of dirty blond hair with intense but tired-looking blue eyes. He was slighter than he had seemed in the library, and young, probably in his early twenties.

"Where am I?" Adam asked, his voice like sandpaper.

The man didn't answer, and Adam didn't waste his breath asking again.

Glancing around, Adam found himself in the living

area of a tiny apartment. The man's chair was crammed into one corner. His own equally threadbare sofa was crammed into another. A decrepit radiator stood against the wall between them. Above the sputtering radiator threadbare curtains—bedsheets actually—covered the only window. Nearby, a black-and-white television sat on a small table. A newscaster was talking about the ethnic fighting in Kosovo. He spoke Serbian, or possibly Croatian, or maybe even Bosnian. All three languages were essentially the same, except that the speakers of each hated the speakers of the other two.

In the same wall as the giant crack there was a door—the entry, based on the adjacent coat rack. To the right of the door, an opening led into a cramped kitchen. An old gas stove stood in the middle of the room leaving barely enough space for a small dinette set.

Another door in the wall to his left promptly swung open, and a woman emerged from the darkened room on the other side. She wore a pair of faded blue jeans and a T-shirt. Her black hair was pulled back into a ponytail. She could have been a female student in any one of Adam's freshman Western civilization lectures, except that she seemed to draw all the shadows in the room toward her. Her movements created a slight sense of vertigo. Adam's heart pounded as he realized what she was.

"Dr. Mire," she said, "so glad to see you're finally awake. I trust your trip was a pleasant one?"

"I'd answer, but I'm afraid I don't remember much of it." Adam's hand went to the crucifix around his neck, only to discover it missing. He shoved his other hand into his pocket. His knife was gone as well. He glared at the man seated in the chair, who simply grinned.

"Now, don't look like that, Dr. Mire," the woman said.

"You'll get your toys back when you leave."

"Whether and how I leave is exactly what I'm worried about."

She smiled. "You needn't worry."

He wasn't sure if her words were meant to comfort him or not.

"Bogdan," she said to the man in the chair, "would you mind giving us some privacy, just for a few hours?"

Bogdan's grin melted. He hesitated, as if to ask her if she was certain, before he wordlessly stood and trudged out of the apartment. He slammed the door behind him.

She walked over to the television and turned it off before taking a seat in the dilapidated chair Bogdan had just vacated. Every move she made was deliberate, performed with a fluid grace that contradicted everything about her surroundings. "You've been busy, haven't you, Dr. Mire? Confronting a vampire as formidable as Yasamin. Challenging Süleyman's Blade. And coming out of the whole affair alive. Quite impressive."

"Who are you?" Adam asked.

Her mouth twisted into an amused quirk. "My name is Elena."

"Where am I?"

"Sarajevo."

Adam's mind went to a day in Prague a few weeks earlier. He was seated in a sidewalk café, drinking his coffee and smoking a cigarette, when his waiter slipped him an envelope. Inside was a clipping from *Liberation*, Sarajevo's daily newspaper. It was dated 16 March 1994, during the height of the siege of the city. The article recounted several deaths that could not be explained by the daily bombardment of shells from the Yugoslav army. Among other things, the victims were found completely drained of blood.

The waiter couldn't remember who handed him the envelope, but Adam knew, even though he caught only a glimpse of her as she walked away, it was Yasamin. And now he found himself speaking with another beguiling, raven-haired vampire. He remembered Stoker's words from *Dracula*.

Two were dark, and one was fair ...

"Why did you bring me here?" he asked.

"You could thank me for saving your life."

"Saving my life? How so?"

"Did you honestly think you could keep up the charade of Edvard Novak forever? If I could find you, then others could as well. It was only a matter of time."

"So I'm supposed to be grateful?"

"I thought you might be."

"Why?"

"Because I need your help, Dr. Mire."

Adam barely suppressed a laugh. "My help? Really?"

"You speak nine languages. You've published four books. You're not even forty, and you're one of the world's leading experts on Eastern Europe during the Middle Ages ... and on artifacts from the time period. Again, quite impressive."

"What's your point?"

"During your pas-de-deux with Süleyman's Blade, you made a show of searching for a medallion depicting a dragon, formed into a circle, with a cross on its back—"

Adam shook his head. "I don't know where it is. I can't help you find it."

Dracula's medallion, the one he wore as a member of the Order of the Dragon, missing for centuries. In a mad plan to avenge the death of the woman he loved, Adam had used rumors of the medallion's reappearance to lure the leader of Süleyman's Blade into the deadly clutches of a vampire, Yasamin, one of Dracula's legendary Brides.

But the medallion really was out there somewhere. He had almost all the clues to its whereabouts. He had spent much of his time in Prague trying to decipher them, but he always met with dead ends.

Elena cocked an eyebrow. "I'm not asking you to help me find it."

"Then what—"

"There are others who want it, who mustn't have it."

"You're not the first to feed me that line."

She glanced at the television set. "They say the war in Kosovo is over now. They've been saying the same thing for six hundred years. Tell me, Dr. Mire, who do you think won the original Battle of Kosovo all those years ago?"

Adam replied without even thinking. "The Turks. Their victory on Kosovo Field paved the way for Ottoman domination of the Balkans for the next five hundred years."

"You know the Serbs say they won."

"I know that nineteenth-century nationalists mythologized the battle to make a claim for the righteousness of the Serbian nation, but that doesn't change the facts."

"Doesn't it, Dr. Mire? Can't events happening now affect the past, just as the past affects the present? I was there in 1989 at the rally to commemorate the six-hundredth anniversary of the Battle of Kosovo, along with a million others. There were icons placed around the stage—of Jesus Christ, St. Sava, King Milutin ... and Slobodan Milošević. It was as if those intervening years had never occurred. All the speeches I had heard before, in one form or another. I knew that day what was to come, because it had already happened."

"Given the history of the Balkans, a lot of us felt what happened was inevitable."

She shook her head. "No, Dr. Mire. You misunderstand. I don't mean similar events have happened in the past. I mean the same events. Your problem is that despite all the time you've spent here among the Byzantines, you still think of time as the path of an arrow—straight and moving in only one direction. You've yet to learn that time is a circle. What is happening now has happened before and will happen again. 1389 is 1689 is 1989 is today. The past, the present, and the future are just different names for fate. To understand my story, you have to understand that."

FIVE

Gračanica, Kosovo
14 September 1689 Old Style

GJON STOPPED AGAIN AND SAT down on the hard ground. "I'm sorry, Elena. I just ... I just need to rest for a few minutes."

Elena struggled to mask her exasperation. "Please, Gjon, it's going to be dark soon. We need to hurry."

It wasn't his fault, Elena knew. It had been a hard journey for him. Though they had walked only a few miles, it had taken them all day. Really, what frustrated her was that the old imam said he couldn't help Gjon anymore. The boy sat by the side of the road, coughing and wheezing, fighting to catch his breath. No one, it seemed, could help him—not the priest in the white robes who sometimes visited their house to give them communion, not the priests in the black robes at the monastery nearby, not the old Gypsy woman who had camped by the river the previous summer, and not an ancient king whose remains rested in a church two days away by horse.

And her brother was only getting worse.

"Please, Gjon," she said again, "please try. We don't have much farther to go. You can rest all you need when we get home."

Reluctantly, he stood, and they continued on their way as quickly as Gjon could walk. The farmhouse rested in a small hollow near the edge of the plain. Its thatched roof finally came into sight just as the orange sun touched the rolling pastureland behind it.

When Elena and Gjon entered the house, their mother was sitting by the fire mending clothes while their sister Irina helped. Slumped in a chair by the table, the remains of his dinner still in front of him, their father had already passed out and was snoring. Their mother glanced up only briefly as the two of them stepped through the door before she returned to her mending. Gjon gave Elena a weary smile and went to his bed in the other room.

Elena stood for a moment, watching her mother work by the light of the fire. Its flickering glow emphasized the hard creases in her face.

"The imam can't do anything more for Gjon," Elena said.

Her mother didn't respond.

"He said he has tried every remedy known to him to help Gjon breathe better and to keep him from coughing. There is nothing left for him to try. He said God didn't create any disease for which he didn't also create a cure, but sometimes it's God's will for the cure not to be found."

The silence was broken only by the crackling of the fire and her father's snoring. Her mother's hands nimbly worked the needle and thread to fix a hole in a pair of her trousers. Elena wanted to cry, but she couldn't, not there, not in front of them.

Men didn't cry.

She went back outside. The moon had risen, bathing the countryside in its silver-blue glow. She walked around to the back of the house under the pretense of checking to make sure the chicken coop was secure. Her sister had a habit of leaving it unlatched, making the chickens easy prey for any fox that managed to squeeze under the fence. Once she made sure the coop was shut properly, she walked out to the new barn just a few yards from the house, a barn she herself had helped to build. The building made of logs and stones was meant to house the two sheep and two goats she had worked so hard to buy. They were returning with the herdsmen from the summer pastures in a few weeks. The barn was small, but she was proud of it.

Whenever she looked down at the baggy men's clothes she wore or felt her closely cropped hair, however, she was forced to admit to herself the sacrifice it had taken to achieve what she had. Neither of her parents had forgiven her for becoming a Sworn Virgin, denouncing her life as a woman to live as a man, but she had done it to save her brother and sister.

She opened the door to the barn and went inside. There, she sat in the fresh hay and began to sob. There were still days when she questioned whether she had made the right decision.

SHE REMEMBERED THE NIGHT VIVIDLY, though more than a year had passed. She sat in her bed after everyone else was asleep, the knife poised in her hand. She hesitated just for a second, thinking somehow there might be another way, but she knew there wasn't. She cut her hair until it was as short as her brother's and took some of his clothes. Then she made the oath to herself that she would be a virgin the rest of her life.

Her father had arranged for her to marry Gjeorgje, the son of Burim Bej, a wealthier neighbor. She would have had to go live with his family, and she couldn't allow that. She couldn't leave Gjon and Irina in that house by themselves—especially not Irina, as she grew older—but refusing Gjeorgje outright would have dishonored his family and started another blood feud. Only by becoming a Sworn Virgin was she able to get out of the marriage.

When she revealed to her parents what she had done, her father screamed at her, called her names, and threatened her. "Do you realize what you've done? Burim Bej is a wealthy man. You've thrown away your future! You've thrown away our future! I'll kill you!"

That day, though, Elena did something she had never done before. She stood her ground. Perhaps it was the clothes. "You won't do a thing. Your hand shakes so much, you can't point a gun straight anymore. And I haven't thrown away our future. You have. You're a coward and a drunkard. You won't leave the house to work, and you force three women and a sickly boy to do everything for you."

She regretted what she said as soon as the words left her lips, but only because of the hurt look on Gjon's face.

Her father's mouth twisted into a snarl. "You'll pay for that remark, girl!"

Elena shook her head. "I'm no longer a girl, and you're too drunk to stand without holding onto something, much less do anything to hurt me. You said that once we moved down from the mountains our lives would be better. You said that even though you were still in blood that you would no longer have to hide. No one would travel this far to take revenge. But you lied. You're still hiding, and we're all slowly dying. If you won't be the man of the house, then I will."

Her father lunged at her. She dodged him easily, but he lost his balance and crashed to the floor. Her mother rushed to his side to help him up. He hadn't tried to touch her since, but he was certainly drunk much more of the time. Her mother stopped speaking to her that day.

Even so, she worked hard. As a man, she could do business with the other farmers in the valley. She could go into town, sell their surplus crops and buy what they needed. Because of her they were not going hungry.

The one thing she couldn't do, though, was save her brother.

SHE DIDN'T KNOW HOW LONG she had been sitting there when she heard the crash coming from the direction of the house. She smelled smoke and sprinted from the barn. By the time she reached the front of the house, flames were already leaping from every window. She called for her brother and sister. Her first thought was that the blood feud had found them. Through the haze of the smoke, her father came running toward her, yelling for her to get away from the house.

"Where's Gjon?" she asked. "Where's Irina?"

He grabbed her by the arm. "This way, we have to get to the neighbor's as fast as we can. We won't be safe until we do." She tried to yank her arm free, but her father gripped her tighter and pulled her away from the house. "What are you doing? Didn't you hear me? We have to get away. Now."

"Where are Gjon and Irina?"

"You stupid girl, you're going to get us killed. Let's go."

They were on him a second later. Two of them. Not men from the rival clan but savage monsters. They ripped at her father's flesh with their teeth, their eyes burning with an unnatural red glow that was more than the mere reflection of the fire. She ran, but not toward the neighbor's farm. As fast as her feet would carry her, she sprinted toward the burning house. She wouldn't leave without knowing Gjon and Irina were safe.

She got as near to the inferno as she could. The two monsters, when they were done with her father, turned their attention toward her, though they seemed concerned with staying a good distance from the fire. Hands and mouths smeared in blood, they growled and paced like hungry wolves.

She found herself trapped with the fire at her back and no way to get past the two monsters. Elena's gaze darted about as she searched for any small opening that might save her. Her father was right. She was an idiot. Gjon and Irina were gone. If they hadn't escaped the house before the fire started, they couldn't have made it out alive.

As if to punctuate Elena's despair, the roof of the house collapsed with a roar, sending flames high up into the night and embers raining down. Smoke obscured her vision, though footfalls on the dry leaves told her the monsters still hovered nearby. Her throat burned. She held her arm to her mouth and nose, but it did little good. An ember landed on her sleeve and smoldered, threatening to set her coat on fire. She flung it away, only to see something in the grass glint off its orange light.

She stooped to retrieve the object and discovered it was the silver coin Gjon kept for good luck. Thinking of the monsters, words came to Elena—*lugat, kukudhi*—bogeymen from the stories her mother told her when she was a child, creatures of the night that fed on the blood of the innocent. Though, in the stories the innocent also had ways of fighting back.

The smoke had thickened to the point Elena could no longer see the monsters. She hoped they could no longer see her. She clutched the silver coin in her fist and darted toward the stream and the thicket of trees that separated her family's farm from the neighbor's land. She didn't hear the monsters behind her as she scrambled through the underbrush and had almost convinced herself she could make it when she tripped and fell. The coin flew from her hand. She fumbled for it in the blackness, but it was too dark to see where it went. As she struggled to her feet, fingers clamped around her wrist. She inhaled to scream, but a hand covered her mouth. She thrashed about until a familiar voice whispered in her ear.

"Stop it, Elena," Gjon said, "or you'll get us both killed."

Her brother pulled her into the shadow of a nearby tree. She helped him up into its branches and then climbed up herself. There they stayed for most of the night in complete silence, arms wrapped around one another for warmth, watching and waiting, but the things never came back.

When the sky began to lighten in the east, Elena gathered up enough courage to speak, though she was still afraid to do so above a whisper. "What happened, Gjon? Where are Irina and Mother?"

Gjon didn't answer right away, and when he did, he didn't look at her. "Gone."

Elena fought the tremor in her lower lip. "What happened? What were those things?"

Gjon shook his head. "I don't know. I heard them when they came to the door. They said they were travelers and had gotten lost. They were both very charming, actually. Mother invited them in, but once they were inside, I heard Mother and Irina both scream. Father ran into the room. He grabbed me and practically tossed me through the window. He told me to run to the neighbor's house and not to look back. I asked where you were. He said you were probably dead."

Gjon started coughing. He coughed so much that he spat up a tiny bit of blood. Elena had to get him somewhere to rest.

"I did as I was told," Gjon continued, "except that I looked back once. I heard a crash, and I glanced over my shoulder to see the fire already spreading. I ran into the woods, but I had to stop because I couldn't breathe."

The sky continued to grow lighter, though the shadows still loomed all around them. Elena hopped down from the tree and motioned for Gjon to do the same.

"Where are we going?" he asked.

"To the monastery," Elena replied as she helped him down.

"Again? They said they couldn't help me."

"You're going to stay there this time, Gjon. You need to be cared for."

"Why? What are you going to do? Why can't you care for me?"

"I'm going to come back to the farm."

"I don't want to be apart from you."

"It's only for a little while, Gjon. I promise. Please do this, for me."

Gjon nodded.

She helped him along, clearing the brush as best she could as they made their way through the forest, and when it was too thick, she helped him to climb over the brambles and thorns. Elena wasn't as sure as she had made herself sound. She was hungry. She was tired. All she wanted was to lie down on the ground in the damp bed of leaves and sleep, forgetting the night had ever happened, but she continued to put one foot in front of the other because she didn't know how to do anything else.

The sky had turned the pale blue of morning by the time they reached the clearing where the monastery stood. Though she had visited it before, she was always awed by the grandness of it, compared to their tiny home. The sun rising behind the domes gave the building a magical glow.

Elena stepped into the clearing and turned to Gjon. She watched in horror as a hand reached out of the shadows and grabbed her brother. Elena screamed and rushed toward him, but the hand dragged him back into the woods. Gjon reached for her, his eyes wide with terror as another hand covered his mouth. The creature's face appeared, eyes burning like hellfire and mouth filled with razor-sharp fangs. It sunk its teeth into Gjon's neck, and deep-red blood spurted over them both. They vanished into the shadows just as the sun topped the monastery's highest dome.

SIX

Sarajevo, Bosnia and Herzegovina
7 October 1999

ADAM STUDIED THE MOTH-EATEN CARPET, deliberately avoiding Elena's gaze. "Vampires murdered your family."

"One of the many tragedies of my life," Elena replied.

She had a voice like smoked glass. Her lilac perfume was beginning to make him light-headed, or it could have been her proximity to him on the sofa. He didn't remember when she had moved there from the chair in the corner. He struggled to keep his head clear. "And yet here you are. How is that?"

"What do you mean, Dr. Mire?"

"I mean, when did you know? Was it before or after you agreed to be turned?"

Her eyes narrowed. "What does it matter to you?"

"It matters."

"There were a great many things I didn't know until ... later."

"You must have had some idea."

"If you'll just let me finish telling you the rest of the story—"

He shook his head. "I don't need to hear it."

Her voice took on a tone of mock hurt. "How can you say that, Dr. Mire?"

"Very easily. Whatever fight this is, it's not mine."

Her fingers brushed his bicep. "But there must be something I can do to convince you."

"There is not a thing you can do that would make me want to help you."

"Not even if I could get your life back for you?"

He snorted. "How exactly do you propose to do that?"

She chuckled. "I have resources."

"All of Interpol is probably looking for me."

"No doubt."

"And the Chetniks are still out there. Not to mention a screwed-up serial killer who paints his victims' hands green. You're telling me you can just snap your fingers and make all that go away?"

"Well, it will require more than snapping my fingers, and I can't make them go away, but I can fix it so that they're not looking for you anymore."

"So that they're not looking for me? How?" he asked.

She leaned forward and whispered in his ear. "No one tends to look for dead people."

Adam leapt off the sofa, but she was faster. She intercepted him before he could reach the door. "I don't mean what you think, Dr. Mire." She pressed a hand on his chest where his heart pounded. "Trust me, you're much more useful to me alive. No, we just have to convince everyone else that you're dead."

"And how does that get my life back? I'm not even sure

there's enough left worth saving."

She smiled. As she talked, she pushed him away from the door, back toward the sofa. "It depends on what's important to you, but don't ponder for too long. All the pieces are already in motion on the board. If you hesitate, you may find you no longer have any options."

SEVEN

Thessaloniki, Greece
7 October 1999

THE GENTLEMAN PLACED A GLOVED hand on the body sprawled across the floor of the dark basement room. As he lifted it from the pool of thick, almost dried blood, the body made a sucking noise that would have sickened anyone else. He traced a finger across a small bullet hole in the dead man's chest. The bullet had torn through the heart, killing him instantly. The same went for the other body in the room.

He sighed. So much blood.

A shame it had all gone to waste.

At the sound of footsteps in the hallway, he turned his head toward the door. By the time the doorknob turned, he had hidden himself in the corner. A flashlight's beam swept across the floor, and another man cautiously entered. His gaze darted from side to side along with the flashlight. He had dark hair and small close-set eyes in a round face. The sleeves of his shirt were rolled up, revealing a tattoo of a wolf covering one forearm along with the words "Freedom or Death" in Serbian.

A Chetnik.

"Filip? Viko?" the Chetnik called. "Are you here? We were expecting you yesterday."

He stepped farther into the room, and the flashlight's beam fell on the body on the floor. The Chetnik gasped. In a blur of motion, the gentleman slammed the door closed and swatted the flashlight out of the Chetnik's hand. The cheap plastic casing shattered on the floor, plunging the room into absolute darkness again. Fortunately, the darkness was never a problem for him.

"What was that?" the Chetnik shouted. "Who's there?"

The man let out a low chuckle.

The Chetnik groped for the door, but in the darkness, he was hopelessly disoriented. He tripped over the body, tumbled to the floor and immediately jumped up, screaming. His hands and face were covered in sticky blood. Eyes wide with panic, he began flailing, feeling for the door, his terror growing every second until it practically pulsed through the room.

"Let me out!" the Chetnik shouted. "Please. I don't know anything. Please just let me go."

The gentleman grabbed the Chetnik by the shirt and shoved him against the wall. "Do you think any of this concerns me?" the gentleman asked. "Your petty factions? If you could only understand."

"Who ... who are you?"

"Does it matter?"

"Please. Let me go."

"Oh, but I can't do that." The gentleman flexed his jaw as his eyeteeth pushed through his gums, growing into fangs. The pain of it only made him more excited. "I'm hungry."

The Chetnik screamed as jagged teeth tore through his throat. Blood spurted into the gentleman's mouth and ran down his chin. For the next several minutes, he lost himself in the images flooding his mind as he drained the Chetnik of life. The pathetic man's rage, hatred, and shame—all of it rushed through him, leaving him drunk. When the gentleman was finished, he let the dead body of the Chetnik slump to the floor. He staggered backwards, wiping his chin and licking the blood from his fingers.

EIGHT

Mostar, Bosnia and Herzegovina
7 October 1999

THE SKY IN THE EAST had begun to pale. Clara watched the clouds turn lavender and orange-pink with the coming sunrise. She glanced at Arkady, who had been behind the wheel of the silver Mercedes through the night. His bland smile did little to appease her barely controlled panic. They hadn't spoken much. He had encouraged her to sleep, which she did eventually. When she woke up, she was surprised to learn they had crossed from Greece into Macedonia and then into Bosnia and Herzegovina. She didn't have travel visas for either country, and yet somehow they had crossed into each one without incident. She knew she should ask Arkady about that. At the moment, though, she had other questions.

"Back in the abandoned house in Thessaloniki, I saw claws made of shadows reaching out from underneath the furniture."

"I saw them, too," Arkady said.

"And there was a man. I couldn't see his face. The shadows wrapped around him like a cloak, but his eyes—"

"Yes, I saw that as well." Arkady squeezed the steering wheel with both hands until his knuckles turned white.

"What was happening?"

Arkady sighed. "I don't know exactly."

"But you have an idea."

"When we get to Mostar, I promise I will tell you what I can."

A few minutes later the car crested a ridge, and a battered skyline came into view.

"Mostar, I'm assuming?" Clara asked.

Arkady nodded.

"I remembered the name from the news," Clara said. "It's a World Heritage site, isn't it? But it was almost completely destroyed in the war."

Arkady nodded again. "The name of the city comes from a four-hundred-year-old bridge that spanned the Neretva River. *Stari Most* means 'Old Bridge' in Bosnian, but the bridge was destroyed during the later part of the civil war. There are plans to rebuild it."

"But it won't be old anymore, will it?" Clara gazed at the city, for so long nothing more than an abstraction on the television news, just one more place "over there." Seeing it with her own eyes didn't serve to make it any more real though. It just seemed like some postapocalyptic Emerald City. Steeples and minarets jutted upward at irregular intervals, some halfway constructed and others still in ruins.

"So these Chetniks," she said, "Serbian ultranationalists as you call them, tell me again why they want me."

"I don't really think they want you," Arkady replied. "As I explained, while I was supposed to keep an eye on you in Thessaloniki, my primary goal was to follow the Chetnik Filip. I had no idea they were planning to assassinate a professor or kidnap you. I would have ... done more. They want Adam, and they probably thought they could use you to get to him."

"But how did they know I was looking for him?"

"You haven't exactly been discreet about your inquiries."

She frowned. "I didn't know I needed to be."

"I always tend to err on the side of caution."

"Said the spy."

Arkady raised an eyebrow. "Who said anything about being a spy?"

"You mean you're not?"

"Absolutely not. Spies are employed by the Federal Security Service. I would never lower myself to that level."

"And who employs you then?"

"A higher power."

She looked at him. "Sorry if I offended."

He shrugged. "It's an honest mistake."

"In any event," Clara continued, "I don't know how these Chetniks expected a plan like that to work if they don't even know where Adam is."

"They have a wide network across Eastern Europe they could use to get the word out. He would have heard, somehow."

"And then they would have waited for him to swoop to my rescue."

"In all likelihood."

Clara's gaze fell to her lap. "They might have been waiting a long time."

Arkady glanced sideways at her. "Why? Wouldn't he have tried to save you?"

Clara sighed. "Adam ... doesn't make it easy for a person to get close to him. Sometimes he's the most thoughtful person on the planet, and other times you're lucky if he remembers you're in the same room with him. Still, I thought he loved me."

"Until ..."

"When he left this past summer, I told him I didn't think he should go. He said he had to, but I just couldn't shake this uneasy feeling about the trip. We talked a few times after he left, and things seemed okay, but then something ... changed."

"How so?"

"I'm used to Adam being distracted. This was different. The last time we talked, he was aloof, cold even. And he was evasive about what he was doing, where he was. I asked him if anything was wrong, but he said everything was fine. Then he asked me not to call him again. I thought at the time he was just being a jerk. Now, though, I think he might have been trying to protect me."

"Because of something he'd discovered."

"Professor Tsakalidis said as much before they killed him."

"Did Professor Tsakalidis know what it was?"

"If he did, he didn't have a chance to tell me. Do you know why the Chetniks want Adam?"

Arkady fixed his gaze straight ahead. "I have ideas."

"Why are you looking for him? Why is it so important that you find him? Is it just to stop these Chetniks?"

"That is part of it, but there are other reasons as well."

"Such as?"

He hesitated. "I ... had a brother. His name was Konstantin, Kostya for short. He was killed, while he was with Adam."

"I'm sorry," Clara said.

Arkady clenched his jaw. "So am I."

"What was he doing with Adam? Did he work for the same 'higher power' as you?"

"He did. As far as anyone can tell, he was meeting with Adam because of something Adam knew, or was trying to find out. They found his body in an abandoned warehouse in Banja Luka. I just want to know what happened."

"Banja Luka? Where is that?"

"Also in Bosnia," Arkady answered, "to the north of here."

"So sometime between Budapest and Thessaloniki, Adam might have been in Banja Luka. I'm getting a headache trying to keep all this straight."

"I wish I could tell you there wasn't anything more. I'll try to explain the rest when we get there."

"Was Adam seen in Mostar, too?"

"Not as far as anyone knows."

"Then why are we here? Shouldn't we be going to Banja Luka instead?"

"There is someone here I have to talk to."

Clara huffed. "You think you could be a little more vague?"

Arkady gave her a sidelong glance. "I'll answer the rest of your questions soon, I promise."

For the rest of the ride into the city, they were silent. As the countryside gave way, a heaviness settled over the car. Clara couldn't imagine living in a place so close to death. The war was over, but the scars would probably always remain. Like the Old Bridge, they could rebuild their lives, but nothing would ever be the same.

Arkady stopped the car in front of an apartment building not far from an Orthodox church. He led Clara inside to an apartment on the fourth floor. It struck her as rather bland—generic furniture, no personal effects whatsoever, not even books.

"Is this your apartment?" she asked.

"Not exactly," Arkady replied, "but we'll be safe here."

"From the Chetniks?"

"Among others."

"You said you were going to explain why we're here."

"And I will." He reached underneath a table. With a click, a small hidden drawer popped open. Arkady retrieved several folded pieces of paper from it. "This is a letter, written by someone who was trapped in Mostar during the Second World War. It describes an experience he had one winter night with a vampire."

NINE

From the Journal of Andrej Nešović

Mostar, Independent State of Croatia
28 February 1945

I*N THE WINTER OF 1945, Yugoslav Partisans mounted an operation to take the city of Mostar from the pro-Nazi Ustaše regime. They easily overwhelmed the city's beleaguered defenses and entered Mostar on the night of 14 February without further resistance. Almost immediately, they seized seven Franciscan friars and executed them, then threw their bodies in the Neretva River as an example for the Roman Catholic Croatians.*

However, the secondary goal of the pro-Communist Partisans was the eradication of the Chetniks, who had been waging a guerilla war in the area and whom the Partisans saw as their chief rivals for control of postwar Yugoslavia. In this effort, too, they were mostly successful, but in the days that followed, they encountered a different kind of threat, one no one expected.

THE SNOW WAS RED. A vibrant, brilliant, glistening red in the light of my lantern. I shoved my glove into my mouth to keep from retching, and I followed the trail of blood until it ended on the steps of a townhouse in the shadow of the cathedral.

That he would pick such a place so near holy ground disgusted me, and it only made my resolve stronger. I climbed the steps and pushed the door open. Once inside the darkened house, I paused to listen. There was no sound. The owner of the house had clearly abandoned it, fleeing for the Dalmatian coast, or maybe Italy. Everything was still there—the furniture, the linens, even the silver. A chill passed over me as I entertained another option— that the owners hadn't left at all.

I crept up the stairs, stopping every few steps to listen. Still there was no sound. At the top of the stairs, my lantern threw light on another long hallway. I thought I saw the shadows move in the room at the far end. Easing my hand into my jacket, I pulled out the wooden stake I had spent the last few days fashioning. I closed my eyes and said a prayer. I blew out the lantern and continued down the hallway.

My plan was to surprise him, but of course I should have known better. When I burst into the room, he was waiting for me, sitting in a chair at the foot of the bed. Across the bed lay the body of Boris Petrović, our commanding officer. Blood smeared the bedspread and covered the walls, where it formed some obscene symbol that resembled a serpent eating its own tail.

"Good evening, Andrej," he said. "Is there something I can do for you?"

He was still in his uniform, though it, too, was stained with blood. His name was Dejan, and I had counted him as a friend and a comrade. We had fought together for the cause. We had huddled in trenches together and taken cover from enemy fire together. We had shared meals, drinks, thoughts on the state of the world. I still cringe at some of the things I told him about myself. When I thought he was dead, a part of me died as well.

"This isn't your home," I said.

He looked around the room, feigning shock. "No, no you're right. I don't believe it is."

"What happened to the people who live here?"

He raised his eyebrows. "They're gone."

"Where did they go?"

"I don't know."

"I think you do. I think you're lying."

His features hardened. "Get to your point, Andrej."

"I know what you are," I said. "The night we went into Nevesinje I watched you die. The Chetniks ambushed us. One second the street was perfectly quiet, and then suddenly everything was chaos. When the shooting began, I saw you stagger and clutch your chest, then crumple to the ground. We had no choice but to retreat. We didn't even have a chance to retrieve your body. I'm sorry."

He chuckled. "Don't be."

My anger flared ret hot again at his words. "Then I saw you again a week ago outside our barracks, hiding in the shadows, watching us all come and go. I would have confronted you then, but I wasn't prepared."

"And you think you're prepared now?"

"I've studied."

He laughed. "Books? You think you know what you're dealing with based on what you read in books?" He stood and stepped toward me. "You have no idea. Boris Petrović hunted us. He trained his entire life to fight us. Who knows how many of us he's destroyed? And look at him now. What chance do you have?"

I clenched the wooden stake. Through the window, the dome of the church reflected the pale moonlight. "I have God on my side."

"You do? Well, then, let's just see how much your God cares." As he glared at me, his eyeteeth grew into fangs, and his eyes changed to a burning red. "Run."

I would like to say that I stood my ground and sent him back to the hell he came from, but at that moment, my resolve melted. My legs buckled, and I stumbled back into the hallway. I ran toward the stairs, but I knew I'd never make it out of the house alive.

The shadows seemed to reach for me, grabbing at my arms and legs, attempting to make me stumble. When I reached the stairs, he came out of the bedroom, eyes burning like the devil he was. I clutched the silver crucifix around my neck, pulling so hard I broke the chain. I didn't look back any more after that. I half fell down the stairs, and when I came to the bottom, I sprinted for the door. I had almost reached it when his clawed hand raked my back, and I tumbled to the floor.

He lifted me effortlessly. "A shame. I liked you. I could have seen convincing you to turn."

"Never," I managed to croak. "You should just kill me."

"As you wish."

He opened his mouth, and his jaw seemed to unhinge as he prepared to sink his fangs into my throat. At that moment, I crammed the crucifix in as far as I could. He shrieked and jerked away, his teeth ripping half the flesh from my hand. I nearly fainted from the searing pain, but I fought my way out of the house, outside into the cold night.

He followed me, screaming and growling, struggling to speak with his suddenly useless tongue. His once handsome face was deformed into the demon he was, his jaw hanging, blood dripping from the corners. Even injured he was faster than I was, and in seconds he had caught up to me. With my one good hand, I managed to pull the knife concealed in my boot, and I slashed him across the chest. I knew it wouldn't kill him, but I hoped it would slow him down.

His dark-red blood splattered across the snow again and again as I cut into him. He howled in pain and rage, and in my own pain and rage I joined him. Finally, reduced to little more than a wild animal, he lunged at me. From my jacket I pulled the second wooden stake I had made, and as he came at me, I thrust it into the gaping wound I had opened in his chest. He looked at me, hate in his eyes. I let go, and he collapsed to the ground. Flames engulfed his entire body, and only seconds later there was nothing more than a smoking pile of ash.

I vomited and then stumbled back toward the barracks, leaving behind the black mark in the snow, all there would ever be to commemorate the man who was once my friend.

TEN

Sarajevo, Bosnia and Herzegovina
7 October 1999

"WHAT DO YOU MEAN WHEN you say 'all the pieces are already in motion'?" Adam asked.

Elena shook her head. "Come now, Dr. Mire, you know full well that if I hadn't sent Bogdan to fetch you, someone would have found you sooner or later. Did you really expect to get away scot-free?"

Adam gritted his teeth. "I didn't get away scot-free. I lost everything."

"Not everything. You're still breathing when, by all accounts, you shouldn't be."

He couldn't argue with her on that score. "I knew I couldn't stay in Prague forever, but I was hoping for at least a little more time."

"Time's up. The game you inserted yourself into when you went up against Serhan and Süleyman's Blade, it isn't over."

Adam shot her a glance. "Something's happened, hasn't

it?"

She chuckled. "And now suddenly you're interested."

"Tell me Süleyman's Blade hasn't come back."

"No, Dr. Mire. You managed to deal them what appears to be a fatal blow. The Chetniks on the other hand …"

"What have they done?"

"They are beginning to exert their muscle. They've already seized control of several of the smaller towns between here and Mostar. No one knows for certain what their endgame is, but of course they're not going to stop at a few villages."

"And getting their hands on Dracula's medallion is part of whatever they have planned?"

"I have every reason to believe so."

"What happens if the Chetniks find the medallion?"

"Chaos."

Adam smirked. "It seems to me we have enough of that already."

"Nothing like what would happen. The Chetniks think the medallion will make them invincible. If they are allowed to find it, they will rip this continent apart. Again."

"And why do you care if there's a little more bloodshed?"

She frowned. "I hoped by now you'd realized we are more than bloodthirsty monsters. Yes, strife makes things easier for us in some ways. But in others it's much more difficult. There is a rhythm to human violence. Interfere, and you cause catastrophe. I only want to maintain the natural ebb and flow."

"Because time is a circle."

"You're learning, Dr. Mire."

"Why can't Bogdan be your dayman? It seems like he's

got the minion role down."

She raised an eyebrow. "Bogdan is useful for ... a good many things, but this requires a set of skills I'm afraid he simply doesn't possess. You do."

"If I were to somehow figure out a way to stop the Chetniks, then what? I get my life back, whatever that looks like, and you go away?"

"You'll never see me again."

Adam sucked in a deep breath. "I still don't trust you."

She smiled. "Good, but in this case you should believe me when I tell you I have only the best intentions." She left him and walked into the bedroom, reemerging a moment later with a bag, a familiar one. She tossed his old work satchel full of his books down on the sofa next to him. "Bogdan retrieved it from your apartment in Prague. I thought you might need it. And a room has been booked for you at a hotel nearby. I didn't expect you to be comfortable staying here."

Adam pawed through the satchel, pulling out all his books, making sure nothing was missing. "An accurate assessment."

"So are you going to let me continue now?"

Adam sighed. "I never really thought I had much of a choice."

ELEVEN

—⟡—

Gračanica, Kosovo
15 September 1689 Old Style

ELENA STOOD AT THE WINDOW of a room she had never seen before. Through the trees the monastery's white walls gleamed in the afternoon sun. She had awoken minutes before in a clean bed, a thick blanket covering her. Her old trousers and shirt were gone. She wore instead a dress she discovered lying across the chair next to the bed. She had no recollection of how she had gotten there.

The door creaked as it opened, and Elena turned away from the window. An old woman entered holding a tray of food—crusty bread and soup that filled the room with an earthy aroma. The woman set the tray down on the small table next to the bed and turned to leave.

"Wait," Elena said. "Who are you? Can you tell me how I got here?"

The woman merely shook her head, grunted, and left, shutting the door behind her. Elena eyed the tray of food, suddenly realizing how hungry she was. By the time the woman returned a few minutes later, Elena had devoured all the soup and bread. The old woman raised an eyebrow when she saw the empty tray, but said nothing. Instead, she gestured at the window. Elena's gaze followed where the woman's gnarled finger pointed, but she didn't understand.

After more adamant gesturing and muttering, the old woman finally managed to convey that she wanted Elena to see something outside. Elena went to the window. A man in a monk's cassock stood outside underneath an oak tree. They made brief eye contact before he looked away. Elena turned to ask about him, but the old woman had already left.

As Elena approached the monk where he stood under the oak tree, she realized he was perhaps no older than she was. He had reddish-brown hair and a short beard. Although Elena had seen many young monks like him on her last visit, she was certain she had never seen him. She would have remembered his blue eyes. He smiled when he saw her walking toward him.

"I'm sorry for making you meet me out here," he said in Albanian, to Elena's surprise, "but I can't enter the house of an unmarried woman. My name is Brother Stjepan. I'm a novice here. I was the one who found you this morning, collapsed in the grass on the far side of the courtyard. Are you all right?"

Elena smiled weakly back at him. "I'm doing better. Thank you. My name is Elena."

"Elena," he repeated. "I also should apologize for any impropriety that may have occurred. We didn't know ... The way you were dressed ... We thought you were a ..."

Elena held up her hand. "There is no need to apologize

for that. Just tell me something. How do you know my language? Do all the monks speak it?"

Brother Stjepan shook his head. "Only a few, but I grew up here, and I learned it at an early age. There are quite a few like you who live near the monastery—I mean, those who speak the same language." He added the last part quickly, as his face flushed red. "Do you speak any of my language?"

"A little," she replied in tentative Serbian. "I have to in order to barter in the marketplace in Priština."

"Can you tell me how you came to be here?"

His question hit Elena like a slap in the face. She didn't know how to answer. She hadn't been able to think about what had happened, and now the reality hit her. Everyone was gone. She bit her lip and fought against the emotions threatening to engulf her until she could speak without her voice wavering. "Bandits attacked our farm and set fire to our house. I barely escaped."

Bandits seemed as good a word to call them as any other.

"Your family?"

Her gaze fell to the fallen leaves under their feet. She shook her head.

"I'm sorry," Brother Stjepan said. "You're welcome to stay as long as you like. You'll be safe here with Marija. She is always willing to take in pilgrims to the monastery."

"Thank you," Elena replied.

A rook landed above them on a branch of the oak tree. It cocked its head to the side and croaked at them a few times, then flew away. The momentary distraction seemed to unsettle Brother Stjepan. He glanced over his shoulder, and when he looked back, his face had taken on a definite pallor.

"Is something the matter?" she asked.

"No," he said, "not at all. I need to go before I'm missed. Again, I am truly sorry for what you have been through."

He turned and left without waiting for Elena to reply.

TWELVE

Gračanica, Kosovo
20 September 1689 Old Style

ELENA PASSED THE DAY IN a fog. She sat in the church, staring at the murals adorning the walls. In one of them, an old man sat in a cave. Atop the cave's mouth perched a crow. Another depicted a man dressed in gold and floating in the air, whom she guessed to be the Christ, but she didn't know for sure. She couldn't read the inscription on the parchment he held. Still another mural depicted a line of men and women who all looked vaguely alike. One of them held a model of the monastery itself. She wondered about these figures the most, with their crowns and their halos and their brightly colored, fur-lined robes. It was hard for her to believe such people ever existed.

"You know, they're never going to move, no matter how long you stare at them."

The voice startled her. She turned to find Brother Stjepan standing next to her.

Her cheeks grew hot. "I'm sorry. I was simply admiring them."

"There's no need to apologize. Admire them all you like." Stjepan glanced over his shoulder. "I only have a moment, but I'm happy I've found you. I need to speak with you."

"About what?"

He shook his head. "Not now. Tonight. Will you meet me under the oak tree again, after the vespers service?"

"I suppose I can. What is this about?"

A finely dressed man entered the chapel. His boots echoed on the stone floor as he crossed to an alcove where he knelt in front of the icons presented there. He closed his eyes to pray.

"I have to go now," Stjepan said. "I can't say anything more. Please, it's important. I'll explain it all tonight. Just promise me you'll meet me."

"I promise," Elena replied.

As Stjepan hurried out of the church, Elena glanced at the man praying. She thought she caught him peering back at her.

THE DISSONANT HARMONIES OF THE monks' songs echoed through the trees, carried by the breeze. The vespers service had already lasted more than an hour, with no sign it would end any time soon, giving Elena more than enough time to think about her stay at the monastery and to wonder what was keeping her there.

When the singing finally ended, she waited beneath the tree. Several minutes passed before she saw Stjepan in the moonlight, approaching from the direction of the monastery. She stepped out of the shadows to meet him, but he placed a hand on her elbow and ushered her back underneath the ancient oak.

"I'm sorry to have kept you waiting, but I had to make sure no one saw me," he said. "Thank you for keeping your promise."

She glared. "I take my promises seriously."

Stjepan regarded her in the faint moonlight. "Of course."

"Before you start, will you answer a question for me?"

Stjepan's expression changed to a puzzled frown. "I suppose that's fair."

"Who are the people in the paintings?"

"You mean the murals in the church?"

"Yes."

"Well, the man in the cave is the prophet Elijah—"

"No, the others," Elena interrupted, shaking her head, "the line of people, the ones dressed in purple with crowns and jewels and golden halos."

"Those? They're the Nemanjas. They were all kings, and the saviors of the people. Every last one of them is a saint. King Milutin Nemanja commissioned the building of this monastery more than three hundred years ago, before the Turks, when we were free."

"How can you claim they saved the people? The Turks have overrun everything. They take our crops and our animals and even our brothers whenever they see fit."

Stjepan shook his head. "You're not looking at things the right way. They saved the souls of the people with their piety and their devotion."

"Piety and devotion don't feed anyone."

"Maybe not, but they still offer one thing that isn't in abundance right now."

"And what might that be?"

"Hope."

Elena stifled a laugh. "Hope? For what?"

"Hope for eternal salvation and a place in heaven in the next life."

"But what about *this* life?" Elena threw her hands in the air. "I have watched you all for days now. You monks with your silent comings and goings, your prayers, your rituals, your obediences. I don't understand you. What you do seems so pointless. Your religion is no good to me if you can't make the rain fall so the crops grow or heal people who are sick."

"I'm sorry you feel that way," Stjepan said quietly.

Elena turned away.

"May I say what I wanted to say now?" Stjepan asked.

"Go ahead."

Stjepan inhaled sharply. "I need to apologize to you."

"Apologize? For what?"

"When we spoke a few days ago, I was less than truthful with you."

Elena eyed him. "You lied?"

"By omission. I asked what had happened to you when, in fact, I already knew." He drew his mouth into a grim line. "Elena, bandits didn't attack your family. Or at least not the kind that steal the things bandits normally steal."

"What do you mean?"

"We have heard rumors of several other attacks in the last month, in the more remote villages. People have been found murdered in their homes in … gruesome ways. In every case nothing was taken, not even things of value left in plain sight, and there are no living witnesses. At least not until now."

"But who would do such a thing?"

"I think you know the answer to that."

Elena frowned. "Me? How could I know?"

"You thought a silver coin would keep them away. You had to have at least some idea."

Elena took a step back. "I didn't tell you that. There's no way you could possibly know about the coin."

"The monsters that murdered your family, you have different names for the kind of creature they are, but my people use the word *vampir*."

"I don't understand." The wind rustled the tree branches and sent their shadows dancing in the moonlight. Brother Stjepan's shadow flickered and then vanished, only to return seconds later. She gasped. "You're a *dhampir*!"

Brother Stjepan held up a hand. "Please don't say that word. No one here knows—no one here *can* know—but yes that is what I am. My mother was a mortal. My father ... was one of *them*. I can sense when they're near. Sometimes, I have dreams about the things they do. The night before you appeared, I had a dream about the attack on your family. I saw you running from them while clutching a silver coin."

Elena's legs threatened to give way beneath her. She had to place a hand on the trunk of the oak tree to steady herself, yet even as she grappled with Stjepan's confession another thought pricked her consciousness.

She was no longer alone.

"Why do you think they are making these attacks?" she asked.

Stjepan shook his head. "I don't know, but I have the sense there is a terrible darkness coming. Last night I had another dream, another attack, but this one was different. It happened in the woods, and I think it happened close by. Tomorrow I'll be able to slip away for a few hours. I want to see if I can find the place where it happened.

Would you like to come with me?"

Elena raised an eyebrow. "Why?"

"Because I've watched you the last several days. You've been wandering around in a daze. I can't imagine what you're going through. I can't bring your family back, but I can offer you the chance to help destroy the monsters that took them."

Elena remembered the terror in Gjon's eyes as the clawed hands dragged him away, and she wanted to see the same terror in the eyes of the creature that killed him. She nodded. "I'd like to have that chance."

THIRTEEN

Sarajevo, Bosnia and Herzegovina
7 October 1999

ADAM PINCHED THE BRIDGE OF his nose between his thumb and forefinger. A headache was building behind his eyes. "What does any of this have to do with Dracula's medallion? How do I find it?"

Elena let out a brief chuckle. "Impatient?"

"I don't think I can afford to be patient right now."

"Dr. Mire, I haven't survived for over three hundred years without learning to wait."

"And I haven't survived as long as I have by going off half-cocked without knowing what I'm up against. There is more going on than what you're telling me."

She regarded him for a moment in silence, a twisted smile on her face. He studied the crack on the wall to avoid meeting her gaze again.

"Much more," she said, her voice even. "It will come as no surprise to you that the Chetniks were on the side of the Serbs and the Yugoslav army during the recent war.

At the height of the siege, there were rumors they had a secret plan to tip the balance in their favor, that Sarajevo was going to fall."

"But the city didn't fall."

"It came close, closer than anyone will ever admit."

"And what was the Chetniks' secret plan?"

"Actually, the better question is, '*Who* was the Chetniks' plan?'"

A chill passed over Adam. "Another vampire." He dug through his satchel until he found the newspaper clipping from the *Liberation* describing the exsanguinated bodies found in the midst of the siege. He handed it to Elena. "You mean this wasn't you?"

Elena took the scrap of paper from him and scanned the article. "No, Dr. Mire, this wasn't me."

"There must have been so many. Would you even remember?"

Her eyes narrowed. "I remember everything. Besides, your article talks about a woman, a young mother. I would never feed on someone like that."

Adam couldn't stop himself from laughing out loud. "A vampire with a code of ethics?"

"You can call it whatever you want, Dr. Mire, but it is how I choose to conduct my business."

"Did you try to find this other vampire?" Adam asked.

"Of course, but as you know, we are very good at hiding, even from each other."

"And now this vampire has come back."

She nodded. "There is something about the Chetniks' recent activities beyond their usual disaffected rumblings. It seems some dark intelligence is behind their movements."

"So, not only am I up against an ultranational paramilitary group armed to the teeth, I'm also facing off against a vampire."

"I never said you had an easy task."

"But how—"

She placed a hand on his knee. "Dr. Mire, you have had a long trip. I suggest you try to get some rest now."

His headache had progressed to a pounding at his temples. He wanted to stay, to learn all he could, but Elena was not likely to share any more secrets at the moment, and he could use some time to clear his head. Something about Elena's story nagged at him. Elena was a monster. She had murdered countless people, but from what he had seen of her, she was also careful, deliberate, controlled. He couldn't imagine her going on a rampage. If this mystery vampire had returned, then the chances of another rash of violent attacks like the one during the war had suddenly increased by an order of magnitude. The fear and mistrust would spread. In her words—*chaos.*

FOURTEEN

Mostar, Bosnia and Herzegovina
7 October 1999

"A VAMPIRE ATTACK," CLARA SAID, searching Arkady's expression for any indication he was being less than serious. "You want me to keep an open mind about a vampire attack."

"I know it's a difficult thing to accept."

"Difficult? Really? I'm not going to accept anything. This is crazy."

"But you saw with your own eyes the house in Thessaloniki."

"I saw shadows move, but admitting I saw something I can't explain and believing in vampires—those are two entirely different things. Besides, assuming it was a vampire, why didn't it attack us?"

He shook his head. "I don't know, but I don't like the implications. The vampire wanted us to know it was there. Otherwise it wouldn't have riled up the shadows so."

Clara's gaze darted around the room. The generic décor, devoid of any character, began to take on a sinister note in her mind, and Arkady's grave expression suddenly seemed menacing. "I'm going back."

She went for the door, but Arkady stepped in her way. "You can't."

"Step aside," she said through clenched teeth.

"But the Chetniks—"

"How do I even know you were telling the truth about them?"

"Clara, you saw what they did. They murdered someone in front of you and tried to kidnap you. Whether or not I can convince you to believe in vampires, I'm not lying when I say that you are in a great amount of danger."

Her resolve began to crumble. She still wanted to shove him into a wall, but she couldn't deny the violence she had witnessed.

"Clara, please," he continued. "We're both tired and hungry. Stay here and rest and let me go get some food for us. I want to reach out to my contacts here as well. If you're serious about leaving and giving up on finding Adam, maybe we can arrange to get you back to the States safely."

CLARA STOOD AT THE WINDOW surveying the skyline of the bruised city. Arkady had been gone for more than an hour. Her hunger clawed at her stomach, and she felt light-headed. She had found the refrigerator empty, not that she expected anything. The spotless shelves were perfectly in keeping with the soulless interior of the rest of the apartment. Likewise, the pantry was bare. She went back into the living room, straight to the couch, and picked up all the perfect, white pillows and hurled them across the room. When that failed to make her feel any better, she collapsed on the couch and buried her face in the cushion, trying to avoid thinking about the knot of hunger in her midsection.

Another half hour passed before she finally made up her mind. She couldn't stay. She had to find a way to get out of there. All she needed to do was to find a telephone. She could call her brother—he would help. But first, she had to find something to eat. There was an outdoor café on the ground level of the building across the street. Suspecting her credit cards would be useless, she dug into her bag only to find a few Greek drachmae. She doubted they'd take those, but then she remembered her coat. She had a layover in Frankfurt on her trip from the States. In one coat pocket she found some leftover German marks. They might prove more useful.

She stuffed them back inside her coat and left the apartment. Outside, the midday sun shone overhead. The café was busy. Most of the tables along the sidewalk were taken, and a small crowd huddled around the display case full of pastries. Few people paid her attention as she took a place in line, which she was grateful for, but glancing at the chalkboard menu above the counter sent her into a momentary panic. The writing was all in Bosnian. She hoped smiling and pointing could get her by.

The stout, middle-aged woman behind the counter moved faster than Clara thought she should be capable of. Wisps of salt-and-pepper hair escaped from the kerchief tied around her head. When there was only one more customer in front of Clara, her panic began to rise again.

"If you've never had *jabukovača* before, you should definitely try it. It's very good."

Clara stiffened at the sound of the voice behind her and

twisted her head to look at the café's new patron. A tall, wiry man with light-brown hair and a scruffy beard, probably in his mid-twenties, he carried an oversized backpack and was dressed exactly like any of the thousands of other backpackers she had seen. His demeanor, though, was far from that of the happy-go-lucky hostel dwellers. He looked haggard.

"How did you know I spoke English?" she asked.

He laughed. "Americans are always easy to spot, if you know what to look for, but I didn't need to use any powers of deduction, Dr. MacIntosh."

Her blood ran cold. "Stay back," she said. "Stay back or I'll scream."

He held out a pleading hand. "Wait. I'm not trying to scare you. I just want to help."

"You'll pardon me if I don't believe you."

"Nevertheless, it's the truth." He unshouldered his backpack and, reaching into a pocket on the side, pulled out a slender book and handed it to her. "Here, please. Take this."

Hesitantly, her hand closed around the book. "What is it?"

"Something you're going to need. And one other thing. You mustn't trust the Russian. His duty is not to protect you."

"I don't trust him," Clara said.

He raised his eyebrows. "Good."

He slung his backpack over his shoulders again and turned to walk away.

"Wait," Clara said. "Who are you?"

He left without answering. Clara slipped the book into her bag and watched him walk down the street until a barked request redirected her attention back to the café owner. She stood frozen for a moment, unable to respond to the woman glaring at her, when suddenly another voice replied from behind her. The woman nodded at the newcomer and went to the pastry display. Clara turned to her side to see Arkady standing next to her. He held two large paper bags.

"The *jabukovača* here is amazing. You have to try it," he said.

Clara waited while Arkady paid and the woman handed over the pastries and two cups of black coffee. He motioned to a nearby open table.

"Did I see you talking to someone?" he asked when they were seated.

"No," Clara said.

"That backpacker—"

"He was lost. He asked me for directions."

Arkady glanced sideways at her. "I see."

Clara bit into the *jabukovača*, which turned out to be some sort of apple Danish. Arkady and the mysterious man were both right. The unpronounceable pastry was indeed amazing. Meanwhile, the strong coffee warmed her from the inside, calming her frantic state of mind.

"So, what was your plan?" Arkady asked.

"I was going to find a phone and call my brother and get him to wire me money. Then I was going to the American embassy in Sarajevo."

Arkady sipped his coffee. "I wouldn't recommend that."

"Why not?"

"Do you honestly think any of your country's diplomats unlucky enough to get themselves stationed here are going to be equipped to handle vampires?"

She leveled an angry gaze at him. "They don't need to be equipped to handle vampires."

"So you're ready to give up on finding Adam then?"

Clara didn't have a real answer. "I'm not ready to give up on finding him, especially if he's in danger, but I never bargained for what I've been through in the last twenty-four hours. And there's still so much I don't know about you."

He took another sip of his coffee. "What do you want to know?"

"Who is the higher power you work for?"

"The Russian Orthodox Church."

"In the vampire movies it's always the Catholic Church."

Arkady frowned. "Proof that there truly is no justice in the world. Do you know how many Orthodox Christians there are? There's a world beyond America, you know."

"Adam used to say that all the time. So does that make you a priest?"

"Actually, yes."

"And your brother?"

"He was as well."

Clara smirked. "Do they give you classes in proper wooden-stake technique?"

Arkady huffed. "Clara, the monsters don't care if you believe in them. They'll kill you just the same."

Clara stared into her empty coffee cup. "What are you planning to do now that we're here?"

"There's a reason we're in Mostar," Arkady replied. "There was … an incident a few days ago that may be related to what's going on. I'm here to see what I can uncover. I also made some inquiries today while I was out. The Chetniks' little stunt yesterday in Thessaloniki is having some repercussions. Police agencies all over Eastern Europe are on alert now. If any of our Chetnik friends so much as sneeze, I'll know about it." He paused. "I also pulled some strings. If you still want to go, I think we can get you out safely."

Clara thought back to the last time she had seen Adam, the frown on his face he always had when concentrating. He was reading through a copy of an old, marked-up book, nothing unusual for him. He had barely spoken to her. Though at the time his ambivalence hurt her, she couldn't say she didn't have her own obsessions. "I can't give up on Adam yet."

Arkady nodded. "I think for the rest of the day we should both try to rest. I have an appointment to keep tomorrow morning. It shouldn't take long, though."

"I want to come with you."

"Clara, you can't."

"I don't want to stay by myself anymore. And I hate feeling useless. Maybe I can help."

Arkady eyed her. "What can you do?"

She shrugged. "You never know. I *am* a psychiatrist."

"So that's what kind of doctor you are? I had assumed you were an academic like Adam."

"Maybe you shouldn't be so quick to judge."

He sighed. "Fine. There's not much you don't already know anyway."

Clara smiled, but the words of the backpacker remained in the back of her mind.

You mustn't trust the Russian.

FIFTEEN

Sarajevo, Bosnia and Herzegovina
8 October 1999

THE SUN WAS ALREADY HIGH in the sky by the time Adam left the small hotel on Titova Street where Elena, true to her word, had arranged a room. She'd even gone to the trouble of getting him toiletries and a few changes of clothes, again courtesy of Bogdan's visit to his apartment in Prague. When he had arrived the previous evening, he had collapsed immediately on the bed, the last part of his conversation with Elena still echoing in his head. When he woke up, he found someone had slipped a note under his door, a small slip of paper bearing an address and nothing else. Once he'd showered and eaten breakfast at the café downstairs, he called a taxi. The address wound up being in the New City, at an abandoned construction site surrounded by a high wooden fence. Adam walked the perimeter, searching for any reason he might have been directed there.

More than once he wondered what he was doing there

at all. He should have just found a way to get back to Prague, but he knew it wouldn't be that easy. Elena was right. Someone would come for him eventually. He had convinced himself he could make a new life, but it was all play-acting. Everything would have come to an end sooner or later.

After only a few minutes, he spotted a person across the street, a tall man with a buzz cut and a tattoo peeking out from underneath the collar of his shirt. A Chetnik. As Adam kept walking, he picked more suspicious figures out of the crowd. All young men with short military-style haircuts or shaved heads, all with tattoos. Every few minutes, he would pass by one of them. Interestingly enough, they didn't seem to be paying much attention to him. Rather, they all seemed to be focused on the construction site itself. Just in case, he pulled the collar of his jacket up around his face.

As he rounded the corner onto a street with much less traffic, Adam noticed a section of the fence that was lower than the rest. He glanced around, then jumped up and managed to grasp the top of the fence with his fingertips. With some effort, he lifted himself over and landed on the other side. When he turned around, he faced a scene that would have been the perfect setting for a horror movie. The rust-colored metal skeleton of a building pushed up through the ground, stopping abruptly after only a few stories. Other debris scattered the site—metal beams, plywood, bags of cement. Strangely enough, nature had begun to reclaim the spot there in the middle of the city. Grass grew among the metal columns. Saplings pushed out of the ground here and there. Even the city sounds seemed muted.

Adam trod farther in, careful to watch his step. Whatever had the Chetniks interested in this place, Adam couldn't even begin to guess. It didn't seem especially noteworthy. Adam couldn't even tell what the building was supposed to be—an apartment building, a warehouse, an office building—it could have been anything. Now it was nothing.

At the scuffling sounds behind him, Adam glanced over his shoulder. Several of the men he had identified as Chetniks appeared over the top of the fence. As quickly as he could, he found a place to hide in the shadow of the building's incomplete form. The men fanned out over the site. Surprisingly, they didn't seem to be looking for him, but rather someone or something else. Still he didn't want to think about what they would do to him if they found him.

He ventured deeper into the structure, deeper into the shadows. Examining the building, he spotted other signs that the construction was halted hastily. There were abandoned tools, even a few hardhats. The eerie scene stood the hairs on the back of his neck on end. He decided he might have been too hasty in his earlier conclusion that there was nothing remarkable about the site. A lot of abandoned construction dotted the city. Somehow this site was different.

As Adam hid and waited, the air around him grew colder. A slight breeze picked up and carried with it whispers, but not from the Chetniks. The voice belonged to someone else and came from somewhere else. Adam couldn't make out any of the words, but he knew they were not kind and welcoming. He was thankful it was still daylight, though the shadows remained.

He clutched the rosary in his pocket. The voice diminished, but it didn't go away. The words pulled him toward the center of the unfinished building. Checking for any sign of the Chetniks, Adam left his hiding spot and crept deeper inside. His rosary wasn't his only weapon. He ran his fingers across the front of his jacket and felt the reassuring bumps of a wooden stake on one side and his Glock pistol on the other.

The shadows were heavy in the center of the building, covering everything in a twilight gloom except where shafts of daylight pierced through the partially finished floors above. There Adam found what he hadn't known he was looking for. To most, the giant dragon with its tail wrapped around its neck would just seem like elaborate graffiti, but Adam immediately recognized the symbol of the Order of the Dragon, the same symbol depicted on Dracula's medallion. The red paint dripping down the wall even resembled blood.

It was a message, but for whom and from whom—that remained a mystery.

The cold tip of the knife in the small of his back jolted him out of his thoughts.

"Who are you?" a man's voice barked in Serbian.

"I'm nobody," Adam replied.

"Okay, nobody. Why are you here?" the man asked.

Adam kept his voice even. "Why should I tell you?"

"Because I have the knife."

The corner of Adam's mouth twitched. He spun around, grabbing the arm that held the knife and slamming a knee into his would-be attacker's groin. The man went sprawling onto the ground. Adam twisted the man's arm behind his back until his wrist popped and he let go of the knife. Adam snatched it up and held the blade before him. The man tried to stand, but let out a cry as he attempted to put weight on his broken wrist. Adam drew his

Glock, but it seemed all the man could do was sit and rock, cradling his useless hand. Adam took a closer look. His would-be attacker, barely out of his teens, was hardly a man at all. The shaved head and the tattoos told Adam what else he needed to know.

"You're a Chetnik," he said.

The man glared at him.

"Did you make this symbol?" Adam asked.

The Chetnik still didn't answer.

Adam sighed. "Do I need to remind you who has the gun? I'll ask again. Did you make this symbol?"

The Chetnik shook his head.

"Do you know who did?"

The young man shook his head again.

Just then, Adam heard a short gasp from behind him. The Chetnik heard it as well. Adam risked a glance over his shoulder, but couldn't see anything.

He looked back toward the Chetnik. "My apologies, but I can't exactly let you go."

He stepped forward and slammed the butt of his pistol into the back of the man's head. The Chetnik crumpled to the ground, unconscious. With the Glock still drawn, Adam made his way out of the building. He found the body by a pile of cement bags he had passed when he entered. Another Chetnik, the first one he had spotted, the one with a buzz cut. Blood pooled around his head from the gash in his throat. Adam swore as he scanned the construction site, but he couldn't see anyone else. By then it was late afternoon, and the sun was slipping lower in the sky. He dashed across the open space to the fence. Reluctantly he reholstered his gun and climbed over. Three blocks away he hailed a cab. He needed answers, and only one person had them.

SIXTEEN

Sarajevo, Bosnia and Herzegovina
8 October 1999

ELENA'S APARTMENT BUILDING WAS A concrete-slab eyesore left over from the heady days when there was still optimism that the Communist dream would come true—even if that optimism was state-mandated. Stark and cold, the grey façade was the ideal of conformity. The only thing that probably differentiated Elena's apartment from the ninety-nine others in the building was the crack in the plaster wall. Bogdan, hair disheveled and wearing only a pair of sweatpants, let Adam inside. Without saying a word, he went back into the bedroom. A few minutes later he came out, fully dressed. He glared at Adam one last time for good measure and left the apartment.

Seconds later, Elena appeared, looking as if she had just stepped off a photo shoot. Unlike before, she wore her hair down, her raven curls falling past her shoulders. Her simple grey skirt and white blouse drew attention to the curves of her body while still leaving something to the imagination. She smiled at him, and for all he could tell it was actually genuine.

"You came back," she said.

"I didn't have much of a choice."

"Nonsense." She entered the room and sat in the chair opposite him, her every move grace itself. Adam couldn't stop watching her. "You always have a choice."

"But you knew I'd come back, after what I saw today. You knew I'd have questions and that I wouldn't be able stop until I had answers."

She laughed. "What did you see today, Dr. Mire?"

"I went to the address you gave me—the construction site. The image spray-painted on the wall. You knew it was there. You wanted me to see it."

"I thought you'd prefer to explore during the day."

"When did you discover it?"

"A little over a week ago."

"How?"

"I was … out. I walked past a bar just in time to watch a man scream at his girlfriend and slap her across the face. He stalked away from her, leaving her sitting on the street, sobbing, a purple bruise blooming around her right eye. She yelled after him, begging him to at least give her money for a bus ride home. He didn't respond. He didn't even look back."

"And you decided you were going to teach him a lesson."

"I followed him for a few blocks. His path took him past the construction site. I drew closer, ready to 'teach him a lesson' as you say, but then I heard a voice coming from inside the site."

"I'd expect that to happen fairly often. You deal in

whispers and shadows after all."

"The voice said my name."

"Interesting," Adam said.

"Disconcerting," she corrected. "I broke off my hunt and went looking for the source of the voice."

"But you found the symbol instead."

"And more. Someone else was there."

He raised an eyebrow. "You saw someone?"

"Felt. Another vampire. I'm certain of it."

"What did you do?" Adam asked.

"I left. I found the man I'd been following, and I taught him his lesson."

"That's rather anticlimactic."

"But prudent. Whatever was there that night was dark and dangerous, and I had no idea what it was. I had no intention of confronting something I knew nothing about."

"What was located at that site before?"

She shrugged. "A block of townhouses. Nothing remarkable."

"But why would Dracula's symbol show up here? And why now?"

"Questions I need your help to answer, Dr. Mire."

"I'm starting to take a strong dislike to these intrigues."

She chuckled. "Intrigues made this city. Trust me, I would like nothing more than to leave well enough alone. I have all I need. I'm not interested in upsetting the status quo—but no one can have the medallion."

"Are you sure you don't want it for yourself?"

She shot him a withering glare. "What good would it do me?"

"It might lead you to Dracula."

She pursed her lips. "I don't care about him. He can stay wherever he has gone."

Her reply was not the reaction Adam had expected. "Really, now? That's a little surprising."

"It wouldn't be if you knew the entire story."

"Then tell me."

She smiled again, showing her teeth.

SEVENTEEN

Gračanica, Kosovo
21 September 1689 Old Style

STJEPAN APPEARED AGAIN THAT MORNING underneath the oak tree. This time he held the reins of a horse.

"He is beautiful," Elena said as she pet the chestnut flank of the animal. "Where did you get him?"

"He belongs to the monastery," Stjepan replied.

"He would demand quite a bit of coin if you wanted to sell him."

Stjepan shook his head. "He's a good workhorse. Besides, we have little use for money."

"Yours sounds like a nice fantasy to live in."

His eyes narrowed, but there was a hint of a smile at the corners of his mouth. "It is, most of the time."

He climbed on the horse's back and then helped Elena up.

"Where are we going?" she asked.

"I'm not sure. In my dream I saw a road I think is near the monastery, but I don't know exactly where. I thought we would try first looking to the north, on the approach from Priština."

The horse ambled down the path that led away from Marija's house. Elena held onto Stjepan's waist.

"Are you allowed to ride horseback with an unmarried woman?" Elena asked.

"I don't believe the others would approve," Stjepan said, "but they don't know."

"How long have you lived at the monastery?"

"My mother put me in the care of the monks when I was still a boy. She was extremely devout. She thought that growing up in the monastery would help to suppress my father's nature in me."

"Has it?"

"I am grateful to the monks who raised me for the lessons they've taught me, but I can't deny that I'm different. Even when I was younger, I knew. I was twice as strong as the other boys. I could run for miles without getting tired. Even now I need only one or two hours of sleep in a night. And I can see in the dark." He paused. "Yet every time I asked questions, I was met with silence—or worse yet, extra chores."

"How did you learn about ... what you are then?"

"The monastery has a library, but the books there go beyond subjects the Church would approve of. I used to sneak out at night when everyone else was asleep and look through the books on history and superstitions, trying to find something, anything that could explain what I was. During those long nights I learned about all the different names for the creature called the vampire, the creature my father was. And the books also taught me something else—

all the ways to destroy them."

"How many vampires have you killed?"

"None."

Elena frowned. "None? Then how do you know you can?"

"Because I'm the only one who can. Only I have the speed, the strength, and the stamina to stop them. It's my calling, and God doesn't call us to do things without giving us the tools to do them. When the time comes, I trust I will know what to do."

Elena didn't respond. She wished she could afford to have the same faith.

For the next hour or so, they explored the roads around the monastery. The steady gait of the horse and the easy, rolling terrain threatened to lull her to sleep. Elena pulled her arms tighter around Stjepan's waist. The roads took them past open fields lined with low stone walls, over rushing streams, and through the woods where the leaves of the trees were starting to turn red, gold, and orange. Elena had spent her entire life within just a few miles of the monastery, and yet she found herself taking in every sight, every sound as if it were new to her. As they traveled through a heavily wooded area where the road narrowed to little more than a track, Stjepan signaled for the horse to come to a halt.

"Here," he said. "My dream. Whatever it was. It happened here."

He dismounted and then helped Elena down. The horse, which he tied to a tree, neighed quietly.

"What did you see?" Elena asked.

"I saw a man on horseback, a wealthy one judging by the ermine lining his cloak. By the way the shadows of the trees lay on top of one another on the path, I would guess it was late afternoon. The man's horse was extremely skittish. It whinnied nervously and started at almost every sound. The man seemed to be in a hurry. He tried to get the horse to move faster, but nothing worked. The lower the sun sank in the sky, the more anxious he and the animal both grew." Stjepan pointed to a hawthorn tree at the edge of the road. "A rook lighted in this tree right here and cried out."

"That's why you seemed so troubled by the rook when it landed in the tree above our heads yesterday."

Stjepan nodded. "It sounded like it said, '*Vuk! Vuk! Vuk!*' The man brought the horse to a halt. 'Who's that?' he called. 'Who said my name?'"

"Vuk?"

"It's a fairly common name. It means 'wolf.'"

"If a rook says your name, it means you're going to die."

Stjepan raised an eyebrow. "The man prodded the horse, but it wouldn't move. He swore, but no matter how many times he jerked at the reins or how many times he dug his heels into its sides, the horse would not budge. And then he saw something that drained the color from his face."

"What could that be?"

Stjepan scanned the area until he spotted what he was searching for. Elena tried to follow his gaze. He ventured off the road into the underbrush and, pulling back some branches, revealed the trunk of a yew tree. Someone had carved a symbol into the trunk—a dragon, with its tail wrapped around its neck. Deep-red sap still ran down the trunk like blood.

"This," Stjepan said. "He was so busy staring that he didn't see the hooded figure in black appear on the path in front of him. When he did, he yelped and fumbled to draw his sword. He told the hooded man to let him pass because he was an important man and would be missed should anything happen to him. The black figure remained still and silent. The rich man's resolve faltered, and he tried a different tactic. He said he was a religious pilgrim and was not carrying much of any value. 'Please let a pious man pass,' he entreated."

Elena snorted. "I've met his kind. I have yet to meet one who's pious."

"I don't think the hooded man believed him either. He didn't move from his place in the road, and a low chuckle rose from his throat. The rich man's anger at the thought of being mocked was apparently enough to overcome his fear. He challenged the hooded man to try to rob him if he intended to do so."

"A challenge I'm sure he regretted." Elena said.

"For a short amount of time at least. The hooded man leapt in the air and launched himself at the rich traveler with a speed I would consider impossible had I not seen it. The rich man screamed. I can still hear his gurgling cries as he died."

EIGHTEEN

Mostar, Bosnia and Herzegovina
8 October 1999

AFTER ANOTHER BREAKFAST OF JABUKOVAČA and strong coffee, Arkady and Clara set out on a walk through the medieval heart of Mostar. Arkady kept a brisk pace, forcing Clara to struggle to keep up. At times it occurred to her he might be trying to lose her in the warren of narrow cobblestone streets and sand-colored stone buildings.

At one point their path skirted the river, and Clara caught a glimpse of the scaffolding being erected to reconstruct the Old Bridge. After about twenty minutes, they came to a street lined with the same squat stone buildings but away from the more populated tourist area. Halfway down the street was a building with a door painted bright blue, the word "POLICIJA" written across the top in bold capital letters. Clara shot Arkady a puzzled look. He pushed the door open and held it for her.

Clara stepped into a small room, barely large enough

for the desk there, let alone the two chairs facing it or the portly man seated behind it. He pounded away on an electric typewriter, the rhythmic clicks stopping as they entered. He glanced up, the grim line of his mouth deepening into a scowl, and when his gazed shifted to Clara, an eyebrow ticked up. He grumbled something in Bosnian.

"Please, Vasilije, for the sake of our guest, could you speak English?" Arkady asked.

Vasilije's eyes narrowed as he scrutinized her. "Who is she?"

Arkady turned to Clara. "Dr. Clara MacIntosh, meet Police Inspector Vasilije Abramović."

Clara mustered a smile and held out her hand. "A pleasure, Mr. Abramović."

Vasilije glared. "Arkady, I tolerate you in my city only because I'm told I have to, but if you pull one more stunt like this, I swear I will toss you off a bridge." He pointed to the door. "Get her out of here."

"She's in trouble, Vasilije."

He snorted. "Aren't they all?"

"She's been through a lot in the last twenty-four hours. She was almost kidnapped by the Chetniks."

"And I'm guessing you swooped in and saved her. Very chivalrous. What do the Chetniks want with her?"

Arkady shot Clara a glance. "She's an acquaintance of Adam Mire. She's been looking for him."

Vasilije laughed. "Girlfriend, I assume? Well, I think we'd all like to have a chance to chat with your boyfriend, Dr. MacIntosh."

"Not to mention, when we were in Thessaloniki, the two of us had an odd encounter of a different nature," Arkady said.

Again Vasilije's ample eyebrows conveyed his surprise.

"You mean ..."

Arkady set his jaw. "She already knows."

"But it's okay, because I don't actually believe in vampires," Clara added.

He eyed her again. "Fine, but if anything happens to her, it'll be your funeral, too, Arkady. Do you understand?"

"Perfectly."

"Good," Vasilije said. "Have a seat."

Once they were seated, Vasilije reached into a drawer in the desk and pulled out a manila folder, which he tossed to Arkady. Clara looked over his shoulder as he opened the folder to reveal photographs of a cozy bedroom, complete with frilly pillows and paintings of flowers on the walls. The scene would have been downright restful if not for the mutilated body on the bed and the blood smeared on the wall. Clara had seen a lot of horrible things in her daily work, but with every successive picture she struggled more and more not to look away.

"His name was Georg Lazarović," Vasilije said. "He was young. He had only been with us a year, but he had a lot of promise."

"Us?" Clara asked. "You mean the police?"

"He means the network of law enforcement agencies in this part of Europe who monitor supernatural activities," Arkady replied.

"Monitor and contain," Vasilije corrected.

"Unless it's too big of a problem. Then they call in the Russians."

Vasilije's grimace grew. "Because that's worked out so well for everyone in the past."

Arkady grinned. "Think what you want. I'm still here to help. Tell me what happened."

Vasilije glowered. "It was a week ago exactly. The last

time anyone saw Georg alive was in a pub on Kneza Višeslava Street that evening."

"What was he doing there?" Arkady asked.

Vasilije shrugged. "Getting a drink after work, I suppose."

"So he wasn't there on business."

"Not officially," Vasilije replied. "Around eight o'clock he paid his tab and left alone. His wife found him several hours later when she returned with their daughter from visiting her mother."

Arkady studied the pictures. "So this is his bedroom?"

"Indeed it is."

"He would have had to invite in whoever did this."

Vasilije grunted. "Exactly."

"And I assume he was trained to resist psychic charms."

Vasilije nodded.

Arkady shot Vasilije a curious glance. "So why would he invite his killer in?"

Vasilije held up his hands. "I suppose that's what you're here to find out."

"Wait," Clara said, "are you talking about the legends where a vampire can't enter a home unless invited? You actually believe a vampire did this?"

"Isn't it obvious?" Vasilije asked.

"You're ignoring the obvious." Clara snatched the pictures from Arkady. "All the classic signs of a sociopath are here. A human one. No vampires needed."

Vasilije smirked. "Please elaborate, Doctor."

Clara laid out the photos one by one on the desk. "Sociopaths are narcissistic. They tend to have an overinflated sense of their own importance and their own intelligence." She pointed to one of the photos, a close-up of the blood smeared on the wall. "This isn't spatter. The killer painted what looks like some sort of symbol on the wall after he murdered Mr. Lazarović. It's a taunt. He thinks he's smarter than the police."

"Why do you say 'he'?" asked Vasilije.

"Statistical probability. Most sociopaths are male."

Vasilije crossed his arms. "What else do you see?" His tone was still mocking, but a tiny spark of interest flashed in his eyes.

"The violence inflicted on the body suggests poor impulse control, and the fact that the killer laid him out on the bed for Mr. Lazarović's wife to find suggests a definite lack of empathy—two more hallmarks of a sociopath. Humans are just as capable of being monsters. Why do you have to make them up?"

His barely contained contempt evident, Vasilije glared at her for almost a full minute before responding. "We're not making them up. I can show you proof."

"No, you can't," Clara said.

His chair scraped the floor as he stood. "Come with me."

Arkady jumped to his feet as well. "Vasilije, you can't be serious."

"As the grave, my friend. She wants to be part of this, then she should really know what we're up against."

Arkady shook his head. "No. I can't allow it."

"But I want to see his proof," Clara said as she rose.

Arkady grabbed her arm. "Clara—"

"No," she said, pulling away. "No more 'knight in shining armor' routine. Would you be objecting like this if I were a man?"

Arkady stared at her for a moment, then sighed and backed away, his hands raised. Vasilije retrieved a flashlight from the desk and proceeded to a door opposite the entry. He motioned for Clara to follow. On the other side of the door, a set of stairs led down into darkness.

"Watch your step," Vasilije said as he switched on the flashlight.

Clara followed Vasilije, with Arkady close behind. She could feel his glare boring into the back of her head. Within the flashlight's beam, Clara caught glimpses of dirty concrete walls covered in indecipherable graffiti, which struck her as out of place for a police station. She was about to ask Vasilije about the graffiti when he stopped abruptly. She ran into him, nearly sending them both tumbling down the stairs.

"Where are we?" she asked.

From somewhere ahead in the darkness, Clara heard something that sounded like a growl. Vasilije shined the light on a door. It was also covered in graffiti, but in the center a string of letters stood out that definitely hadn't been spray-painted by some extraordinarily brazen vandals. The letters reminded Clara of the ornate Cyrillic script in some of Adam's books or on the painted icons she had seen in Orthodox churches.

Another growl reverberated from the other side of the door.

"Something's wrong," Arkady said. "Clara, I need you to go back upstairs."

"He said he had proof."

"I am not going to debate this with you."

"And I'm not going back upstairs."

Swearing, he descended the rest of the stairs, pushing past her and Vasilije. "Fine, then stand back."

"What are you going to do?" she asked.

Instead of answering, Arkady charged directly at the

door. His boot hit the lock, and the door flew inward, colliding with something on the other side. He shouted in a language Clara assumed was Russian and held something in his outstretched hand. The narrow beam of Vasilije's flashlight revealed another person in the room, cowering on the floor, as if terrified. He had an unhealthy pallor, and his clothes hung in rags off his emaciated frame. Broken manacles encircled his wrists. The man was a prisoner.

Clara gasped, attracting the man's attention.

She had made a mistake.

He wasn't a man.

Fangs like a wolf's gleamed in the flashlight's beam, and the creature's eyes burned with a red light all their own. He rushed at her, moving faster than a person should. When he came to the steps, he lunged for her, his clawed hand coming within inches of her throat before Arkady tackled him and dragged him back toward the basement room. Still chanting in Russian, Arkady held aloft what Clara could now see was a small painted wooden icon. The creature screamed and tried to hide his face.

And then Arkady stopped chanting. He lowered the icon, and he waited.

"What are you doing?" she asked.

She could only watch in horror as the thing rose up from the floor, crimson malevolence shining from its eyes. Fangs bared, he threw himself at Arkady.

"No!" Clara screamed.

But the creature didn't rip out Arkady's throat. He stopped short, mouth agape and eyes wide open in shock. He staggered back from Arkady, allowing Clara to see the wooden icon protruding from his chest. Arkady had unfolded the icon into a stake.

Without warning, the creature burst into flames, like the vampire in the letter Arkady had read to her. The fire died just as soon as it bloomed though, and the body disintegrated into ashes, the manacles clanging on the concrete floor. Clara's knees gave way underneath her. She half fell, half sat down on the steps.

Vasilije turned around and knelt in front of her. "Now do you understand?"

She nodded.

"I'm sorry you had to see that," Arkady said.

Clara struggled to breathe. "Was that ... that a ..."

"Vampire," Arkady offered.

"Why was he down here?" Clara turned to Vasilije. "Did you trap him down here?"

Vasilije shrugged. "Better than him being loose in the city."

"And all you had to restrain him was a pair of manacles?" Arkady asked.

"No. We had him in a cage." Vasilije swept the flashlight to reveal a metal cage at the far end of the basement room. The door had been torn off its hinges.

Arkady clicked his tongue. "Clearly you need to rethink your security system."

Vasilije glared. "We had him down here because we thought we could get some information from him before we destroyed him."

"Did you?" Arkady asked.

Vasilije shook his head. "He was too far gone."

Clara looked from Vasilije to Arkady. "What does that mean?"

"Some of them, over time, become more animal than human," Arkady explained, "especially if they don't feed on a regular basis."

Clara peered into the dark basement room. "Any chance this was the one who killed your friend?"

"Not likely," Arkady answered. "He wouldn't have had the presence of mind to put the symbol on the wall or arrange the body."

"Not to mention the fact that as hungry as he was, there wouldn't have been much of a body left," Vasilije added.

"So are there more like that running around?" Clara asked.

Arkady's steel-blue eyes carried a conviction that unnerved her. "I'm certain of it."

Clara shivered and hugged herself. "This dangerous information Adam uncovered, it's related to something these vampires have planned, isn't it?"

"One vampire, actually," Arkady said.

Clara looked up at him. "What do you mean?"

Arkady cocked an eyebrow. "The symbol on the wall. Did you happen to notice what it was?"

Clara frowned. "It looked like a snake curved into a circle. Or maybe a—"

"Dragon?" Arkady interjected. "With its tail wrapped around its neck?"

Something registered in the back of Clara's mind, something Adam had shown her once.

"The symbol of the Order of the Dragon," Arkady continued.

The word escaped Clara's lips before she even realized she'd spoken. "Dracula."

NINETEEN

Sarajevo, Bosnia and Herzegovina
8 October 1999

STANDING OVER THE BODY OF yet another dead Chetnik, the gentleman swore under his breath. He knelt down and closed the man's sightless eyes with a gloved hand. He couldn't help but feel a step behind, a notion he didn't particularly relish. He stood again and strode across the construction site toward the half-finished building.

He didn't care that the Chetniks were dead. What bothered him more than anything was that he wasn't the one killing them. The timing was off. He had always planned to let the Chetniks lead him to the medallion before he took care of them. To have them being picked off as they were now, it wouldn't do. There simply wouldn't be any left.

His thoughts went to Adam Mire, the American, and his thoughts were less than charitable. He had helped Mire once, but since that night in Thessaloniki months earlier, he had spent time regretting his actions. Others may still have thought Mire useful, but he considered the American professor too unpredictable. And he hated nothing more than surprises.

But this ... this was different. None of the events of the last few days had any of the hallmarks of one of Mire's schemes.

As the gentleman crept farther into the abandoned structure, drawn by a force even he didn't understand, an image on a wall resolved itself. Despite the utter blackness of the night, he had no trouble seeing it, and the sight of the dragon painted in red on the wall filled him with a rage he hadn't experienced in a very long time. No one had the right to invoke the power of the Dragon's Son in such a way. He clenched his hands into fists and let out every curse he could think of in his native tongue—until a noise off to his right interrupted him.

Someone else lay on the ground. Someone alive. The gentleman smiled. The figure groaned and sat up. A young man. Another Chetnik. When their gazes met, the Chetnik's eyes grew wide in fear.

"Who ... who are you?" the Chetnik asked.

"Who I am is the least of your concerns," the gentleman said.

Without another word, he pounced. The Chetnik didn't even have time to move. The gentleman sunk his fangs into the Chetnik's throat and let the hot blood splash across his face. As always, the images flooded his mind. He had learned to block them, or at least ignore them if he wanted, but sometimes—sometimes the psychic link created from feeding helped in other ways.

Just as the Chetnik's heartbeat slowed to a stop, the gentleman saw a series of images that reignited his rage.

The dyed-blond hair and the blue-colored contact lenses might have been enough to fool most, but not him. The last person the unfortunate Chetnik had seen was Adam Mire.

TWENTY

Sarajevo, Bosnia and Herzegovina
9 October 1999

She was not as difficult to find as Adam thought she might be. Posing as a reporter for a German newspaper, he tracked Tamara Janković down to the café where she worked. She was the widow of Igor Janković, who was killed by a shell during the civil war. At least, the official report said he was killed by a shell. His name was listed in the article from the *Liberation* among the victims who died under strange circumstances.

It was one of those perfect October days—not too hot and not too cold, the sun shining out of a clear, deep azure sky. People were out, enjoying the pleasant weather, as if Sarajevo were a normal city. He spotted her, hair tied into a bun, wearing an apron and carrying two coffees to a couple seated at a table on the sidewalk. She lingered a moment to chat with them. She smiled, even laughed, but the crease in her brow and the dark circles under her eyes spoke to days of worry and nights without sleep. He took a table nearby. When she glanced in his direction, he waved to her. After she took her leave of the couple, she walked over.

"Good afternoon, sir," she said. "What would you like?"

He smiled. "I'll have a coffee. And when you get a chance, I'd like to speak with you, Mrs. Janković."

She paused and eyed him warily. "Who are you?"

"My name is Edvard Novak. I'm a reporter."

"What do you want to talk about?" she asked, her jaw set.

Adam didn't see any point in sidestepping the issue. "It's about your husband."

She tensed, drawing in a sharp breath. As the seconds ticked by, Adam watched her internal struggle play across her features, but finally, she exhaled.

"Not here," she said. "I'm finished with my shift in a half hour. Then we can go somewhere to talk."

"Thank you," Adam replied.

She left and returned with his coffee a few minutes later. For the next half hour he watched her attend the other customers. Occasionally she made eye contact with him and then glanced over her shoulder, as if checking to see if anyone was watching. Finally, she emerged from inside the café, a small satchel slung over her shoulder. Her apron was gone, and her hair, free of the bun, was pulled into a loose ponytail. Signaling to him with a quick nod of her head, she left and began walking down the sidewalk. A few seconds later, Adam stood and followed her. After a block and a half, he caught up with her.

"I appreciate your willingness to talk to me," Adam said.

She glanced at him. "One condition."

"Name it."

"You have to publish the truth."

"Of course. That goes without saying."

She let out a mirthless laugh. "That's exactly what the reporter from the *Liberation* said. And when the story appeared, it was nothing even close to the truth. Suspicious deaths. Mysterious circumstances. Rubbish, all of it."

"Then what *is* the truth, Mrs. Janković?"

"Igor was murdered. And I even told them who did it."

Adam stopped. "You know who did it?"

She nodded. "I do. His name is Dragomir Sokolović."

"Why haven't you reported this to the police?"

"I did. Nothing happened. That's why I spoke to the *Liberation*. Maybe you can do what they didn't, Mr. Novak. Maybe if you publish the truth, they won't have any choice but to bring Igor's killer to justice."

A pang of guilt tied Adam's stomach into a knot. "I can't promise anything, but I'll do my best. Why do you think this Dragomir Sokolović killed your husband?"

"Because everything was fine until Igor met him."

"Why do you say that?"

"Igor had dreams of being a famous filmmaker one day. He even went to school to learn about it. Mr. Sokolović encouraged those dreams."

Adam raised an eyebrow. "And you disapproved?"

"I wanted my husband to be happy, Mr. Novak. Of course I wanted him to be able to pursue his passion one day, but I've always been practical, and we had bills to pay."

"How did your husband meet this Sokolović person?"

"Igor worked at a bookshop near the university. One evening a few months before he died, he came home excited. He said a man had come into the shop just before closing, wanting to speak with him. He said his name was

Dragomir Sokolović. He had seen a few of Igor's short films at the university and was impressed. He wanted to work with Igor on a film project. He promised it would make Igor's name."

"Did your husband say what this project was?"

She pursed her lips. "It was supposed to be a secret."

"I take it that didn't sit well with you."

"Keeping secrets was only the beginning. After that night Igor was gone all the time. When he wasn't working, he was meeting with Mr. Sokolović so they could talk about this project. We had a few fights about it. If I had known …" Her voice almost broke. Almost.

"Did you ever meet Mr. Sokolović?"

"Never. I asked if I could, but there was always an excuse. It wasn't a good time. He had other engagements."

"So then you don't know what he looks like."

"Unfortunately not."

"Still," Adam said, "I'm not exactly following why you think Mr. Sokolović murdered your husband."

"I'm getting to that. About a week before he died, everything changed. Igor came home early. He was shaken. I asked him what was wrong. He said he didn't feel well and just wanted to go to bed. The next day he came home early again, and every day after that, always well before sunset. There were no more late-night meetings."

"But?"

She sighed. "I still didn't get my husband back, Mr. Novak."

"How so?" Adam asked.

She glanced around before leaning in closer. "You should have seen his eyes," she said in hushed tones. "There was something in them I can't describe. It was like he was being hunted. He was constantly jumpy, always looking over his shoulder. And he still wouldn't talk to me about this film project. That's what made the night he died so odd. He called me and told me he'd be late because he had another meeting with Mr. Sokolović. We fought again. I hung up on him. I found out the next day about the shell that hit the cinema on Radićeva Street, and that Igor was inside."

"It could just be an unfortunate incident."

"Then where is the body of Dragomir Sokolović?"

He glanced sideways at her. "With all due respect, Mrs. Janković, there is something you're not telling me."

She was silent for a moment. "I suppose no harm can come from it now."

"Come from what?"

"Igor was good at … procuring things. Before the war, he used the bookshop to smuggle in goods from outside Yugoslavia. After the fighting broke out, he turned to trying to get things past the blockade."

"And you think Mr. Sokolović was trying to get something smuggled into the city and turned to your husband for help."

"Smuggle something in, or something out."

"You think their deal went sour, and he killed your husband."

"I know in my heart that's what happened."

They stopped in front of a brick townhouse on a street lined with nice, upscale residences. There were even flowers in the window boxes, a far cry from Elena's apartment.

"Thank you for being honest with me," Adam said. "Is there anything else you can think of that maybe you found strange or out of the ordinary?"

She looked past Adam, over his shoulder. "Interesting you should ask. The police inspector who told me about what happened to Igor, he said something strange to me when he brought me back home from identifying the body at the morgue. He walked me to my door, and he warned me not to invite any strangers into my house."

"Do you remember this police inspector's name?"

She shook her head. "I'm sorry, I don't."

"Well, thank you for your time."

She nodded and smiled, though to Adam the smile seemed forced.

As he walked away, he took the tattered news article from his pocket. Elena had gone to the trouble of underlining the names of the victims she took responsibility for. The others she swore were the work of the other vampire. Adam folded up the piece of paper and put it away again. It had been his idea to try to find out more about the victims, a thin lead, but at least he was doing something. A part of him still recoiled at the idea of working for a vampire, but Elena's parting words still echoed in his mind.

You may very well find deals with the devil aren't so bad, Dr. Mire.

TWENTY-ONE

Gračanica, Kosovo
23 September 1689 Old Style

A WHISPER WOKE ELENA. IN the darkened room several seconds passed before she remembered where she was. She lay still, listening to the night noises, but she didn't hear the whisper again. She began to drift to sleep when the voice spoke a second time.

Elena.

She sat up, scanning the dark bedroom. No one was there.

Elena.

She recognized the voice. She pushed back the quilt and stumbled to the window where she could make out a vague figure in a monk's cassock standing under the oak tree. He didn't carry a lantern.

"Stjepan? What do you want?" she asked.

"I want you to come with me," he replied. "Something's happening at the monastery."

"What is it?"

"I don't have time to explain. I need to show you."

She joined Stjepan a few minutes later under the oak tree, having dressed as quickly as she could. Trouncing through the cold, damp grass to the monastery, Elena wished she had her boots. As it was, she was forced to make do with the slippers Marija had given her to wear, and they were soon soaked through. Her heavy skirt also thoroughly frustrated her after she stepped on the hem for the third time. When they reached the iron gates in the monastery's outer wall, Stjepan pushed them open just wide enough for the pair to slip through. He held an index finger in front of his lips and motioned for her to follow. They skirted the courtyard, staying in the shadows. Stjepan moved without a sound, and on more than one occasion he blended in so well Elena actually lost sight of him. She wondered if he was deliberately trying to hide himself or if it was an instinctive part of being a dhampir.

Stjepan came to a halt in front of a nondescript wooden door in the back of the monastery. Flickering light emanated from around the edges, and the muffled sound of voices carried through the wood. Stjepan placed his finger over his lips again and motioned toward the door with a jerk of his head. Together they listened. One male voice stood out. It spoke, and other voices responded.

"We die with Christ," the first voice said.

"To live forever," the others replied in unison.

From there, the call-and-response continued.

"Do you choose a heavenly kingdom or an earthly kingdom?"

"An earthly kingdom lasts only a little time, but a heavenly kingdom lasts forever."

"Our Prince chose a heavenly kingdom. We honor his decision tonight. Because of his sacrifice, Heavenly Serbia will last for eternity and its centuries."

"We will bring Heavenly Serbia to Earth. Now is the time."

"Fortunate were the twelve loyal lords."

"Fortunate will be the twelve loyal lords."

"All will be holy. All will be honorable."

"And the goodness of God will be fulfilled."

A momentary silence was followed by the sound of shuffling boots on a stone floor. The flickering light shifted, and the door opened. Out filed the men, one by one. Stjepan and Elena flattened themselves against the wall of the church. As they did so, Stjepan grabbed Elena's hand. Her entire body tingled. Her heart slowed. She was suddenly able to see as clearly as if the noonday sun shone down. She could hear every footfall as the men trudged away from the church, every rustle of clothing, every breath. She could hear the animals in the stables, the monks in their cells, Stjepan's heartbeat next to her.

Though she could have reached out and touched each man as he passed by, none of them noticed her or Stjepan. Elena counted nine, their solemn faces illuminated by the lanterns they carried. They all wore furs and jewels set in gold rings and boots made of fine leather. One of them was the man Elena had seen in the church a few days earlier. They continued their march toward the guesthouse. When they were far enough away, Stjepan let go of Elena's hand, and her world returned to normal.

"Who are those men?" she asked.

"I don't know exactly," Stjepan replied. "They all arrived in recent days. They're all obviously wealthy, and they all traveled here alone. It's been a long time since the monastery has had so many visitors, but I don't think they're here for spiritual renewal."

"What sort of chant was that?"

Stjepan shook his head. "No liturgy I've ever heard."

"Why did you want to show me this? What do these men have to do with the monsters that attacked my family?"

"The same sort of monster attacked the man on the road, the one I believe was headed here. I'm positive he intended to meet with these others."

"They said something about twelve loyal lords, but there were only nine of them. If he was part of this group, then where are the other two?"

"Maybe they're dead as well, and I'm afraid they won't be the last unless we—"

"No, not 'we.' I can't help you."

"Why do you say that?"

"I don't know these men, and they don't know me. They wouldn't care about me if they did. Why should I care if they die? Why do you care if they die for that matter? And if you've never fought a vampire before, what makes you think you can?"

"Faith."

Exactly the answer Elena expected. It disappointed her. "Faith is not something I've ever found to be reliable."

"Then I suppose I'll have to do my best to change your—"

He staggered and placed a hand on the wall of the church for support. His eyes lost focus, and his jaw went slack.

"Stjepan?" Elena asked. "Stjepan, what's wrong?"

He blinked. "Oh, God, no. Not here. How can that be?"

"What are you talking about?"

He didn't answer. Instead, he took off in a dead run in

the same direction the men had gone. Elena chased after him as fast as she could, again cursing her long skirt. When she caught up with Stjepan, she found him staring at the trunk of a yew tree at the edge of the courtyard. Carved into the bark was the same symbol as the one carved into the yew tree in the forest by the road, where the wealthy traveler had met his end. Again it seemed to be some kind of serpent or salamander with its body curved into a circle so that its tail was wrapped around its neck. The red sap dripping from the gashes in the bark made it look like the tree was bleeding.

"This is a very old tree," Stjepan said. "It was here when King Milutin laid the foundation for the monastery."

"You had a vision, didn't you?"

He nodded. "The vampires are here, on the grounds of the monastery. I didn't think that was even possible."

The hairs on the back of Elena's neck stood on end. If what Stjepan said was true, they could have been nearby even then, lurking in the darkness, waiting to strike. She shivered and stepped closer to him, her hand brushing his arm. "What happened?"

Stjepan gestured toward the guesthouse. "I saw one of our pilgrims, a squat man of about fifty, approaching the tree. The glossy sap must have caught his lantern light. He reached out a shaky hand to touch the carving and immediately jerked away, the sap covering his fingers. Then a gloved hand closed over his mouth, and his lantern went out."

"So you don't know if he's actually dead," Elena said.

"He's dead," Stjepan replied.

"How can you be so certain?"

Stjepan knelt. "There's blood here on the ground. A lot of it."

"You can see it?"

He gazed up at her. "I can smell it."

Elena squinted to see the image in blood-red sap oozing from the wounded trunk of the tree. "It's not a serpent or a salamander. It's a dragon."

Stjepan stood to look at the yew tree again. "Does that mean anything to you?"

"Only that you're right. There is more death to come."

TWENTY-TWO

Mostar, Bosnia and Herzegovina
9 October 1999

CLARA SAT ON THE BED, studying the slender book the stranger had given her. The edges of the faded blue cloth cover were worn and tattered. Ostentatious Gothic letters spelled out the book's title: *The Giaour*. Inside, the pages had begun to yellow. The old-fashioned type reminded her of the grammar primer from the 1920s she had found at her grandmother's house once, and in fact the printing date was 1926. From her vague recollections of English literature in college, she knew *The Giaour* was an epic poem by Lord Byron about a love triangle between an Ottoman aristocrat, a Westerner, and a harem girl.

It also introduced Western readers to the concept of the vampire.

As she read, she remembered why she disliked it. The poem told an overwrought, melodramatic, sentimental story of betrayal and revenge. Even as a student, she had thought the whole idea rather naïve and silly. But Clara doubted the stranger had given her the book just because he liked it and wanted her to read it. Annotations covered every page. There were notes in the margins, underlined passages, circled words, and sometimes just circled letters. And unlike the poem itself, none of the annotations were in English. The language looked vaguely Italian, but having spent a college semester abroad in Italy, she knew it wasn't. She guessed it might be Romanian. Adam would have known.

The afternoon sun streamed in through the window. She had pushed back the curtains, skittish at the thought of not having a patch of sunlight available. Thinking about the sunset in a few hours tied her stomach in knots. The previous night had not been a good one. Every time she closed her eyes, she saw the face of the vampire in the basement of the police station.

About halfway through the book, the words on the pages began to swim. The warm sun conspired with her exhaustion to make her drowsy. Her eyes were fluttering shut when she heard a noise outside her room. She assumed it was Arkady, but then there was another noise and a loud crash.

"Arkady," she called. "Arkady what's going on?"

She jumped out of her bed, ran to the door, and was about to open it when she saw the smoke creeping underneath into the room. Yellow-white billows curled around her bare feet, and a caustic smell began to tickle her nose. Tear gas. She backed away.

From the other side came Arkady's muffled voice. "Clara! Stay back."

The door burst open, and Arkady rolled into the room, a rag over his face. He slammed the door behind him, grabbed Clara, and put a wet rag over her nose and mouth before she could say anything.

"We can't stay here," he said, removing his rag briefly.

"Where are we going?" Clara asked.

He shook his head. "I'm not sure yet. Please just get ready as fast as you can."

Clara slipped on her shoes and gathered up the few things she had, being sure to hide the book from Arkady as she tucked it in her bag.

"How are we going to get out of here?" she asked before starting to choke. The gas was thick, and the rag was drying out.

"We're going to have to go through the smoke. They'll expect us to climb out a window. If we do that, we're as good as dead."

"Who are they?"

"Who do you think? Please, right now just take my hand and whatever you do, don't let go."

Clara placed her hand in his.

"Are you ready?" he asked.

She nodded. He threw the door open again, and the thick yellow smoke rolled into the room. Clara hesitated, but Arkady surged forward, jerking her with him. She stumbled and nearly gagged on the gas, but Arkady relentlessly pulled her through the apartment. The gas stung her eyes and clawed at her throat. She couldn't see anything in the yellow haze.

Together they fumbled through the living room. Arkady opened the door, and immediately Clara could breathe easier, but Arkady didn't slow down.

"Where are you taking us?" Clara asked.

Arkady glanced back at her, a sly grin on his face. "They don't call it a safe house for nothing."

He led her down a narrow hallway that seemed to be a

dead end, but Arkady shoved a shoulder into the wall, and a portion of it moved. He pushed until he revealed a hidden tunnel. He pulled Clara inside and closed the hidden door behind them, plunging them both into complete darkness and almost causing Clara to hyperventilate. Arkady didn't give her the opportunity to panic, though. He seemed to know where he was going and dragged her through the black corridor. Just when she thought she couldn't take any more fumbling in the dark, Arkady opened another door, and daylight flooded into the tunnel. They were on the ground level in the back of the row of apartments.

"Now you see why I didn't want to park the car directly in front," Arkady said.

They sprinted around the side of the building and directly into the path of a man holding a knife. Clara didn't recognize him, but she didn't have to in order to know what he was. The Chetnik took a swipe at Arkady, but Arkady ducked and seized the man's extended arm, then flipped him over on his back.

"Keep going," he shouted.

He and Clara ran the rest of the way to the car. They were almost there when a bullet whizzed past Clara and threw up small bits of pavement from the road. Arkady was a few steps ahead of her. Just as he reached the car, another gunshot rang out. Arkady lurched and fell to the ground, clutching his leg as a streak of red appeared between his fingers.

"Arkady!" Clara called.

"My leg," he said. "I can't drive. You'll have to do it."

"Me? I can't—"

"You have to, or we're going to die here. Now help me into the car."

Arkady winced in pain as he stood leaning on Clara. He was all compact muscle and weighed more than she expected. They both nearly fell. She halfway tossed him into the passenger's seat and ran around to the driver's side. Arkady dangled the keys toward her. She grabbed them and shoved the car key into the ignition. Several people ran in the direction of the car, all shaved heads and tattoos, all carrying guns. Hoping she remembered enough about operating a stick shift from driving her dad's old pickup truck, Clara put the car into gear. It lurched forward, nearly hitting the car next to it. Arkady groaned and muttered something about lazy Americans and their awful cars.

Clara glared at him and pushed down on the clutch again. This time she was able to maneuver the car out of the space and onto the road. She revved the engine, and the little car sped away. In the rearview mirror she watched clouds of dust rise as the bullets struck the pavement where the car had been.

"Where are we going?" she asked.

Arkady ripped a portion of his bloodied pant leg off and used it as a makeshift tourniquet. "I haven't a clue."

TWENTY-THREE

Sarajevo, Bosnia and Herzegovina
10 October 1999

HER NAME WAS NATALIJA. SHE worked at a fashion boutique not far from Elena's apartment, the kind of shop that sold knock-offs of Western brands. Her sister was one of the victims mentioned in the newspaper article, the one with the young son.

When Adam entered the shop, she was helping a customer, and so he milled about, waiting for her to finish. He watched her out of the corner of his eye while feigning interest in a handbag. She was probably in her late twenties, a few years younger than Adam. Her short hair was dyed red, and she had several earrings in each ear. She smiled and talked to the middle-aged woman who was buying a dress for a dinner party, but the smile seemed forced. She could do little to conceal the lines around her eyes or the fatigued slump of her shoulders.

With the dress purchased, the woman exited the store, and Natalija approached Adam with the same forced smile. "May I help you?" she asked. "Are you looking for something for your wife?"

Adam grinned. "No, not exactly."

"Your girlfriend then?"

Adam shook his head. "Actually, I'm not looking for anything at all. I'm a reporter, and I'm writing a story about life in Sarajevo three years after the siege. Would you mind answering a few questions for me?"

Her smile melted. "I'm sorry, Mr. ..."

"Novak."

"Mr. Novak. I'm busy at the moment. I don't have time to speak with you."

Adam glanced around the empty store. "It will only take a moment."

She shook her head. "I'm sorry," she said and turned to walk away.

"I know about your sister," Adam called after her.

She froze. "Please leave. I don't want to have to call the police."

"Just listen to what I have to say."

She spun around, anger in her eyes. "I've heard it before. Lunatics. Yugoslav sympathizers. Russian spies. Everyone has a theory, but no one knows who killed her. I doubt you do either."

"What's your theory?" Adam asked.

"I don't have one."

"But you know something isn't right about the way she died, that maybe it was something the police weren't equipped to handle."

"There was a war going on, Mr. Novak. The police weren't equipped to do anything."

"I meant something else. Have you ever felt a sudden unexplained chill? Or felt like someone else was with you when you knew you were alone in your house? Or maybe for reasons you can't explain, you avoided driving on a certain street, only to discover later there was a fatal accident at the same time you would have been there? We've all had feelings like that from time to time. I'm willing to bet you had the same sort of feeling about your sister's death, didn't you?"

"Yes," she said quietly.

"Then please give me a little of your time."

"I ... I don't know."

"I don't want the people responsible for her death to be responsible for any others. Please. For your sister?"

She sighed. "What do you want to know?"

"Anything you can tell me about the days leading up to her death. Anything unusual, strange, no matter how inconsequential it might seem."

"There isn't anything I haven't told to others. My sister wasn't a saint by any means. She got pregnant when she was sixteen by some hoodlum. He didn't stay around once the baby arrived. It's probably just as well. I might have killed him myself."

"Was it just the two of you?"

She nodded. "Our parents both died very early. There was an aunt who took care of us, but by the time I was eighteen, she really couldn't anymore. We were pretty much on our own after that." Tears welled in her eyes. "I tried. I tried to be a role model for her, but I suppose I wasn't a very good one."

"Why is that?"

"She was the best mother she could be, but she was just so young. She'd never even experienced life. I didn't approve of many of her friends, and I certainly didn't want Max around them. A few days before she died, I found out that a few of these 'friends' used her apartment to buy and sell drugs. I confronted her about it. She said it wouldn't happen again. I told her she needed to stop spending time with these people. We had a fight."

"Was that the last time you saw her?"

"No. The night she died, she brought Max over for me to watch. She said she had somewhere to be. I asked her where, but she wouldn't tell me. She left before I could say anything else. Maybe the police were right. Maybe she was just in the wrong place at the wrong time. Maybe she saw something she shouldn't have. Maybe she just shouldn't have been spending time with criminals."

"But you can't get past the fact that her body was drained of blood, like some ritual killing."

She shook her head. "I just can't believe that though."

"Why not?"

She let out a chuckle, but there was no mirth in it. "Her friends were all too dumb to do something like that. I'm surprised any of them could remember more than their names." She paused. "Except for one …"

"Who was that?"

"I only met him once, just before the siege. She said his name was Dragomir. He wasn't like the others. He dressed in expensive clothes. He spoke like he was educated … and I'll never forget the look in his eyes."

"Why?"

"There was intelligence there, but something more. It was the same expression a wolf has."

"Can you describe him?"

"He had dark hair. He wore a beard. He had pale eyes, and kind of a hawkish nose."

That description was a familiar one for Adam. "Do you know what happened to him?"

"Like I said, I only met him once. I told my sister he made me uneasy, and she said he had left the city and gone somewhere else."

"Are you familiar at all with the Chetniks?" Adam asked.

She hesitated. "Every schoolchild in Yugoslavia learned about the Chetniks, Mr. Novak."

"But those aren't the ones I mean. Have you heard of them more recently?"

Her eyes darted back and forth. "There are rumors. But there are always rumors. The name comes up every time a mosque burns to the ground."

"Could your sister's friends have been involved with them?"

She pondered the question for a moment. "There were a few who were more bigoted than the rest. I could see them becoming involved in a group like that, if there was someone they could follow."

"Someone like Dragomir?"

Her eyes grew wide. "Oh, God, do you think that's what happened to my sister? Could she really have gotten caught up in a group like that?"

"I think it's very possible. I'm sorry. People who are full of disappointment are sometimes the easiest to take advantage of. All it takes is someone to channel that regret and anger."

The bell on the door rang, and another woman entered the store. Natalija smiled and waved. "My shift is almost over," she said. "I need to hurry home to Max. A neighbor watches him while I'm at work."

Adam bowed slightly. "Thank you for your time."

He turned to go.

"Do you really think it might happen again?" she asked.

He paused. "Not if I can help it."

TWENTY-FOUR

Sarajevo, Bosnia and Herzegovina
10 October 1999

"Dragomir," Adam said. "Does the name sound familiar to you?"

Adam sat with both Elena and Bogdan in the cramped apartment. Bogdan quietly sipped a cup of tea and glared at Adam.

"I'm afraid it doesn't," Elena said. "Bogdan?"

He shook his head.

"The description of him might ring a bell," Adam continued. "Dark hair. Pale eyes. Hawkish nose."

Elena laughed. "Honestly, Dr. Mire. Do you think he'd bother with any of this?"

"He's had five hundred years to scheme."

"It's not him."

"How do you know?" Adam asked.

"I would know."

Adam took a sip from his own teacup. "Then we're back where we started. With nothing to go on."

"Oh, I wouldn't say that. You have the name."

"And what am I supposed to do with it? Find the Chetniks and ask politely if they'll introduce me?"

She raised an eyebrow. "That's one idea."

"You can't be serious."

She glanced at Bogdan. "Bogdan, dear, would you mind terribly running out and taking care of those errands we discussed?"

Without saying a word, Bogdan stood and set the teacup down on the table so hard Adam thought it might break. He marched to the door, grabbed his coat from the hook, and slammed the door on his way out.

"Talkative one there," Adam said. "How do you ever get him to shut up?"

"You'll have to excuse Bogdan. He's the jealous type, but really you have nothing to worry about. His tough-man act is mostly for show."

"What did you do to him?"

"Nothing he didn't want."

"Somehow I find that hard to believe."

"You could ask him."

"You really expect me to take his word?"

She gestured toward the door. "He is free to go anytime he pleases. He just chooses not to."

Adam smirked. "And why is that, I wonder."

A hard edge entered her voice. "Maybe, Dr. Mire, he enjoys my company. Unlike you, maybe some of us don't prefer to be alone."

"I never chose to be alone."

"Didn't you? It seems to me like you've spent your whole life pushing people away, not to mention the fact that you threw away everything in your desperate quest for revenge. It's almost as if you're punishing yourself for something."

"Are you psychoanalyzing me?" Adam asked.

"It's long been a hobby of mine."

"Let me guess. You knew Sigmund Freud."

She laughed again. "Hardly, but I don't need his jargon to know you, Dr. Mire. Your pain is written across your face. Let go of the anger and the regret. You'll feel better for it."

"But what if there isn't anything to take its place?" Adam whispered.

"There isn't," she said.

TWENTY-FIVE

Gračanica, Kosovo
24 September 1689 Old Style

"TONIGHT I'M GOING TO STOP them," Stjepan said.

He and Elena sat together on a low stone wall overlooking the fields near the monastery. The day was clear and crisp with just a few cottony clouds in the sky. Stjepan's horse happily grazed a few feet away. They had spent the morning away from the prying eyes and ears of the monks and the so-called "pilgrims" at the monastery, discussing the strange ritual and apparent death they had witnessed the night before.

Their conversation, though, meandered into other topics. They spoke a little more about Elena's life with her family. She told him about her brother's illness and her strained relationship with her parents, but she refrained from discussing the blood feud. She asked Stjepan about his mother, only to learn little more than she had passed away not long after he came to live at the monastery.

"What makes you think they'll strike tonight?" Elena asked.

"I had another dream," Stjepan answered.

"What did you see?"

"Not very much, only a knife flashing in candlelight and blood on a wooden floor."

A shiver went down Elena's back, and she pulled her shawl tighter around her shoulders. Even though she and Stjepan were out in the open, in the middle of the day, she couldn't help but feel vulnerable.

Elena's gaze fell to the ground. "This is really not my fight."

Stjepan sighed. "I know. I was hasty before. I can't ask you to help. It's too—"

She held up a hand. "You didn't let me finish. This is not my fight, but I want to be there tonight. I want to help, because you're right. These attacks are connected to what happened to my family. I owe it to them to do what I can to stop these monsters."

He grinned. "Did you just concede I was right about something?"

She smiled back. "I wouldn't be so excited. I doubt it will happen again."

He laughed. Not for the first time Elena wondered what she was doing, if she truly believed the words she said or if there was some other reason she stayed at the monastery, when it would make more sense for her to go back to her family's farm and try to salvage what was left. Stjepan had shown her more kindness than anyone, but he was a monk. He had devoted his life to God, and she had made a vow to remain a virgin. He could never be a reason for her to stay.

THAT EVENING AS THE SUN was setting, Elena met Stjepan again under the oak tree. Unlike earlier, his expression was somber. "They've just closed themselves up for another meeting. We don't have much time." He reached into his cassock and pulled out two wooden stakes. One end of each had been whittled to a sharp point. "I carved these, one for you and one for me."

"This will stop a vampire?" Elena took one and examined the sharpened end.

"It should, yes."

"And what if we come up against something that isn't a vampire?"

"A wooden stake would do the job against a normal person as well, I would think, but if it doesn't, I have another plan." Stjepan reached into his cassock once more and produced a six-inch-long dagger. The end of the hilt was carved into a falcon's talons. "This knife belonged to my grandfather. It isn't worth very much, but it does have gold inlaid on the hilt. I know keeping it goes against my vow to rid myself of ties to the world, but I haven't been able to part with it."

Elena let out a chuckle. "Associating with women. Holding onto earthly possessions. You're not a very good monk."

"You're not the first to tell me that."

"But maybe it's impossible to be a good monk and a good vampire hunter," Elena said. "Have you ever thought of that?"

The corners of Stjepan's mouth twitched. "More than once. Come along. We need to hurry."

On the short walk, Stjepan apprised Elena of what he had learned about their new friends. "The man who led the chant was Vasilije Branković," he said. "He has an estate just to the east of here, and he donates a great deal of money to the monastery every year. Bartolomej Bogdanović is a merchant from Prizren. Jakov Vlahović is from one of the old families in Priština. The unfortunate Ilija Dragović came all the way from Peć. The others all have similar backgrounds."

"They're all rich."

Stjepan nodded. "That is one way of saying it, yes. They are also all powerful, influential men in their communities."

"Do you have any idea why they're all here?"

Stjepan drew his mouth into a thin line. "Not yet. I even asked Father Tomas."

"What did he say?"

"He told me they were here for spiritual enlightenment, just like any other pilgrim and that I ought to pay more attention to tending the garden."

"But instead of pulling weeds, you carved stakes." Elena laughed. "A bad monk indeed."

After peering through and checking to make sure the courtyard was empty, Stjepan pushed open the gates again for them to enter. "If anyone asked, I was going to tell them they were stakes for the grapevines."

"And what exactly is our actual plan for using these stakes?"

Stjepan's gaze fell on the church, its domes glowing a deep bronze in the last light of the day. "For now, we watch. The vampires won't do anything before sunset, and I'm fairly certain everyone will be safe inside the church. Once the meeting is finished and they all come out, that's when they'll be vulnerable."

"What do you want me to do?" Elena asked.

"I hope you won't need to do anything. Hopefully I'll be

fast enough and strong enough."

Hopefully. The knot in Elena's stomach tightened at the word. Stjepan was so convinced hope and faith would carry him through. Although she wanted to believe more than anything, she didn't know if she could. So she resolved to rely on what she did believe in—her own resolve.

As they approached the small door in the back of the church, Elena hesitated. "Wait. How are we going to hide from them and stay close enough to fight off vampires? For that matter, how do we hide from the vampires? We're going to be seen, unless you …"

Stjepan frowned. "Unless I what?"

"Unless you do whatever you did the other night, to hide us from them."

His eyes narrowed. "I didn't do anything."

"But I felt … You did *something*."

"What? What did I do?"

"You mean you don't know?"

"No. Tell me. Please." A hint of panic entered his voice.

"You were acting like a vampire."

His expression hardened. "I'm sorry. It's not something I can control."

"You don't need to apologize to me."

She didn't add that the experience left her breathless … and maybe wanting more.

They huddled behind a copse of juniper trees where they could keep an eye on the door and wait for the men on the other side to complete their ritual. The sky shifted from blue to indigo to black. Every night noise sent Elena's heart racing. A breeze caused the fallen leaves to skitter across the courtyard. Nearby, an owl hooted. In the hills, a wolf howled.

"They're near," Stjepan said. "I can feel them."

"Are we in danger?"

He shook his head. "Their attention is not on us, at least for the moment."

A few minutes later, the door opened. The men filed out, just as they had the previous night, only now they numbered eight instead of nine. Stjepan followed parallel, crouching low and keeping the juniper trees between him and the men, while Elena did her best to keep up. At the edge of the row of trees, he paused. Elena slipped her hand into his, and together they flowed into the shadows. It seemed as if her feet barely touched the ground as they crossed the courtyard in complete silence, every movement poised, deliberate, possessed of a fluid grace. The men stood out in detail so fine she could count the hairs in their beards. Stjepan didn't appear any different, except when she glanced at him out of the corner of her eye—some sort of dark, animalistic image clung to him.

Then Elena became aware of other dark shapes in the courtyard. They lurked at the edges, watching. Stjepan must have sensed them as well because he broke into a run, pulling Elena with him.

But no carnage befell the men. They disappeared inside the guesthouse one-by-one. Stjepan and Elena had almost reached the guesthouse door when he came to a halt and dropped her hand. The world returned to normal again. Elena glanced at Stjepan, his face illuminated by the light of the waxing moon. Confusion ruled his expression. "No, this is impossible."

"What?" Elena asked. "What is it?"

"They're gone."

"Who?"

Stjepan's gaze darted around the courtyard. "The vampires. I can't sense them anymore. They've vanished."

"Did we drive them off?"

He let out a short bark of a laugh. "Unlikely. I don't like this. This is wrong."

Stjepan rushed to the guesthouse door and threw it open. On the other side a set of wooden steps led up to the second floor and into darkness. Stjepan's boots made no sound as he bounded forward, taking the steps two at a time. Elena followed, even as she imagined the monsters waiting for them. When they arrived at the passageway at the top of the stairs, Elena heard two men's voices, arguing.

Stjepan paused. He glanced back at Elena and, smiling, offered his hand. Elena grasped it, and he drew her into his in-between world again. They stalked down the door-lined passageway, as silent as prowling cats, until they reached a door about halfway down. It was open a crack, and candlelight spilled into the hallway.

Through the gap, Elena could just barely distinguish the outlines of a cot and a chair. She also caught glimpses of the two men who stood in the small, dim room. One of them was the man she had seen in the chapel the day before. The other had a red beard that shone bronze in the light of the lone candle.

"It is one thing to speak of Heavenly Serbia returning to Earth," the redhead said, "but to predict that the Turks and their allies will be gone by the next full moon is reckless, especially when there is something obviously … wrong."

"That is Bartolomej Bogdanović," Stjepan said. "He is the one from Prizren."

The other man did little to hide the contemptuous smile on his face. "Wrong? There's nothing wrong."

"Vasilije Branković," Stjepan offered.

Elena recognized his voice as the one that had led the strange chant.

"But how can you say such a thing, Vasilije?" Bartolomej's gestures threw wild shadows onto the walls. "The Germans have not moved from Niš in more than a month. How do you know that their assurances are worth anything? And how can everything be falling into place when we ourselves are not whole? The messages we've sent to Vuk Djeordjević and Slobodan Ivanović have gone unanswered. And where is Ilija Dragović? No one has seen him today."

"We all know that Ilija was not as committed to the cause as he should have been," Vasilije replied. "He probably ran back to his farm to hide because he feels his own neck is more important than what we're doing here. Perhaps the others feel the same way. It doesn't matter. Let them cower. Those of us assembled here have the power to resurrect the Serbia of old. And when the Turks are finally gone forever, there will be fewer to share the glory. If you'd like to join them, Bartolomej, you may."

Bartolomej shook his head. "That's not the only problem, Vasilije. The marking they found on the yew tree, it looks like—"

"It looks like nothing. It's probably simply the work of vandals, Albanians, in all likelihood. Who else would be so base as to disregard the sanctity of the grounds of a monastery?"

Bartolomej held Vasilije's gaze for a moment, but then his shoulders slumped. "I hope you're right, Vasilije."

Vasilije placed a hand on Bartolomej's shoulder. "Of course I'm right. You'll see. The whole world will see."

The door opened, and Bartolomej emerged from the

room. Elena and Stjepan each took a step back, but Bartolomej didn't indicate he noticed either of them. He walked down the passageway to his own room and shut the door behind him. Moments later, a sliver of candlelight appeared around the edges. Images suddenly filled Elena's mind, the same scene Stjepan had described to her earlier—moving shadows, a knife flashing in the candlelight as it opened up Bartolomej's throat ... and blood.

Stjepan's eyes widened in a mixture of horror and panic. He let go of Elena's hand and dashed down the corridor, stopping in front of the door to Bartolomej's room. A small pool of blood seeped from underneath. Stjepan tried to push the door open, but something blocked it. He pushed harder, only to slip in the blood. On the third try, he took all his weight and rammed his shoulder hard into the door, shattering the wooden chair that had been wedged against it on the other side. Stjepan and Elena charged into the room only to find it empty. There was no hooded man. There was no body.

"They must be somewhere," Elena said. "People can't simply vanish."

Stjepan shook his head. "*People* can't, but other things can."

"I thought you said you couldn't sense them anymore."

"I couldn't. I still can't. But how else do you explain the empty room?"

Elena strode to the room's sole window and glanced outside. "It's small, but large enough for a man to fit through."

"What is this? Who are you?"

They both spun around at the new voice. Vasilije Branković stood in the ruined doorway, face red, brow furrowed, jaw set. His glare could have melted steel. The others were assembled in the corridor behind him.

Stjepan dropped the stake he still clutched in his hand, and it hit the floor with a hollow clunk. "Vasilije Branković, my name is Brother Stjepan. Please let me explain. You are all in danger."

Vasilije stepped over the broken chair into the room and surveyed the congealing pool of blood. "Where is Bartolomej Bogdanović? What have you done with him?"

"I haven't done anything." Stjepan raised his hands. "You must believe me. I was not the one who killed him."

Vasilije's eyebrows shot up. "Killed? Are you telling me he's dead?"

Stjepan nodded. While he talked, he inched backward toward Elena and the window. "There was someone else here. A hooded man. He slit Bartolomej's throat with a dagger."

"But there's no body here. And I don't see a hooded man. How do you know what happened?"

"I ... I simply know. Please. If you don't listen to me, there are going to be more deaths."

Vasilije's upper lip curled back in a snarl. "Liar."

"Get ready," Stjepan whispered to Elena.

"For what?" Elena asked.

In a blur, Stjepan leapt onto the windowsill. He pitched himself backwards, hooking Elena around the waist as he did and pulling her through as well. Together they fell to the ground, but instead of the bone-breaking impact she expected, Stjepan somehow landed on his feet with only a minor jolt. He set Elena down, and clasping hands, they fled into the night.

TWENTY-SIX

Vrbanja, Bosnia and Herzegovina
10 October 1999

CLARA STOPPED THE CAR IN front of a house she swore was abandoned. There were no lights on in the stone structure, and the entire building looked like it might crumble at any moment. Disintegrating flower boxes on the windows held long-dead plants, and yet ironically a tree had sprouted through a hole in the chimney.

They had come there at Arkady's insistence. He promised someone would be there who could help them. True to his word, a man emerged from the hovel before Clara could even kill the car's engine. He began speaking in rapid-fire Bosnian to her as she climbed out.

"English, you bastard," Arkady called from the passenger side, his breathing labored. "She speaks English."

The man stopped and peered inside the car. He was short, thin, and balding. A pair of round glasses was perched on the end of his nose. "Arkady? Arkady, is that you?"

"It is indeed. I hate to prevail upon you at such a late hour, but I'm afraid we didn't have any other options." Arkady winced. "You still remember how to remove bullets, don't you?"

The man sighed. "Some things never change I suppose." He looked back to Clara. "An Englishwoman, then are you, Miss ..."

"MacIntosh. Clara MacIntosh. And no, actually I'm American."

He raised an eyebrow. "Well, I wouldn't go about advertising that in these parts. Come, help me get this insufferable jerk inside, and we'll get him patched up. After that you can tell me all about how you were unfortunate enough to get mixed up with him."

Clara joined the man on the passenger side of the car. Together they helped Arkady stand and steadied him as he hobbled toward the house. Inside, the man turned on a lamp to reveal a warm, cozy interior, not the dank, musty rooms Clara expected. A small but neat kitchen stood to one side of a living area filled with dark wood and leather. Arkady limped toward an overstuffed leather couch.

"Oh, no you don't," the man said. "You're not getting your filthy blood all over my furniture again." He exited through a door on the far wall.

"Again?" Clara asked.

"We can trust him," Arkady said. "We've been through a lot together. Isn't that right, Stanislav?"

"More than I care to remember," Stanislav said, coming back with a plastic tarp and what looked like an old-fashioned doctor's bag. "And most of it your fault."

He spread the sheet out on the couch, and he and Clara helped Arkady lie down.

"Now, you know that's not completely true," Arkady said. "I can think of a number of times when you've shot first and asked questions later."

Stanislav scowled as he dug into his bag. "Out of necessity, old friend. You and I both know all I've ever wanted to do is retire and become a farmer."

"Sure, that's what you're doing here. Growing turnips."

"And cabbage, and carrots, and squash. It's lovely. And of course I've been diligent in ridding the whole area of vermin."

He and Arkady exchanged glances.

"Now, did you bring a bullet so you'd have something to bite down on while I do this?" Stanislav continued as he pulled forceps, thread, and a suture needle out of his bag.

"I did, but unfortunately it's lodged in my leg right now." Arkady must have seen the horrified look on Clara's face. "He's joking. Tell her you're joking."

"Mostly. All I have is a local numbing gel. I can't guarantee you won't feel anything." Stanislav put on a pair of latex gloves. "Now let's get you cleaned up."

He took a pair of scissors and cut Arkady's leg free from his pants, then cleaned the wound. He applied an antiseptic and the numbing gel before reaching in with the forceps. Arkady grabbed Clara's hand.

"You're lucky," Stanislav said, probing the wound. "The bullet's not that deep. You must have caught a ricochet."

"Funny how I don't feel lucky," Arkady replied through clenched teeth.

Stanislav didn't respond. Brow furrowed, he spent the better part of an hour fishing out the bullet, then sewing the wound closed and bandaging Arkady's leg. The entire time Arkady squeezed Clara's hand.

"I think you both need some rest now." Stanislav pulled

off his gloves and packed up his instruments. "You'll be fit to travel again in a few days."

Arkady shook his head. "Can't stay. We have to leave tomorrow."

"Of course you do. I shouldn't have to tell you what might happen if you tear open that wound again. Are you trying to bleed to death?"

"There's no way we can stay here," Arkady said. "I won't endanger you like that."

Stanislav shrugged. "Let them come. It won't end any differently from the other times we've faced down enemies."

Arkady frowned. "It just might this time."

Stanislav's eyes narrowed. "That bad? Really? Care to tell me what you've gotten yourself into this time?"

Arkady told him the whole story. He didn't leave out anything at all, not the bit about the strange house in Thessaloniki or the vampire in Mostar. Stanislav didn't register any surprise at those parts of the story either. Occasionally he glanced at Clara. From the way he looked at her, she couldn't tell if he was concerned for her or annoyed by her.

When Arkady finished, Stanislav was silent for a moment and then sighed. "Well, at least I can give you breakfast in the morning before you go."

Despite his best efforts to stay awake, Arkady drifted off to sleep a few minutes later. Stanislav motioned for Clara to follow him. They went through the door into the other room. Like the main room, the bedroom was small, but it had the same cozy charm. A small desk next to the bed held a reading lamp. An open book rested spine-up on top.

"I don't sleep much," he said. "You can sleep here tonight. I have a cot."

Clara shook her head. "I don't want to put you out."

"Please. You're my guest. Besides, you'll be safer in here."

"Safer? Do you really think something might happen?"

"I can't tell you something won't happen, so it's better for you to be in here, just in case. And if I were you, I would seriously consider finding a way back to America as soon as you can." He walked over to the desk and opened the drawer, reached in, and retrieved a pistol. At the door he paused. "If you need anything, just yell."

Clara stared at the closed door. She was exhausted, but she couldn't imagine she'd be getting much sleep. She reached into her bag and pulled out the thin edition of *The Giaour*. She opened it up near the end, and a loose piece of paper fluttered to the floor. She stooped to pick it up. Upon seeing the cramped handwriting of what appeared to be a letter, she nearly folded the piece of paper back up and tucked it away again, too tired to attempt deciphering it. The signature at the bottom changed her mind. It matched the printed signature on the frontispiece of the book.

Lord Byron.

And if the letter could be believed, Lord Byron had encountered a real vampire.

TWENTY-SEVEN

―⚇―

A letter from George Gordon, Lord Byron

Ioannina, Ottoman Greece
13 July 1809

I DON'T PRETEND TO UNDERSTAND this country. It is the living, breathing embodiment of contradiction—wealthy beyond belief, yet at the same time stricken with poverty; educated more than any Englishman could hope to be, yet ignorant of so many things; full of kindness, love, and passion, yet also cruel and merciless.

There are wild and wondrous things here, dark things, dangerous things. But what is life without danger? You'll think me mad for telling you what I'm about to tell, but half the world thinks me mad already. Maybe I am.

But perhaps the fact that I'm mad doesn't make what I'm saying any less true.

One night a few weeks ago, a stifling heat settled over the city. It was too hot to sleep, and so I endeavored to take a walk. There was no moon that night, but the sky was cloudless, and the stars illuminated my way. Down the path from the boarding house, there is a small communal garden. I had visited it during the day and had marveled how, when one entered, it completely shut out the city, and one could imagine being on the grounds of some country manor, or even in Arcadia itself.

As soon as I entered, the scent of jasmines filled my nostrils. I followed the short path around the manicured cypress trees to the center, where there is a bench for contemplation. My plan was to sit there and rest for a while. I thought perhaps the exhaustion would overtake me and I would doze, dreaming some dream of that faraway land. Perhaps Calliope would reach down from the heavens and brush me with her hand, granting me inspiration.

As it happened, she did, but not in the manner I expected.

I found the bench already occupied. A woman sat with her back to me. Her raven tresses fell past her bare shoulders.

"Excuse me," I said in Greek. "I didn't mean to intrude."

She turned to face me, and in that moment my heart stopped. I have never seen a vision so perfect. Her pale skin glowed under the light of the stars, and her green eyes sparkled with a vitality I have found to be so rare. Her smile sent my mind reeling.

"Nonsense. You're not intruding at all." She indicated the place next to her on the bench. "Would you care to join me?"

I did, taking no heed that I knew nothing of this woman. At the moment I cared only about getting to know her more.

"My name is George," I said.

"Call me Helen."

If Helen of Troy launched a thousand ships, this Helen could have launched ten thousand.

"Helen," I repeated. "That is an auspicious name for this part of the world."

Her smile continued to beguile me. "You're not from here."

I could only chuckle at her obvious deduction. "No, no I'm not."

"Where are you from?" she asked.

"England," I replied.

"You're far from home."

I shook my head. "Milady, would that I had a place to call home."

She cocked her head to one side. "Why have you come here?"

"I'm looking for … something. Inspiration, I suppose."

"A muse?"

"You could say that. This country, it begs for poetry. It's everywhere—in the wind, in the murmurings of the men praying in the mosques, in the noise of the marketplace—and yet I cannot find the words."

"Perhaps you're looking at the problem all wrong."

I regarded her with a sidelong glance. "What do you mean?"

She leaned toward me, close enough that I could smell her sweet lilac perfume. "Perhaps you need a subject a little more … intimate."

"Such as the Albanian beauty I see before me tonight?"

She gasped. "How did you know?"

"The pattern on your dress. It's not Greek. I've seen it before on Albanian peasants in the country."

Her cheeks bloomed a deep rose. "Can I still be your

inspiration?"

I reached up and gently stroked the side of her face. I know I shouldn't have, but in that moment her beauty overwhelmed me to the point I thought I might break down in tears. "Absolutely. You should be proud of who you are. I have found Albanians as a whole to be a fine, handsome race."

She clasped my hand and removed it from her face, but not in a reproachful way. She intertwined her fingers in mine. I didn't try to stop her.

"What would you write about me?" she asked.

I closed my eyes, and for the first time in a long while, the words came to me. "That you walk in beauty, like the night of cloudless climes and starry skies; and all that's best in dark or bright meet in your aspect and in your eyes."

"That is beautiful," she said. "It's almost a shame."

I opened my eyes and looked at her curiously. "What is almost a shame?"

"That no one else will have the chance to hear your words."

She seized my arm with a strength I never imagined possible and held me fast in place. I would not have been able to move if I had tried, yet at the time, for some reason, I didn't want to. I knew something was wrong, but I didn't want to leave her side. Even as her eyes changed from green to burning red and her teeth grew into sharp needles, I sat captivated by her beauty. The air around us grew cold, and I shivered. She leaned in as if to give me a kiss, but her mouth went to my neck instead. I felt the warmth leave my body when those needle-teeth broke the skin. As my blood oozed out, her tongue lapped it up.

It was an ecstasy I can barely describe.

I saw things. Miraculous things. People I've never met. Places I've never been. She was draining the life out of me, that was certain, but I only wanted more. As the beating of my heart slowed and my vision began to go black, I saw the darkened interior of a church. Faces leered at me from all directions. Frescoes, I realized. And on the stone floor at my feet, my own body, lying in a pool of blood.

Then everything went black.

When I woke up, I lay on the ground, looking into the night sky above, the smell of wet grass tickling my nose. My friend John Hobhouse stood over me, a torch in his hand.

"George," he said. "George, are you all right?"

I tried to sit up but found I hadn't the strength to move. "I may be able to answer you in a few minutes."

John knelt to help me up. "I woke up and you were gone. I came looking for you. I heard you cry out."

I didn't remember crying out.

"Who was that woman?" he asked.

"You mean the Albanian flower? She told me her name was Helen."

"Albanian flower? George, she was attacking you like some sort of wild animal. I don't know any other way to describe it. I managed to scare her off with the torch. You've got blood all over your face and shirt. My God, George, she would've killed you."

I understood what he was saying, but at the same time I didn't understand. All I could think of was how her embrace made me feel, and how much I wanted it again.

TWENTY-EIGHT

Sarajevo, Bosnia and Herzegovina
10 October 1999

THE SMOKE HUNG THICK IN the air above the heads of everyone gathered at the bar. Adam nursed his third beer, waiting for something interesting to happen. So far, despite the eclectic crowd of punk rockers, goths, and others of Sarajevo's fringe elements, he had not spotted anyone he would have branded a Chetnik. It was getting late, and this was his fourth bar. He threw some cash down, put out his cigarette, and stood to leave when three men walked through the door.

The one in the middle had dark hair and wore a long black trench coat. The one to his right had his shirtsleeves rolled up, revealing forearms covered in skull tattoos. The third one, the youngest, had blond hair and a wisp of a beard. He had a ring through the septum of his nose and at least three earrings in each ear.

Adam knew immediately they were Chetniks. It didn't matter what they looked like—tattoos or not, light hair and typical Slavic features or darker complexions—they all held the same hatred in their eyes and contempt for everyone who was not them.

That and they all carried guns.

Everyone else in the place knew they were Chetniks as well and backed away instinctively. The three of them strode to the billiards table in the corner. Adam collected his beer and followed. He found a spot close enough to listen to the conversation, but not so close he might draw attention to himself. They racked up the balls to play 9-ball. Trench Coat broke. Nothing went in, but he didn't set up anything for Skulls either.

"It's haunted, I tell you," Nose Ring was saying, his words slightly slurred. "My cousin used to work for the construction company until he couldn't take it anymore and quit. They never had anything but trouble there. Machines breaking without explanation. Weird shadows. People hearing voices."

Skulls snorted and leaned over the table to take his shot. "What are you talking about? They abandoned the construction because of the war."

Nose Ring held up a finger to the side of his head. "But what if that's what they want you to think? What if they're covering up the real reason?"

Skulls shot. The cue ball bounced off the 1-ball and sent it into a side pocket. "So are you saying Marko was killed by a ghost?"

"Not a ghost. From what I heard he'd been drained of nearly all his blood. A ghost wouldn't have done that."

A chill ran up Adam's spine.

"Gentleman, we're in public," Trench Coat said, glancing around the bar. Adam barely avoided making eye contact with him.

"So what?" said Nose Ring. "What's anyone going to do? Let them try to say something."

"That's enough," said Trench Coat.

They finished the game in silence. Trench Coat won in two more shots when he banked the 2-ball into the 9-ball and knocked it into a corner pocket. They racked up again. This time Skulls sat out. Adam maneuvered himself closer, pretending to be interested in the game. Trench Coat hit the first three balls in one after another before missing on the 4-ball. The cue ball came to rest in an awkward spot.

Nose Ring took some time to consider. He had just set up for his shot when Adam spoke up. "I wouldn't do that if I were you."

All three of them glared at him.

"Who are you?" Nose Ring asked.

"A friend," Adam replied.

Nose Ring eyed him up and down. "I don't need any more friends. Shove off. Private game."

Adam shrugged. "Suit yourself, but if you actually want to win, I'd bank the cue ball off the other side. If you angle it right, you'll glance the 4-ball and send it into the side pocket."

Nose Ring glanced at the table again and then looked back at Adam, who took a swig of his beer. The Chetnik walked around to the other side and leaned over the table. He set up the shot and tapped the cue ball with his cue stick. It barely touched the 4-ball, but the graze was enough to send the ball into the pocket. The cue ball came to rest squarely in front of the 5-ball.

Trench Coat frowned. "So, *friend*, what did you say your name was?"

Adam grinned. "I didn't. It's Edvard."

"And how did you get so knowledgeable about billiards?"

Adam downed the last of his beer and raised his hand to call for another. "Spending a lot of time in places like this."

Trench Coat snorted. "Funny. I've never seen you before."

"I'm new to Sarajevo. I'm from Banja Luka."

All three of them exchanged glances. Banja Luka, the capital of the Serb Republic portion of Bosnia, was the most extreme example of ethnic cleansing. Before the war it had contained a vibrant Muslim community. Now the mosques were destroyed and the Muslims almost all gone.

"Care to join us, Edvard?" Trench Coat asked.

Adam nodded and stood. With a few more suggestions from him, Nose Ring—whose real name happened to be Slobodan—almost won, but he missed on his first attempt to hit the 9-ball, and Trench Coat took the opportunity to sink it in a corner pocket. Slobodan tossed Adam his cue stick.

"So what brings you to Sarajevo?" Trench Coat asked as they racked the balls again.

"Work," Adam replied.

Trench Coat broke, but didn't manage to make any balls in. He raised an eyebrow. "What sort of work?"

Adam leaned over the table and knocked in the 1-ball easily. "Whatever pays the bills. I'm pretty good with a hammer. There's not much work in Banja Luka. Not anymore."

"No," said Trench Coat. "There hasn't been for a while."

"I figured I'd move on to someplace where my prospects would be better. There are a few places around here in need of a hammer."

Trench Coat smiled. It was not a pleasant smile. "I know exactly what you mean."

Adam knocked in the 2-ball. The cue ball came to rest behind the 9-ball, forcing Adam to puzzle over his next shot. Ultimately, he threw it away, hoping Trench Coat would make a mistake. The Chetnik hit the 3-ball in easily. The 4-ball and the 5-ball followed, but the 6-ball came just short of falling into the side pocket Trench Coat had aimed for.

"I will admit that work is not the only reason I came to the city," Adam said as he chalked his cue stick.

Trench Coat grunted. "Is that so?"

"I have a friend here. Or at least he was here the last I heard. His name is Dragomir. Maybe you know him?"

The three of them exchanged glances again.

"Can you describe him?" Trench Coat asked.

"Dark hair. Pale eyes. The last I saw him he had a goatee."

"I knew a Dragomir several years ago," Trench Coat said, "but he left Sarajevo before the war. I haven't seen him since."

Adam knocked in the 6-ball. "That's a shame. I would have liked to see him again."

Trench Coat's eyes narrowed. "How did the two of you meet?"

"We became friends while I was still in school in Belgrade." Adam took a shot. The 7-ball fell into a pocket. "He encouraged me to come to Sarajevo. He said there were plenty of opportunities for men like me here."

Trench Coat had maneuvered around so that he stood between Adam and the exit. "Men like you?"

Adam banked the cue ball to knock in the 8-ball. "Men who don't think it's wrong for Serbs to do what's necessary to defend themselves."

"I thought so," Trench Coat said. "You know there's a bakery not far from here in need of a few hammers. We were going to go later and remedy that. Do you want to join us?"

Adam knocked in the 9-ball without even glancing at the table. "I believe I would."

The three Chetniks, though, looked toward the door as another man entered the bar. He had a crew cut and hard blue eyes and the same general bearing as the others. He was also built like a prizefighter. The newcomer scanned the room until he spotted the group gathered around the billiard table. As he weaved his way through the bar toward them, something triggered a warning in the back of Adam's mind, but he couldn't place the man's face.

Trench Coat nodded as the man approached. "It's about time you got here, Miko."

"Something came up," the newcomer replied. He pointed to Adam. "Who's this?"

"This is our new friend Edvard," Skulls said. "He knows Dragomir."

"Edvard," Miko said, eying him. "Is that a middle name or something? Because I'm pretty sure your real name is Adam Mire."

Adam's world went reeling, as if a sledgehammer slammed into the side of his head. Miko was one of the Chetniks who had abducted Adam in Thessaloniki and who had killed two Hellenic Police officers. Adam tried to run, but Miko's hand clamped around his arm like a vise. Trench Coat's hand drifted toward his gun, as did Slobodan's and Skulls'.

"Let's talk outside," Miko said.

Outside, "talking" consisted of Miko slamming his fist

into Adam's stomach. Adam doubled over and sank to his knees, but Miko jerked him back to his feet and punched him in the jaw. Stars exploded in front of Adam's eyes. He would have gone down again were it not for Trench Coat, who propped him up so Miko could punch him a third time.

"I didn't think we were supposed to kill him," said Slobodan.

"We're not," Miko replied, "but no one said anything about making him wish he was dead."

Blood trickled from Adam's nose, and the salty, coppery taste invaded his mouth. "You're not going to scare me with that. Most days I already wish I were dead."

Miko laughed. "Oh, really? Then let's make this interesting. How about we give you a sporting chance?"

Miko nodded at Trench Coat, who let Adam go. Adam staggered to his feet. Surrounded and outnumbered, he let out a chuckle. A sporting chance. He had paid his way through college competing in the boxing ring. He was going to lose this fight, but he'd take down a few of them with him. Slobodan came at him first. Adam raised a forearm to block the swing and then threw a left hook that connected with the Chetnik's jaw. Adam sidestepped to put Slobodan between him and the other three. When Slobodan came at him again, Adam hit him with a jab to the chin that sent him to the ground. He didn't get up.

Adam wrung his hand. "Sorry, kid. Not your day, I guess."

Skulls leapt over the body of his fallen compatriot and threw a punch, which Adam barely dodged. Skulls couldn't control his follow-through, and he pitched forward. As the Chetnik struggled to regain his balance, Adam locked his arm around Skulls' head and slammed his knee into the Chetnik's stomach. Skulls crumpled to the ground, clutching his midsection.

Trench Coat charged at him next. By then the adrenaline had taken over, and Adam didn't give the Chetnik a chance to swing first. Trench Coat dodged the first three punches before the fourth one connected with his nose. Adam felt the cartilage break. Trench Coat cried out and stumbled backwards, clutching his face as the blood streamed down from his broken nose.

Adam took a moment to catch his breath and wipe the blood from his face. He didn't see the blow that sent him to the pavement. It felt like someone hit him with a bag of bricks. He tried to get up, but it hurt to breathe. Miko hit him again and again, and Adam could do nothing but lie on the pavement. When Miko slammed his boot into Adam's side, the searing pain engulfed him. Adam vomited.

Miko stood over him and pulled him off the ground by a shock of his hair. He encircled Adam's neck with his other arm, and he squeezed.

"Not your lucky day either," he growled.

Adam flailed and grasped at the man's arm, trying to break free, but the effort was futile. He couldn't breathe. Black spots formed at the edges of his vision and grew until everything was hazy and indistinct. His final thought before he blacked out was that at least Miko would catch hell for killing him.

TWENTY-NINE

Sarajevo, Bosnia and Herzegovina
10 October 1999

KEEP MOVING. NO MATTER WHAT, *keep moving. If you stop, you're dead. Don't choose the obvious path. Don't let yourself get cornered.* The training they had drilled into him came rushing to the forefront of his mind as he darted through the deserted streets.

Somewhere behind him, the shadow followed.

Danilo clutched a rosary in one hand and a pistol in the other. Both gave him some degree of comfort. He glanced up at the darkened windows of the townhouses he passed. How many of the people inside those houses knew the stories their parents and grandparents told them as children to scare them were real? As long as they stayed behind their thresholds, they would be safe at least. Unfortunately, he had no quarter, unless he could make it to the grounds of the church that loomed in the distance. The twin spires of the Cathedral of Jesus' Heart rose up into the night, nearly black against the starlit sky. Just a few more blocks, and he would live to see another sunrise.

In his mind, he surveyed the faces of those who had been in the tavern. Most of them were locals, and almost all of them were too drunk to be anything but human. He would have done well, though, to pay more attention to a few of them. A group of Russians, talking closely. A man staring into his drink, muttering under his breath. An angry German tourist definitely not enjoying his holiday. Any of them could have followed him when he left. Having lived in Sarajevo his entire life, he prided himself in knowing the maze of medieval streets that made up the Old City. He knew all the twists and turns, all the doglegs and switchbacks, all the shortcuts. He knew which alleys connected to other streets, and which ones didn't. Maybe he had become overconfident.

Not long after leaving the tavern, he had come upon an intersection, deserted except for him. Or so he thought. Out of the corner of his eye, he saw the air shimmer, like a mirage in the desert heat, though October in Sarajevo meant a distinct chill in the air. The shadows shifted, out of sync with objects in the real world. One shadow in particular stood out, darker than the rest. When Danilo blinked it was gone.

He wheeled around and fled, his heart threatening to pound out of his chest.

The church stood only a few dozen paces away when the darkness massed in front of him, swirling until it coalesced into an all-too-recognizable shape. A man dressed more for 1899 than 1999, wearing a grey double-breasted suit and riding gloves, stepped out of the dark. A streak of white ran through his black hair from his widow's peak to behind his left ear.

Danilo removed the rosary from his pocket and thrust it

forward.

The man continued to advance, paying the cross no attention. "Where is it?" he growled. "Where is the book?"

Danilo prayed Clara MacIntosh was somewhere far, far away with the book he had passed to her in the café in Mostar. "I'll die before I tell you."

The vampire laughed and took another step closer. "No truer words have been spoken."

"Stay back," Danilo stammered, gripping the rosary.

"I know about you, Danilo Grubelić. You think you're doing good in this world." He sneered. "You're accomplishing nothing."

"You're wrong. You don't have the book. That's something, right?"

"Something remedied very soon."

Danilo raised the pistol.

The vampire cocked his head to one side. "You know that won't kill me."

"No, but it'll hurt a whole hell of a lot."

Danilo fired three times into the vampire's head. With each shot, the vampire recoiled until he finally dissolved into the shadows. Danilo sprinted for the church. He was mere steps away from the church grounds when the vampire materialized in front of him again. His face looked like a bloody skull. Ichor flowed from a gaping hole where his left eye had been. His nose was torn away as well. Loose skin hung from his right cheek where the third bullet had ripped through, exposing his teeth.

"You bastard," he slurred. "I was going to make your death quick, but now you're going to suffer."

The vampire's remaining eye flared a brilliant red. Danilo raised the gun again, but the vampire swatted it out of his hand with enough force to break Danilo's wrist.

Searing pain shot up his arm as his useless hand hung limp. The vampire lifted Danilo off the ground and hurled him onto the pavement. The impact knocked the air out of his lungs and sent rosary beads skittering in a dozen different directions. Gasping, he struggled to get up, but in a flash, the vampire was on him. He picked Danilo up again, twisting his right arm behind his back until his shoulder popped out of its socket. The white-hot pain nearly caused Danilo to black out. The vampire threw him again, and he slammed into the brick façade of the adjacent building. Ribs cracked, and when he landed, his left leg snapped.

There was not going to be any sanctuary for him.

When he turned his head to the side though, his gun came into view lying only a few feet away.

Thank the Lord for small mercies.

He began to crawl toward the firearm, pulling with his good arm and pushing with his good leg. His fingers brushed the grip before the vampire slammed a boot on his hand. He knelt down and jerked Danilo upright by his shirt so that the vampire's grotesque, ruined face was only inches from Danilo's own, close enough that Danilo could have felt his breath, if he had any. The vampire's eyeteeth grew long and sharp.

If he fed on Danilo, the vampire would learn about everything—Mihai Iliescu, the medallion, the books, and—worst of all—Clara. He couldn't let that happen.

He yanked the silver crucifix off his neck and shoved it in the vampire's face. Skin and muscle and sinew sizzled at the touch. Shrieking, the vampire jerked away. Danilo lunged for the gun and snatched it up. The cool metal had given him comfort before. It gave him comfort now, only a different sort.

Danilo raised the gun to his own head, and before the

vampire could sink his fangs into Danilo's throat, he pulled the trigger. There was a loud bang, a flashing white light, and then peace.

THIRTY

Sarajevo, Bosnia and Herzegovina
11 October 1999

GONE WAS THE DARKNESS. DIM grey light filtered behind Adam's eyelids. His eyes fluttered open, and he found himself staring at a plaster ceiling. Gone was the cold, hard pavement, replaced by a warm, soft bed. Gone was the noise of the city, replaced by utter silence. And gone was the snarling face of the Chetnik as he prepared to end Adam's life. Instead, her face entered his field of vision, her midnight-black hair tumbling down around her shoulders, a smile on her deep-red lips—one that actually reached her brilliant green eyes.

He tried to sit up. Elena pushed him back down, gently, but with enough force that he couldn't fight her. "You shouldn't do that right now. You likely have a broken rib. I bandaged your side, but I'm afraid you're going to be sore for a while. Bogdan has gone to get you pain-killers. As you may understand, there is not much of a need for them here."

"What happened?" he asked.

"I saved you," she replied, "though it almost wasn't necessary. You were doing so well there until the end."

"You were watching me?"

"Watching over you. Making sure no harm came to you."

"What happened to the Chetniks?"

Elena chuckled. "They won't be bothering anyone anymore."

"What did you do?"

She arched an eyebrow. "What do you think?"

Adam's gaze darted around the room. Apart from the bed, there was no other furniture. The walls were bare, the whiteness broken only by cracks in the paint. "Where am I?"

"My apartment."

"You brought me all the way back here?"

"Where else would I take you?" she asked, a spark of amusement in her eyes.

Adam glanced down at the bandage around his midsection. "Where's my shirt?"

"I'm afraid you got a little blood on it. Don't worry. We'll get you a clean one." Elena's chest gently rose and fell as she ran her fingers through his hair, brushing it away from his face.

He grabbed her hand before she could pull it away. "Your hand. It feels warm. And you're breathing. You're using a glamour on me."

She jerked her hand from his grip as her smile melted. "I would not do that to you."

"Then how do you explain—"

"We don't explain, Dr. Mire. I will only remind you that I have just fed—and fed well." She brushed her fingers through his hair again, her smile returning. "But that is something you don't need to worry about now. You just need to rest and regain your strength."

"But—"

Elena pressed her finger on Adam's lips. "Listen, Dr. Mire, and perhaps I will tell you another story."

THIRTY-ONE

Gračanica, Kosovo
25 September 1689 Old Style

ELENA PULLED ON HER TROUSERS and then her shirt. Not without some difficulty had she requested her old clothes from Marija. At first, the old woman had outright refused, pointing out the pretty bright skirts and blouses she had given Elena to wear, but Elena persisted, and in the end Marija relented, though her scowl remained. When Elena finally received her clothes, she was surprised to find Marija had washed them. She relished the feeling of the clean fabric, knowing it wouldn't last long. She paused at the kitchen before she left, where Marija busied herself cutting vegetables for stew.

"Thank you," she said, "for the hospitality you've given me. I owe you a debt. Maybe one day, I'll be able to repay it."

The old woman didn't reply. Early in her stay Elena had determined Marija was deaf. She stepped outside and strolled to the oak tree where she picked out a small branch with a golden leaf and a cluster of acorns still attached. She broke it off and carried it with her as she made her way down the path that led to the main road, away from the monastery and back toward her farm.

LEAVES AND ASHES MINGLED IN piles in the corners of the rooms. Of Elena's family home, only the stone walls stood. The fire had destroyed everything else. Fortunately, the barn had not caught fire, and her neighbors, unsure if anyone might return, had tended the garden in her absence. She could survive the winter on her own and live in the barn until she was able to rebuild the house. In a few days, the sheep and goats would return with the shepherds from the summer pastures. The animals would keep her warm. It wasn't the best arrangement, but she could manage.

That night she sat hunched over a fire pit she dug several feet from the barn. She had just started a fire so that she could cook her supper when she heard the crunch of dry leaves behind her. She grabbed the knife beside her and spun around only to see Brother Stjepan standing there. He was not wearing his cassock. In fact, he was dressed in clothes almost identical to hers.

"What are you doing here?" she asked.

He motioned toward the still outstretched knife. "It's good to see you again, too, Elena."

"I thought you were another brigand. You're lucky I didn't kill you."

"I'm sorry. I didn't mean to startle you. Could you please just put the knife down?"

Elena did so, slowly. "Now, answer my question. What

are you doing here?"

"You left. You didn't wait for me."

"Was I supposed to wait for you?" Elena asked.

"I thought you might."

"Why?"

Stjepan took a deep breath. "I want to talk about what happened last night."

"You threw me out a window."

"I threw us both out a window," Stjepan corrected. "It was the only way."

"No one seemed terribly grateful for the effort you made."

Stjepan shook his head. "They don't understand. If they did—"

"If they did, then what? Are you sure these men are even worth saving?"

"How could you ask such a question?"

"They talked about the Turks being gone from here in less than a month," Elena said. "That's reckless—actually it's more than reckless. It's insane. They'll bring the Turks down on all our heads."

"But haven't you thought about what life would be like without the Turks?" Stjepan asked. "Every time I see the crumbling façade of the monastery, I think about how wonderful it would be if we were allowed to repair it. Also, there would be no more taxes, no more harassment, no more fear."

Elena rolled her eyes. "And you. You're insane if you believe them."

"Don't worry. I know the difference between what's real and what's a daydream. The Turks will never be driven out in my lifetime, much less in a month. Still, I think it is something *they* genuinely believe."

"What of it?"

"Their hearts are in the right place."

Elena snorted.

Stjepan glared. "Regardless, hunting down the vampires is still the right thing to do."

"The right thing for you perhaps, but not for me. I thought I could convince myself otherwise, but I was wrong. If I had stayed, if I had waited for you, I would have been turning my back on my own life, on everything I have worked so hard for."

Stjepan swept his arm around, encompassing the barn and the burnt-out house. "You mean this?"

Elena's face grew hot. "It may not look like much, but it's mine."

"I see you're dressed as a man again."

"By the oath I took I am one."

Stjepan crossed his arms and narrowed his eyes. "But you're not. Not really. I can't imagine you prefer to dress that way."

"Actually, I do, but it doesn't matter what I prefer. This is the life that has been chosen for me, and this is the life I must live."

"It wasn't easy to find you," Stjepan said, "and I've risked a great deal to come here."

Elena sighed. "Fine, then, since you're already here. What do you want to discuss?"

"I don't know how, but I know you saw the same vision I did when we clasped hands in the corridor. Did you notice the hilt of the dagger the hooded man used to slit Bartolomej's throat?"

Elena thought back to the vision of Bartolomej's murder, to the moment the dagger opened up the bright red line across his neck, and briefly, just before the hooded man's cloak engulfed the knife, the hilt caught the candlelight. It bore an eagle embossed in gold.

"An eagle," Elena said.

Stjepan nodded. "Do you have any idea what it could mean?"

Elena shrugged. "Any number of things. An eagle can be a symbol of power, courage, protection."

"Protection?"

"I'll tell you a story," Elena said. "There was a boy once who saved an eaglet from a snake. The eaglet's grateful mother blessed him with her strength and her eyesight, and when the eaglet grew up, he always flew overhead, to protect the boy. When the boy grew into a man, he became a very brave hunter and warrior, so much so that the people made him their king and called him the Son of the Eagle. The people became known as the People of the Eagle. We are those people. The eagle has always protected the Albanians."

"Are you telling me the killer is Albanian?"

"I don't know." She fixed Stjepan with a glare. "Would it matter to you?"

"It might help to explain why these murders are occurring."

Elena stiffened. "Or it might not. What reason would an Albanian have, any more than one of your own people? Don't tell me you believe what Vasilije said about us."

"Of course I know what he said isn't true," Stjepan said quickly. "The Albanians who visit the monastery, whether they're followers of Muhammad or the Roman Pope, are often more respectful than the faithful who come."

"We know the monastery is a holy place, even if it isn't one of ours."

"Still ... what you've told me, I suppose it could be useful information."

"I'm sorry I can't help you anymore, Stjepan. I'm sorry you've come all this way. I don't have very much, but you're welcome to share a meal with me before you return to the monastery."

Stjepan hesitated before he answered. "I can't go back."

Elena frowned. "What do you mean?"

"I left the monastery. After I took you back to Marija's house, I didn't return. Maybe it was a cowardly thing to do. Maybe I should have gone back and faced Vasilije and the rest, but I thought about what you said, about how maybe it was impossible to be a good vampire hunter and a good monk at the same time. There is truth there. I've been fighting my heritage my entire life. Maybe it's time to stop."

"Aren't you a little afraid to explore that heritage?"

"A little, but these dreams, I have to learn to use them. Otherwise, what good are they? And I have to learn how to fight the vampires. How to *really* fight them. The books were only able to teach me so much. The rest, I need to seek out elsewhere, and I can't do that if I stay at the monastery pretending to be a monk."

"Where do you plan to go?"

Stjepan shook his head. "I don't know yet."

"Do you have a place to stay this evening?"

He raised an eyebrow. "Are you offering me one?"

"There are rules that we live by. It would be disrespectful if I turned you away."

Stjepan grinned. "Thank you."

With his smile, Elena's pulse quickened. She looked away. "But as I said, I can't offer you much. Just boiled vegetables for supper, not even bread, and a bed of hay in the barn."

"It will be enough," Stjepan said.

They ate mostly in silence, sitting on the ground facing the fire. The world around them—the fields, the woods, the ruins of the house, the barn—it all slowly faded into blackness until only the two of them were left.

"Why did you come back here?" Stjepan asked finally.

"As opposed to staying at the monastery? I told you why."

"No, I mean why here? Why come back here? This is where you lost everything."

"Not everything. I have the land. I get what I need from it."

"But you must miss your family."

Elena bit her lip. "I do."

Stjepan leaned closer. "I would think being here would constantly remind you of what happened to them."

Elena took a stick and made a show of tending to the fire. "Not at all. Being here keeps me near them, and in a way, I'm keeping my promise to them. I'm keeping our family going."

Stjepan hesitated before he asked the next question. "Is that why you did what you did, for them?"

"Someone had to make sure we were all fed, but only men are allowed to own property or do business. My father wouldn't work. I became a man so I could do the things he wouldn't. It's not that uncommon among us, for a woman to do what I've done for her family. And someone had to protect Irina and Gjon from my father. My mother certainly wasn't going to do it." She stabbed at the fire with the stick. "She didn't protect me."

"Do you regret the decision you made?"

"It's done. There's no use wasting energy on regret. I saw what that did to my father. I vowed I would never be like him."

"What did he regret?"

"His life. All of it. I think he blamed himself for the blood feud that forced us to leave the mountains and move down here."

Stjepan frowned. "I don't understand your blood feuds."

"An outsider wouldn't," Elena replied, jutting out her chin.

"They seem so arbitrary, as if anything or nothing at all can set one off."

"That's not true. There are rules that must be followed in how a *gjakmarrja*, a blood feud, is declared, how it is conducted, and how it is ended."

"Is that what's happening at the monastery? Is an Albanian responsible after all? Has there perhaps been a blood feud declared against these men?"

"No," Elena said. "Outsiders are exempt."

"And who came up with these rules?"

"They're all part of the *Kanun* of Lek Dukagjin. He laid out the rules for how all of us should conduct ourselves, and not just in blood feuds, but in our lives—the proper roles of men and women, the hospitality we extend to guests, everything. He was the first to bring all the clans together. Before him, there was chaos."

"It seems as if there is still chaos."

"Only an outsider would think so."

When Stjepan didn't respond right away, Elena peered at him. He stared back at her, the firelight dancing in his pale blue eyes.

"You're very beautiful," he said, "even dressed as a man. It's a shame you can't live as a woman."

Elena bristled and silently cursed herself for letting her guard down again. "I can't break my promises as easily as you. I would be killed for going back on my vows. I'm letting you stay the night, but in the morning, I would like you to leave."

Neither of them said anything more as they both sat and watched the fire slowly dwindle.

THIRTY-TWO

Gračanica, Kosovo
2 October 1689 Old Style

ELENA WOKE TO THE SHEEP bleating in their stall. The sun had not yet risen, and she could barely see in the dim light. Still, she made her way to the nervous animals. She patted the muzzle of the one nearest her, trying to calm it. She couldn't figure out why they seemed frightened until she heard the whines and barks outside the barn. She peered through one of the slits between the wooden planks in the door to see glowing yellow eyes and flashes of grey fur.

For a long time, she listened to the wolves prowling around the barn. She expected them to lose interest when they couldn't get inside, but they didn't leave until just before dawn. Elena waited until the sunlight flowed through the barn's high windows before she opened the door and led her little flock up the path and over the rise to their winter pasture.

She met one of her neighbors there and asked him if he

had seen or heard the wolves during the night, but he had not. She returned to the barn, grabbed a rag and a water pail, and walked down to the creek. She set the full pail down behind the barn, where she couldn't be seen from the path, and stripped off her clothes to bathe. The cold water shocked her, but the more she dipped the rag into the pail and let the water run over her, the better she felt. Her muscles began to relax. She closed her eyes, and she took several deep, long breaths.

The wolf's growl sounded as if it came from right next to her. She opened her eyes and searched around frantically. There was no wolf, but still, she felt something or someone close by, watching her. Shadows moved at the edge of her vision. Leaves crunched. It could have been anything—the wind, some small animal, or simply her imagination—but then as a cloud passed in front of the sun, someone whispered her name. It was a man's voice, low and rough like a wolf's.

"Who's there?" she called. "Show yourself! Or would you rather remain a coward?"

No one answered. The sun emerged from behind the cloud. Elena was alone.

THAT NIGHT, AFTER ELENA PUT the sheep and the goats in their stalls, the wolves returned. She did her best to calm the animals once more, but she herself was unsettled. The wolves were also more active—growling, snarling, howling. The sheep and goats jostled one another. Their instinct was to run, but there was nowhere for them to go.

There was nowhere for Elena to go either.

In an instant, silence replaced the barks and growls, but Elena's animals failed to settle down. Elena had just sat on the hay-covered floor, trying to soothe the sheep in her lap, when a knock came at the door. Her blood froze. She didn't move. She didn't respond. After a few moments the knock came again.

"Please," a man called. "It's late, and I need a place to stay for the night. Is there anyone in there? Can you let me in?"

Elena didn't reply. She couldn't make her voice work. Gjon's words from the night everyone died came back to her. The monsters that murdered her family had posed as travelers needing a place to stay.

"Please," the man called again. "Is anyone there?"

If the monsters had come back, she would kill them. She grabbed the nearest weapon she could find, a pitchfork, and threw open the door. She thrust the pitchfork at the man standing there, the tines coming within inches of his face.

"How do I know you're a traveler and not a brigand come to rob and kill me?"

The man, though obviously shocked, didn't move. "Is this how you show hospitality? I'm not a brigand. I only need a place to stay for the night."

"Swear it," Elena said. "Swear you've never been here before."

"I swear to you I am not a brigand, but I can't swear I've never been here before. It has been a long time, but I was here once, before your family ever came to this valley, Elena."

She thrust the pitchfork at him again, forcing him to step back.

"Tell me who you are," she demanded.

"You may call me Lek," the man answered.

Elena tried to see his features in the scant light. He

was not very tall, but he was powerfully built. He had a full black beard and mustache and a hawkish nose.

"How do you know my name?" she asked.

"I've met you before. You were no doubt too young to remember, but I was a good friend of your father."

He must have been much older than he looked, if he knew her father before they moved down from the mountains.

"How is your father?" Lek asked.

"He's dead," Elena replied.

Lek placed a hand over his heart. "I'm sorry to hear that. Your mother must live every day with a broken heart. As I remember, she was very beautiful. I recognized you because I see her in you."

"She is dead also."

"I am doubly sorry then," he said, bowing his head. "It feels like the day your family left the mountains. Only then, there was the hope I might see them again someday. It pains me to know I will never have the opportunity."

Elena still held the pitchfork aloft, but she began to waver. Something about him made her want to believe him, to trust him. Also tempting was the opportunity to find out what her father was like before the blood feud ruined all their lives.

"I can only offer you a bed of hay," she said.

Lek smiled. "To my tired body, it will be like sleeping on down. I am grateful. Thank you."

Elena lowered the pitchfork, and let the man called Lek step over the threshold.

THIRTY-THREE

Sarajevo, Bosnia and Herzegovina
11 October 1999

SILENCE RETURNED TO THE DIM bedroom, and Elena allowed it to linger for several minutes. She looked away from him, a wistful expression on her face, but there was no way to truly tell what she was thinking. Adam studied her features—her narrow, slightly upturned nose, her small mouth, full red lips, her pale skin set off by her pitch-black hair.

He closed his eyes.

Hail Mary, full of grace ...

When he opened his eyes again, she was staring at him.

"Why did you come here?" Adam asked.

She cocked her head to one side. "What do you mean?"

"Why did you choose Sarajevo?"

"I like it here."

"A battered city, the capitol of a nation torn to pieces by hate and bigotry."

"It wasn't always so."

"I know. At one time it was a crossroads of culture. A mixture of East and West. Different cultures, races, and religions living side by side."

"It can be that way again."

Adam shook his head. "Not in my lifetime."

"I wouldn't be so certain, Dr. Mire. Who knows how long your lifetime will be?" She placed a hand on his chest. "You've got a strong, healthy heart."

Adam struggled to focus. "These brigands who murdered your family, could one of them have survived all this time? Could he be here in Sarajevo?"

She shrugged. "Anything is possible."

"I was able to confirm that Dragomir is involved with the Chetniks, but I didn't get the chance to find anything else out, and now I'm not sure what else to do."

"Maybe you've done enough for now."

Adam tried to sit up again. "What?"

Elena ran a finger along his jawline and down his neck. "Let me take care of you."

"I don't know if I can afford to let you do that."

She sighed. "Now Dr. Mire. After all you've been through, you should know that we're more than monsters. We care, in our own way."

She leaned down and kissed him on the lips. She tasted like lavender and honey. After a few seconds of ecstasy, she pulled away, but he cupped a hand behind her head, pressing himself to her as she sat up. The pain in his side was like being stabbed with a hot poker, but he didn't care. He just didn't want the kiss to end.

Just then the door opened, and Bogdan stepped into the room. He stopped and gaped, his eyes wide. Then his brows furrowed in rage. He dropped the bag he was carrying and charged at Adam, snarling like a wild animal. He tore Adam away from Elena and lifted him off the bed like a rag doll. A searing pain spread out from Adam's side as Bogdan slammed him against the bedroom wall, hard enough for the entire apartment to shake. He cocked his arm, ready to slam his fist into Adam's face.

"Bogdan," Elena said as if talking to a naughty child. "That's enough."

For the first time, it seemed, Bogdan remembered she was in the room. He met her gaze and, after several long seconds, let Adam go. Adam hesitated only to catch his breath before he bolted out of the bedroom. Snatching a coat off the rack next to the door, he ran out of the apartment, making a silent vow never to return.

THIRTY-FOUR

Vrbanja, Bosnia and Herzegovina
11 October 1999

CLARA WOKE TO THE SMELL of cooking sausage and brewing coffee. Her stomach rumbled, reminding her she hadn't eaten anything in almost twenty-four hours. She dressed quickly and peeked out of the bedroom to find Stanislav in the kitchen in front of the stove. Arkady was seated at the small table, a plate of mostly eaten breakfast in front of him.

When Arkady saw Clara, he waved. "Oh, good, you're up. Come, get something to eat. We're going to need to leave soon."

"How's your leg?" she asked.

"It'll do," he replied.

Stanislav snorted. "You'll be lucky if he doesn't tear the stitches out before you get to the main road."

Arkady glared at him. "It'll have to do." He turned his attention to Clara. "Do you think you're up to driving some more?"

Stanislav handed her a plate full of sausages and a hunk of bread. She tore into it without ceremony. "If you'll tell me where we're going."

"Sarajevo," Arkady replied.

The doctor stiffened. "Arkady, I really don't think—"

"We've already had this conversation. There's no other choice."

"You think we'll be able to find out more about what happened to Adam there?" Clara asked.

"I have some contacts in the city," Arkady replied. "I can ask around."

"Arkady, God knows I can't stop you from doing anything idiotic, but it's not just you this time. You're endangering her as well."

"I can take care of myself," Clara said.

Stanislav shot her a withering glance. "Can you?"

Arkady glared. "Please don't. I'd rather not have to kick your ass for being ungentlemanly to the lady."

"Arkady, if there's a vampire—"

"Then I'll deal with it," Arkady said. "Besides, it could have been pure chance Vasilije had one caged up in the basement."

Stanislav laughed. "You know there's no such thing as chance. I warned you. I warned both you and Kostya that it was a bad idea to go after Dracula's medallion."

"We had intelligence that Süleyman's Blade was going after it."

"From who? A green recruit."

Arkady balled his hands into fists. "Anna Fyodorovna had impeccable credentials."

"And look where those credentials got her," Stanislav replied. "Not to mention Kostya."

"Which is why I have to finish this, Stanislav. For him.

Süleyman's Blade may be done, but the Chetniks are still out there."

Stanislav shook his head. "Bastards. We should have killed them all when we had the chance."

"There would have been more. There always are."

The two of them seemed to have forgotten about Clara, but, her questions were piling up by the second. She glanced back toward the door to the bedroom, where she had left *The Giaour* and Lord Byron's letter. There were other things in the book, things she didn't understand. She wondered if it might not be a good idea to tell Arkady about it.

Before she could say anything though, the door flew open, and three men burst into the room, guns drawn. The one in the middle, a tall man who reminded Clara a little of Dolph Lundgren, barked something in Serbian. Arkady and the doctor put their hands up. Clara followed suit. Dolph looked at Clara and grinned. He barked another order.

"What did he say?" Clara asked.

"He says if you go with them, they won't shoot anyone," Arkady replied.

Clara eyed the three men. "Do you believe that?"

Arkady frowned. "Not in a million years."

Dolph shouted something else.

"He says now," Arkady translated.

Clara glared. "Tell him to come and get me."

Arkady glanced at her. "I really don't think that's—"

"Just do it. And be ready."

Arkady paused, then replied to Dolph in Serbian. The Chetnik sighed, lowered his gun, and marched toward Clara. The other two kept their guns trained on Stanislav and Arkady. Dolph jerked her up by the arm and dragged her toward the door. She flailed and kicked, doing everything she could to resist. When she passed the stove, she grabbed the pan full of hot grease from the sausage and flung it at Dolph. As the scalding liquid hit his face, he screamed and let go of her. She swung the pan at another Chetnik. The man dodged, but Clara's distraction served its purpose.

Her ears rang when two gunshots echoed through the small room. The other two Chetniks crumpled to the floor, one of them clutching his shoulder as a red bloom spread across his shirt. The other writhed and shrieked in pain, grasping at the bloody hole where one of his kneecaps had been. Clara turned to Arkady, his gun drawn.

"Behind you," he called.

Dolph staggered back to his feet, the side of his face red and blistered. He reached for his gun, but Clara slammed the frying pan down on the back of his head. He fell to the floor and didn't move again.

Arkady limped over to the Chetnik he had shot in the leg and grabbed him by a shock of hair. Clara guessed what followed was supposed to be an interrogation, though it mainly consisted of Arkady banging the man's head on the floor until he blacked out.

Arkady stood and glanced at Clara. "Get your things. We need to leave now."

"Are you sure there aren't more of them out there waiting?" Clara asked.

Arkady's gaze went to the open door. "It's doubtful. With all the noise we just made, they'd have come storming in already."

Then he spun and shot Stanislav in the foot.

The doctor fell to his knees. "What was that for?" he asked, grimacing.

"You know exactly what that was for," Arkady snarled. "I should do more to you for tipping them off, but given our past friendship, I'll leave it at that."

"How did you know?"

"Educated guess. Someone had to do it."

Stanislav clenched his teeth. "I didn't have a choice in the matter. The Chetniks are the only thing close to law and order we have around here. They would have found out eventually. You all but signed my death warrant by bringing her here."

"When did you sell out?"

Stanislav glared. "When all of us sold out. You know there was a time when we would have been on the side of the Chetniks."

"Times change," Arkady said, his jaw set.

"As if your goals are so much nobler. What are you going to do with the medallion if you find it, Arkady?"

Arkady spat something in Russian and then looked at Clara. "Please hurry and get your things."

"What's going to happen to them?" she asked.

Arkady stepped over the body of the unconscious Chetnik. "Let their friends take care of them."

THIRTY-FIVE

Sarajevo, Bosnia and Herzegovina
11 October 1999

THE "HIGH-LOW" WAIL OF A siren grew louder and then receded as a police car sped past outside on Titova Street. Adam lay on the bed in his hotel room, staring at the ceiling.

A few years earlier, he would have been listening to the sound of incendiary shells exploding all around as the Yugoslav People's Army bombarded the city. During the Bosnian War, forces loyal to Milošević surrounded the city, blew up the roads leading out, and cut off the water and the electricity. For four years, they rained hell down on Sarajevo, but they never could take the city. Its people refused to bow.

But there was, as there is always, a price.

On a sweltering August day in 1992, just before the start of the fall term, he received the call. Adam was in his last year as a graduate student and preparing to defend his dissertation. Adam's compatriots, not having grown up enduring the fiery summers Adam did, all sealed themselves up in their dormitories with the air conditioning on high. Adam had his window open. He told people he preferred the fresh air.

Adam didn't leave the windows open anymore.

Just as he was getting ready to pack it in for the night and try to get some sleep, the telephone rang. When he answered, he was greeted with only static, but after a few seconds, a man's voice cut through the noise.

"Adam! Thank God the connection went through."

Adam recognized the voice immediately. It took him a few seconds to remember he needed to say something back. "Radovan?" he managed to spit out. "Radovan, is that you?"

"Indeed," the man replied through more static.

Radovan Marković was a professor at the University of Sarajevo. They had met on one of Adam's research trips. Radovan was a scholar of medieval Eastern Europe as well, and their paths had once crossed quite a bit, but since the war started Adam had heard nothing at all.

"Radovan! I can't tell you how unbelievably good it is to hear your voice," Adam said. "Are you okay? How did you get a phone call through?"

"It's good to hear your voice as well," Radovan replied, "and am I physically okay? Yes, I'm fine. As for how I'm able to talk to you, let's just say it helps to have friends in the government."

Adam chuckled. If anyone could find a way, it would be Radovan. More than a few times Radovan had proven invaluable in helping Adam hack through the bureaucracy of the Yugoslav government. Because Radovan's area of study was the medieval Bosnian Church, a touchy subject in the officially atheist country, he had become quite proficient in skating around the rules. Adam found himself almost wishing those days would come back.

"It must be horrible what you're going through," he said.

"It's been a rough year."

Something in Radovan's voice made Adam pause. "There's something else wrong."

Radovan let out a long, weary sigh. "I don't know how long this connection is going to last, so I'll just say it. Someone outside needs to know. They bombed the library in the middle of the night. It's gone. Everything is destroyed."

The Bosnia National and University Library, the storehouse for Bosnia's cultural legacy, housed hundreds of irreplaceable manuscripts, some dating back to the tenth century. Adam had visited it on at least a dozen occasions, and in fact, he had plans for another trip before the civil war cancelled them.

"Tell me you're not serious," Adam said.

"As serious as the grave, my friend."

"Oh, my God."

"I'm afraid it gets worse."

"How's that?"

There was silence on the other end of the line. For a second, Adam thought the connection had been lost.

"The bastards," Radovan said finally, "they did it on purpose."

A month later, Radovan died when a shell hit his house in Sarajevo's western suburb of Ilidža. Adam wouldn't know of his friend's death for three years.

The destruction of the Bosnia National and University Library made Adam realize just how tenuous a hold humanity had on its own history. Mankind's living memory reached only a hundred years or so into the past. Any earlier event of any significance had to be decoded, discerned, deduced, or in some cases divined from what people left behind. Piecing the past together was a messy process, and as facts receded into the distance, they became more and more indistinct, able to be shaped to further the agenda of a person such as Slobodan Milošević.

In 1989, he gathered hundreds of thousands at the monastery of Gračanica, on the Plain of Kosovo. There he took a heroic story out of Serbia's past and twisted it to his own ends. The real history behind the 1389 Battle of Kosovo was more finely nuanced than the plot of a Russian novel, and like a good Russian tragedy, the battle itself didn't even prove to be decisive in the end, but Milošević and those like him made it into a simplistic morality play—good versus evil, white versus black, we versus they.

Tens of thousands died in the war that ripped Yugoslavia apart, a war that completed the circle of history as Elena had explained it, a war, Adam believed, that could have been avoided if the myths had not overtaken the facts. If the people who had been there were somehow able to tell their stories in their own words, then maybe the facts could prevail again.

Traveling back in time was impossible, though.

Adam dozed off thinking about those days. He opened his eyes to find Bogdan seated in the chair at the foot of his bed.

"Please, I need to talk to you," Bogdan said in heavily accented English. He smelled like cheap plum brandy.

"How did you get in here?" Adam asked.

"I picked the lock."

Adam clutched at the crucifix around his neck.

Bogdan snorted. "Look above the door. Your holy wafer

hasn't moved. I'm not one of them."

Adam looked up to see the small circular disk propped against the wall on top of the doorframe. He was right. A vampire couldn't have crossed the threshold of the room with the holy wafer resting where it was.

"You can speak English?" Adam asked.

"A little," Bogdan replied, "though usually it's better to pretend I don't."

"What are you doing here?"

"As I said, I need to talk to you."

Adam looked at the clock on the nightstand. It was two forty-five in the morning. "It's late. Can't this wait until tomorrow?"

Bogdan shook his head.

"Why?" Adam asked.

"She doesn't want me anymore."

"Elena? Why not?"

Bogdan glared at him. "Why do you think?"

"What happened at the apartment wasn't my doing."

"No, but the result is just the same."

He pulled a gun from his coat pocket.

Adam thought often—understandably—about his own death. He knew he could die in a way that he could do little to prevent, quickly in an airplane crash or a natural disaster, or slowly from cancer. He liked to think, though, that in other situations, he might be able to stave off the cutting of his mortal thread. It was why he carried the holy water, the wafers, the rosary, and the crucifix on a chain around his neck. Even though being shot was a mundane way to die by comparison, he didn't think of himself as the type of person who would simply put his hands in the air or lie down on the ground and let someone pull the trigger.

Bogdan didn't give Adam the chance to find out what type of person he was, though. He turned the gun around and took it by the muzzle, then held it out with the handle toward Adam. His hand shook.

"Please," he said. "Please, you have to kill me."

Adam didn't take his eyes off the gun. "I have to what?"

"Kill me. I can't do it myself. You have to do it for me, and you have to do it so that I don't come back."

So that I don't come back. Very few people in the world had to worry about such things. Adam counted himself among the fortunate who didn't.

"Please," Bogdan said, his voice almost inaudible. "I don't know what else to do."

Adam stared at him in silence. A man had just asked him to kill him, as a favor. *Bogdan* meant "gift from God."

God's sense of humor could be dark sometimes.

"Bogdan, when did you meet Elena?" he asked.

"Almost four years ago."

"Tell me about it."

Bogdan hesitated. Adam could see in his eyes the debate going on inside his head. "I was at the University of Belgrade," he began finally. "It was autumn. I had just begun my third year there. I was studying in the library late one night. As I was leaving, she came up to me. She said she was lost and needed directions. She was the most beautiful woman I had ever seen. I don't remember too much after that."

"What did you receive your degree in?"

"I didn't finish."

"Because you followed her here."

Bogdan nodded.

"How long ago did you come here?"

"Three years."

"Right after the siege lifted, then."

Bogdan nodded again.

"Do you know why?"

"I don't." He paused and looked at Adam quizzically. "Why are you asking me all of these questions? Why do you care?"

"Bogdan—"

"You're not going to do it are you?"

Adam shook his head.

He started to sob. "Please. Just do it! Do it now!"

"Bogdan, there has to be another way."

"There isn't."

"Yes, there is. There always is."

"Maybe in America. Not in Bosnia."

"Bogdan, I can't just shoot you here in this hotel room. Think about it. How would I explain it?"

"Very simply," Bogdan replied. "I tried to rob you, and you tried to wrestle the gun from me. In the struggle, it went off. As I said, this is Bosnia, not the United States. The police here, they would accept that. There wouldn't be any more questions."

"Why me, Bogdan?"

"Why you? You're the only other one I've ever met."

"Other what?"

"You know what she is, and she let you live. I can't think of a single other person who can claim that." He pointed to Adam and then himself. "We're brothers, you and me."

"I don't think so," Adam said flatly.

"Then you're fooling yourself. You're attracted to them."

Adam shook his head. "You're wrong."

"When Elena and I make love, it's like trying to hold on

to a lightning bolt. I don't know any other way to describe it. It sounds ironic, but it's the only time I feel alive. Any time she says my name, any time she looks at me, any time she touches me. That's when I exist. Any other time, I'm just a shadow. There's nothing inside. If I do something wrong, she'll go days without talking to me. It hurts. I long after her so much it physically pains me. Sometimes, I cut myself, here on my arms, and I let the blood drip onto the floor as a distraction. You know the same feeling. You get a thrill by just being in the same room with one of them. For you, every time you walk away alive, it's an adrenaline rush. You'll do it again. You can't stop any more than I can."

He sat looking defiant, but he still trembled as he held the gun toward Adam.

"That's not the reason I talk to them," Adam said.

"Isn't it?"

"I'm not going to kill you, Bogdan. You should leave now."

Bogdan didn't move. "I saved your life. The other day at the construction site. I killed a Chetnik who was about to shoot you."

"The one I found? You did that?" Adam narrowed his eyes. "You were following me. Did she tell you to, or did you take it upon yourself?"

"What difference does it make? You're not dead thanks to me." He thrust the gun toward Adam again. "You owe me."

Adam didn't want to meet Bogdan's gaze. "Please leave," he whispered.

Slowly and without a word, Bogdan lowered his arm. He stood and trudged toward the door, but with his hand on the doorknob, he paused and looked back toward

Adam.

"You don't get off that easily," he spat as he placed the muzzle of the gun to the side of his own head and pulled the trigger.

THIRTY-SIX

Banja Luka, Bosnia and Herzegovina
11 October 1999

"THIS ISN'T SARAJEVO, IS IT?" Clara asked. Abandoned buildings—windows boarded, walls covered in graffiti—lined the street they drove. Though the sun had not quite set, the street was deserted save for a stray dog scavenging for a meal.

"No, it certainly is not," Arkady replied from the passenger seat.

"Where are we, then?"

"Banja Luka." Arkady pointed as they passed an empty lot filled with rubble. "See that? That used to be a mosque. There were sixteen of them here. Now they all look exactly like that one."

Clara stopped the car at an intersection so an elderly man wearing a fez could cross. Their eyes met briefly before the man averted his gaze. In his face Clara saw fear. "This is where you said your brother died. Is that why you brought us here?"

"Partly. But the day after Georg Lazarović was killed, there was another murder here. In fact, there have been four murders in the last week, all the same. Body mutilated. A symbol painted on the wall in blood."

"Dracula's symbol."

Arkady nodded. "As you say."

"It seems to me someone's targeting vampire hunters," Clara said.

"I came to the same conclusion, but it's not that simple. You'll recall that in the letter I read to you, the vampire painted the same symbol on the wall of the house in Mostar. That was in 1942. Since then, there have been a dozen or so identical murders throughout Yugoslavia. There was one in Banja Luka in the 1960s."

"That's why you think your murderer is a vampire."

"Yes, but the timing is … curious. The murders all seem to happen at the same time the Chetniks decide to cause trouble."

"You think the Chetniks are allied with a vampire?"

"Or rather, a vampire is using the Chetniks for its own ends. Vampires, as a rule, don't play well with others, not even their own kind."

Clara smirked. "Typical sociopath. Do you have anything you can share with me about this murder that happened in the '60s? Maybe I could help find a pattern."

Arkady shrugged. "I don't see what the harm could be."

"You were in Thessaloniki tracking the Chetniks?"

"It was odd. They normally don't operate outside the former Yugoslavia."

Clara spent a few minutes working up the courage to ask the question she had wanted to ask ever since leaving Mostar. "So is finding Adam a priority for you at all? It seems like I'm just along for the ride here."

Arkady tensed. "I said there were four murders. I could have picked one of the others to investigate. Instead I chose to come here—because of my brother, and because of Adam. I promise, we will try to find him."

An uneasy silence settled over the car as they continued their way through the empty streets, the buildings casting long shadows across their path.

Clara broke first. "How did ... how did it happen?"

"You mean how did my brother die? No one knows for certain. His body was found in an abandoned warehouse, a bullet through his back."

"Did the Chetniks kill him?"

"No, Süleyman's Blade did."

"The other group Stanislav mentioned. Who are they?"

"Islamist fanatics. They were also ... interested in Dracula's legacy."

Clara gave him a sidelong glance. "Were?"

"About a week after Kostya was murdered, the entire organization imploded," explained Arkady. "Their leader, Serhan, was killed in a brutal attack. After that, they just fell apart."

"Do you think Adam—"

"I don't see how. There's no way he could have taken down the entire organization, not by himself."

"What if he had help?"

"Who would be helping him?"

"What about the other person Stanislav mentioned—a woman?"

Arkady shook his head. "Anya disappeared only a few days after Kostya was killed. No one has heard from her since."

"Just like Adam. What if she's still out there somewhere? What if they're together?"

An unexpected pang of anxiety accompanied the last suggestion. It was ridiculous, but Clara really hoped Adam wasn't with Anya.

"Serhan's body was found mangled and dumped in the middle of a construction site in Berlin. Crushed bones, compound fractures, a punctured lung, a ruptured spleen. Any one of his injuries would have killed him given enough time, if not for the giant knife sticking out of his back. Do you think Adam would have been capable of any of that?"

Clara couldn't picture it. Adam went to a boxing gym a few times a week. She had watched him spar once, but that was different. Adam was always controlled, calculating. He never threw a punch he didn't need to. He was never brutal, never excessive.

"I suppose not," she said. "What about this medallion Stanislav talked about?"

Arkady shifted in his seat. "Dracula's legacy. The Chetniks are looking for it, as was Süleyman's Blade."

"And you?"

"And me," he said quietly.

"What does it do?"

"It doesn't do anything. It's nothing more than an historical artifact. A trinket."

"Then why does everyone want it?"

"Because of what it represents. The medallion is dangerous not for what it does, but for what everyone believes it can do. The Chetniks think the medallion will make them invulnerable. If they get their hands on it, they could unleash a wave of violence that would make the devastation of the war seem tame."

"And what do you want with the medallion?"

"I just want to keep the Chetniks from getting it."

"That's it?"

He held up a hand. "That's it."

The car came to another intersection. "Where are we going?" Clara asked.

"Another safe house," replied Arkady. "Turn left. We're almost there."

This new street was lined with townhouses on either side, and while Clara still wouldn't have called them upscale, they didn't look quite so neglected. "Is it safer than the last one?"

Arkady glared. "No one knows we're in Banja Luka."

"How did they know we were in Mostar?"

"I'm still working that out. You can park here. It's the third row house on the right."

Clara eased the car into a parking space on the street. "You're not inspiring much confidence, you know."

"I have kept you alive thus far, haven't I?"

"With the help of a frying pan."

He scowled. "Look. I'm asking you to please trust me for a little while longer. There's a good chance we may find out more about what happened to Adam while we're here."

He climbed out of the car. Clara hesitated for a moment before following. The setting sun turned the sky a blazing orange, and the shadows crept along the ground and up the façade of the townhouse.

"I just hope we *have* a little while longer," she muttered.

THIRTY-SEVEN

Sarajevo, Bosnia and Herzegovina
12 October 1999

THE POLICE INSPECTOR INTERROGATING ADAM had an altogether clownish appearance—big rosy cheeks, a small nose, close-set black eyes, and mid-length black hair that fell in ringlets around his pudgy face. Adam had to believe the look was deliberate. It was hard to take a character out of an Italian street play seriously, but at some point in his third hour of questioning, he wished he had told the inspector the story Bogdan suggested he tell.

The inspector's eyes gave him away. They belied a particular cunning. Within thirty seconds of entering the room, he had scanned the entire scene and taken in every detail, to the point Adam felt sure the cameras employed by some of the other police officers were superfluous. The inspector, who had introduced himself as Nikola Gavrilović, also had a way of filling in the subtext of his questions by where he let his gaze rest.

Adam hadn't called the police, but they had arrived regardless, mere minutes after Bogdan blew off half his head, spattering grey matter and blood all over the walls. Currently, three police officers scoured the room with cotton swabs while the inspector questioned Adam. He was beginning to think the inspector was a veteran of the UDBA, Yugoslavia's secret police.

"So you say he may have been from Belgrade," the inspector said. "What makes you think that?"

"He said he went to university there," Adam replied.

"Did he say anything else, anything about his family, or a wife, maybe?"

"No."

"Friends, then, a female companion?"

"No." Adam hoped the inspector didn't notice his slight hesitation in answering.

"So you say you woke up at around two forty-five to find him in your room?"

"Yes."

"And that he told you he was going to kill himself?"

"Yes."

"What happened next?"

"He killed himself." Adam failed to contain his sarcasm.

"That's all?" the inspector asked, glancing at the pattern of blood spatter across the wall near the door.

"Should there be more?"

"The chambermaid who was down the hall said there was a delay of at least ten minutes between the time he entered your room and the time the shot was fired."

"I tried to talk him out of it."

"Why would he come to you?"

"I don't know."

The inspector let his gaze wander around the room

again. He paused briefly at the strings of garlic around the windows and the holy wafer over the door, his only reaction to Adam's precautions. "What is it you do, Mr. Mire?"

"It's 'Doctor,'" Adam corrected, "and like I've already said, I'm a history professor. My interest is medieval and Renaissance Eastern Europe."

"And what are you doing in our lovely country in particular?" As the inspector asked the question, he looked past Adam at an officer who was taking a picture of Bogdan's revolver.

"I'm researching a book."

"And what is it you're researching?"

"The everyday lives of Christian peasants in the Balkans in the seventeenth century."

It wasn't exactly a lie.

"You admit you've met this man before."

Adam looked over at Bogdan's corpse. "Yes. He was part of the interview I conducted yesterday."

"Are you sure you didn't discover that you and he shared ... similar interests? Perhaps he came here so that you and he could engage in those interests? Perhaps something went wrong?" His eyes wandered to the unmade bed.

Adam's eyes widened as the inspector's meaning became clear. "What? No."

"I can understand your embarrassment, Dr. Mire, but lying will only make things worse for you."

Adam thrust his hands toward the inspector. "Here, take my fingerprints. Test my hands for gunshot residue. I didn't kill him. Whatever you have to do, just do it."

"Are you sure? You know, you would have to come with us to the station in order for us to do those sorts of tests. I cannot guarantee how long it would take to verify the results. There will be paperwork. It could take weeks, even months, and I also cannot guarantee that word of what has happened here won't leak out. On the other hand, if you were to just tell me the truth, then matters could perhaps be handled a little more discreetly. Are you entirely certain it didn't happen the way I just described? Are you sure it wasn't just an unfortunate accident?" The inspector fixed his gaze on the holy wafer above the door. "You may have even been defending yourself?"

"Yes, I'm sure. I think I'm finished talking. You do what you need to do. In the meantime, you're going to allow me to call the American embassy."

Adam reached for the telephone. The inspector caught his arm. For a tense minute neither of them moved.

Then the inspector leaned close and whispered in Adam's ear in German, *"Ich versuche Ihnen zu helfen, mein Freund. 'Denn die Todten reiten schnell.'"*

For the dead travel fast. The same quote from *Dracula* the Hellenic Police officer in Thessaloniki had said.

Adam didn't take his eyes off the inspector. "You're right. I'm sorry," he said, loud enough for the others to hear. "It happened exactly as you just said. We arranged to meet here tonight. Only, when he arrived, he tried to rob me. We struggled for the gun. As we were fighting, it went off."

The inspector smiled and stood. "There now, wasn't that easy?"

He said something in Bosnian, too quickly for Adam to understand. A few of the other police officers began to take Adam's books and papers and stack them in boxes.

"What are they doing?" Adam asked.

"We'll need a forwarding address for you so that we'll know where to send your things when we're finished with them," said the inspector.

Adam started to panic. "Wait ... no. These are my notes, my research. I need all of this."

He stood and tried to take one of the boxes from the hands of the officer carrying it out of the room. Another one efficiently restrained him.

The inspector held up his hands. "I'm afraid all of this is evidence, Dr. Mire. I have to take everything, including the clothes you're wearing. You'll need to take them off. Of course, we won't leave you naked."

He gave another order. One of the officers opened a dresser drawer, picked a pair of pants and a shirt out at random, and threw them both at Adam.

"You may use the bathroom to change, if you're modest," the inspector said.

Without a word, Adam took the clothes and trudged to the bathroom. A few minutes later, he handed his old clothes to the inspector.

The inspector smiled as he handed off the clothes to one of his subordinates. "It's a pity, you know, that you're leaving our city tomorrow. You won't have time to visit our beautiful Cathedral of Jesus' Heart. They've done a wonderful job restoring it. You can't even tell where the shells damaged it."

Adam started to explain that he had nowhere to go, but he caught himself. "Yes, it certainly is a pity."

THIRTY-EIGHT

Banja Luka, Bosnia and Herzegovina
12 October 1999

CLARA NEVER EXPECTED TO BE standing at a crime scene, admiring a picture painted in blood. As disturbing as the thought was, the murderer's artistry impressed her. Up close, the picture held an incredible amount of detail. The dragon even had scales. Underneath, words scrawled in Latin spanned the wall: *O Quam Misericors est Deus, Pius et Justus.*

"O how merciful is God, faithful and just," Arkady translated. "It was the motto of the Order of the Dragon."

Three of them stood in the bedroom of the townhouse—Clara, Arkady, and Boris Kalinić, a local police inspector and a member of the same secret order as Vasilije Abramović. Other than the body, which had long been removed, nothing about the room had been altered. The bloody bedspread remained with the imprint of the victim, a man named Goran Subotić. Clara had seen the pictures of him though, sprawled across the bed, arms outstretched, throat ripped out, eyes frozen wide open in terror.

"He was found by his brother," said the police inspector.

Boris Kalinić was a short, willowy man. Wisps of grey-blond hair fringed his otherwise bald head. Maybe in his prime he could have gone toe to toe with a vampire, but even then, Clara had trouble picturing the actual scenario.

Arkady had already looked under the bed and behind the wardrobe, run latex-glove-covered fingers through the carpet, and looked at the blood on the wall with a jeweler's loupe. He scanned the room again. "Displayed like a trophy in his own home. The same as the rest."

Boris nodded. "He invited the thing inside."

"Was he working on anything?" Arkady asked.

"Officially, no," Boris replied.

Arkady cocked an eyebrow. "But unofficially?"

Boris glanced at Clara. "I don't like speaking out of turn."

Arkady jabbed a finger at the bloody dragon. "It's not speaking out of turn if it keeps something like this from happening again."

The inspector pursed his lips. "There have been rumors of a ... a dark presence in the city. But you have to understand they are only rumors, nothing substantial. After that awful business a few months ago—"

"I am well aware of that awful business, Boris," Arkady said, drawing his mouth into a grim line.

Boris let his gaze fall to the floor. "I'm sorry. You have my condolences. Understandably, everyone has been on edge. A few days before his murder, Goran came to me about these rumors. I told him he was being paranoid. It happens a lot with the newer ones, but he insisted he wasn't, that there was a real threat."

"Did he give you any more details than that?"

"Unfortunately, no." Boris took off his glasses and buffed them on his sleeve. "I told him not to pursue it, that I would relay what he said through the proper channels, and that we would come up with a plan. I was very adamant."

Arkady examined the room's window, poking at the crevices with a small pocketknife. "Obviously he didn't listen."

"No," Boris said, "he apparently went digging on his own."

"And he unearthed a vampire. Clearly he wasn't prepared."

"As I said, he was new to ... our line of work."

"And how does one get into your line of work?" Clara asked.

"By chance, more or less," Boris replied. "Generally, we are all police officers who encountered the unexplained in our jobs."

"And survived the encounter," Arkady interjected.

Boris shot him an annoyed glance. "Yes, that. Most of those who do survive find a way to rationalize it, dismiss it, even forget it, but there are others who can't. The nightmares don't go away. They start to ask questions. That's usually when they come to our attention."

Clara glanced down at the outline on the bedspread. "And how did Goran come to your attention?"

"There was a murder about a year ago. A young woman was attacked late at night. Goran was the first on the scene, the first to notice the puncture wounds on the woman's neck and the lack of blood. I interviewed him myself afterwards. He saw a demon, he said, a shadow darker than the other shadows, flying away."

"Was he involved in the 'awful business' of my brother's death?" Arkady asked.

"He helped a little with the cleanup," Boris answered. "A few members of Süleyman's Blade tried to cause some trouble. We stopped them."

"Would he have known about Dracula's medallion?" Clara asked.

The two men looked at her in surprise. Boris frowned. "Why do you ask?"

"Because Adam and Kostya were here, looking for the medallion. You said Süleyman's Blade was looking for it, too. Could Goran have learned something about it? Maybe a clue to its whereabouts?"

"It's possible," Boris said, crossing his arms, "but unlikely."

She gestured toward the symbol on the wall. "You said that the medallion is dangerous because of what people believe it can do, right?"

Arkady nodded. "If the Chetniks believe it will make them unstoppable, there's no telling what kind of carnage they could unleash on this part of the world. And I can tell you, given the current climate between my country and yours, the violence will spread."

Clara almost laughed out loud at the thought that came to her. It was absurd—even more absurd than believing in vampires—but it also made perfect sense. "What if you're wrong?"

Arkady narrowed his eyes. "What do you mean?"

"What if the medallion is powerful in its own right?"

Boris scoffed. "Ludicrous."

Clara smiled. "It is, isn't it? But think about it. These murders seem like they're just opportunistic, like the killer is eliminating vampire hunters whenever he has the chance, but they aren't random killings. They can't be. Goran had the opportunity to learn about the medallion. I'm willing to bet Georg Lazarović was at that tavern in Mostar because he was meeting someone to talk about it as well. In both cases the killer was looking for information. He's after the medallion, too."

"But what makes you think it has power?" Boris asked.

"Because why else would a vampire have use for it?" Clara replied. "If everything you've told me is true, what does a vampire care about politics or religion?"

Arkady looked to Boris. "She has a point."

Boris shook his head. "Violence and chaos would cover a vampire's activities rather well."

"True, but that's a bit like swatting a fly with a sledgehammer." Clara looked from one confused face to another. "A vampire needs a safe place to stay during the day, right? Rioting in the streets puts a vampire in almost as much danger as a human. If a vampire wants the medallion, it must be for some reason other than what people believe it can do. He must want it for what it actually *can* do."

"What reason would that be?" Arkady asked.

She grinned. "You tell me. You're the vampire expert."

CLARA RAN HER HAND OVER the pristine, white bedspread, a contrast to the bloodstained one in the bedroom of Goran Subotić. Only a few months earlier, Adam had visited Banja Luka. He had stayed at the same safe house and slept in the same bed. Closing her eyes, she tried to imagine him there, to sense his former presence, but she couldn't. She sat alone in the still, quiet room.

"Oh, Adam, what were you thinking?" she whispered.

A knock at the door brought her out of her thoughts.

"Clara? May I enter?" Arkady asked.

She hesitated before answering. "Come in."

Arkady pushed open the door and slipped into the room. "It's late. I would have expected you to be in bed by now."

She mustered a weary smile. "I'm not sleeping anytime soon."

"Still, you should get some rest. You've had a rough several days."

"I'd go with a much stronger word than *rough*."

"I'm going out in the morning," Arkady said. "I just wanted to let you know in case I'm not here when you wake up."

"Where are you going?"

"I'm going out," he repeated, his face an unreadable mask.

Clara balled her hands into fists and pounded the bedspread. She wanted to wrap her hands around his throat. The only other person she'd ever wanted to choke was Adam. "Dammit, Arkady. I thought we were past this."

"Clara please—"

"No. No more. I'm tired of being kept in the dark."

Arkady pointed to a stack of papers on the bed next to her. "You asked about the murders that happened here in the 1960s. I've given you the documents we have on them. I even translated them for you."

"But you're keeping something from me. I could see it today when we were with Boris. You were worried he would let something slip. The same thing happened with Vasilije the other day when Adam's name came up." She pointed a finger at him. "And don't you dare tell me I'm being paranoid. Why was Adam here? What was he doing? And where did he go?"

Arkady sighed. "Clara, there are some things you shouldn't know."

She glared. "Why."

"For your protection."

"I don't need your protection," she said through clenched teeth. "What I need is to find Adam. And to start with, I need you to tell me where you're going tomorrow."

Arkady stared at her, the weariness evident in his eyes. "I'm meeting with an old Muslim man, one of the few who can remember what it was like here just before World War II."

"Why are you meeting with him?"

Arkady slumped into the chair in the corner of the room. "There was another murder last month. Another old Muslim named Ibrahim Zorić. His throat was slit, and his right hand was painted green."

"And you think Adam knows something about it?"

"It was not the only murder of the kind. There was a string of them—Budapest, here, Dubrovnik, Thessaloniki, and Berlin."

"But what would Adam have to do with that?"

"I don't know, but when we find him, I plan to ask him."

"You don't honestly think …? Adam would never do such a thing."

"The world is full of people who would never do such a thing … until they do."

Clara stood. "That's absurd. You're insane if you think Adam was involved in any way with those murders."

"Still, you have to admit, there's a lot of death in your ex-boyfriend's wake. Don't you want to know why?"

Clara didn't answer, staring straight ahead as she

fought back tears. He was right. Adam seemed to attract death, and it scared her.

"There's something else," Arkady continued. "I think you're right about the medallion."

"Then you do believe it has some kind of power?"

"I still believe it has the power to make others believe. But I also think Georg and Goran were murdered because they knew something about it. I'm sure Boris would have a fit if he knew I was telling you this, but when we apprehended some of the members of Süleyman's Blade, they made mention of clues to the location of the medallion."

"What sort of clues?"

"Journals. Letters. They really weren't more forthcoming than that. They were lower-level members, and Serhan liked to hold his cards close to his vest."

Clara smirked. "And I'm sure you asked as nicely as you could."

"We do what we must," Arkady replied.

"Do you think Adam was following these clues?"

"It's likely. And if they led him to Mr. Zorić …"

Clara nodded. "I understand."

"When we find Adam, I promise I'll do my best to keep him safe and ensure he's treated fairly, but things might be a little rough for him for a while."

"Thank you," Clara said.

"Now please, get some sleep." Arkady stood and started for the door. "I'll see you tomorrow."

Clara stared after him. She had no intention of leaving it up to Arkady to make sure Adam was treated fairly. She picked up the documents lying on the bed next to her. If she couldn't sleep, she might as well try to find something to keep her a step ahead of the vampires—and the vampire hunters.

THIRTY-NINE

From the Journal of Vasko Kurjak

Banja Luka, Yugoslavia
9 November 1969

O<small>N 26 AND 27 OCTOBER 1969,</small> *two devastating earthquakes hit the city of Banja Luka, registering magnitudes of 6.0 and 6.4 on the Richter scale. While the loss of life was relatively small, the damage to property was extensive. Tens of thousands were displaced from their homes, forced to live in trailers and tents while facing the harshest winter in memory. Aid poured in from all parts of Yugoslavia and the rest of the world, and the city was rebuilt, but as with all human tragedy, there were those who would take advantage.*

I SHOVED MY HANDS FARTHER down into my coat pockets. My breath came out in white puffs. Not for the first time I thought to myself what a strange place it was to meet, an alleyway behind a collapsed building, in the dead of night. Still, it wasn't my place to question. After almost twenty minutes of waiting, I started walking in circles.

"What are you doing?" Toma asked.

"Trying to stay warm," I replied.

"That will never work," he said. "You're only going to tire yourself out."

I shrugged. "I have to do something."

After a few minutes I gave up. I was as cold as ever. To add insult to injury, it began to snow.

"He's almost a half hour late," I said.

Toma continued to gaze down the street. "He'll be here."

"My apartment is warm and dry."

"What of it?"

"I'm giving him five more minutes, and then I'm going home."

He whipped his head around. "Vasko, you can't do that."

"Watch me."

After six minutes of Toma fretting over whether I'd follow through with my threat, the third member of our party finally appeared. If I didn't know better, I would say he simply materialized from the shadows, but of course, it had to be a trick of the light.

"Dragomir, where have you been?" I asked. "It's freezing."

"Really?" he replied. "I hadn't noticed." He remained stone-faced, his voice even. I couldn't tell if he meant what he said to be a joke.

In any event, I was in no mood for jokes. "What's the point in dragging us out here in the middle of the night? We're not exactly blending in. If a policeman rounds the corner, we're done for. Why couldn't we use a pub to pass messages the way we normally do? The one on Jevrejska Street wasn't damaged. At least then I'd have a beer in me to warm me up."

Dragomir shook his head. "Our people are still scattered because of the earthquake. I couldn't be certain any message would get to you uncompromised. Besides, this is too important. We can't risk UDBA taking notice."

"UDBA is already taking notice," I said. "I spotted someone watching my apartment last week, and then just yesterday, I'm sure someone was following me. I was able to lose him, but if someone followed me here—"

"No one followed you, either of you."

"How do you know?" Toma asked.

Dragomir turned his cold gaze to Toma. "I'm certain of it."

"What's so important then?" I asked.

"We are moving the timetable ahead."

I laughed, hoping he had made another joke. "What? You can't be serious. We're not ready. You yourself just said that our people are still scattered."

"Everyone who matters is in place. But it has to happen tonight. Sergej Cvijić dies."

Sergej Cvijić was merely a petty local official, but he had connections in Belgrade and would not be a petty official for long. He had proven a thorn in the side of the Chetniks, and Dragomir deemed him enough of a priority that we spent months preparing for the assassination and the following cover-up.

I let my jaw drop. "Tonight? You're insane. How can you say that?"

He handed us each a slip of paper. "You are to go to these addresses tonight and wait."

I took the paper from him. "Wait for what?"

"You'll know."

I didn't recognize the address I read. "I don't like this. There's something you're not telling us. What's going on?"

Dragomir's eyes narrowed. "Of course there's something I'm not telling you. It's safer for all of us that way. What's the matter? You've never questioned orders before."

"I've never had a reason to."

"You're being paranoid."

"Yes, and that's the reason I've survived as long as I have."

Anger flashed in his eyes, but then his expression softened, and the corners of his mouth turned up in an almost-smile. "Do you remember when we first met? How many years ago was it?"

"Ten."

"The blink of an eye, but so much has happened. Do you remember the very first assignment I sent you on?"

"Running guns to Skopje. How could I forget? I nearly died. The leader of the Chetniks in Macedonia was a government mole."

"But you didn't die, and you proved yourself by taking care of him. I knew that day what kind of person you are. The Chetniks have had a long and proud history of defending the Serbian nation against its enemies. I have never doubted your devotion to that cause. Your role is vital. Believe me when I say so. No one can replace you. I would never think of such." He turned to Toma. "And you, Toma, what were you doing when I met you?"

Toma looked down at his shoes. "I was working in a factory."

"For pennies," Dragomir added. "And now where are you?"

"At the Agricultural Ministry."

"You have money enough to support your family, and you have a purpose. Have I ever lied to you?"

Toma lifted his head and met Dragomir's gaze. "Never."

"So I'm asking you both to trust me tonight. Go to the addresses I've given you and wait. You'll know what to do."

And with that he turned and crossed the street, glancing over his shoulder before he stepped into a shadow and disappeared. Again, I know it must have been a trick of the light, but when he turned to face me, his eyes reflected a fiery red glow.

Toma and I parted ways. The address Dragomir gave me was a warehouse, the only intact building on the entire street. And of course, there was no power, meaning no heat. I found a place sheltered from the wind at least, and I did what I was told. I waited.

An hour later, in the darkest part of the night, a siren wailed. Not an uncommon sound in the city, but many of the streets were still blocked. The piercing howl grew louder, and the siren was joined by others. I found a set of stairs and climbed up to the second floor of the building where I peered out a window. Darkness enveloped most of the city, but one bright glow dominated the skyline. Some distance away, orange flames leapt up into the indigo sky. A few mental calculations gave me a good estimate of the fire's location.

And then I remembered Dragomir's words. *You'll know.*

I dashed down the stairs and out into the cold night, tripping and stumbling as I went. By the third block, I was gasping for breath, but I didn't dare stop.

I could come within only a few blocks of the fire. Just as I suspected, the home of the local head of the secret service was engulfed. It didn't make sense. He was not the intended target of our plot, not yet in any event. Of course Dragomir was right. The timing was perfect. The fire would be blamed on a gas leak because of the earthquake, and the Chetniks would be freer to operate without him, but the hairs on the back of my neck prickled.

Dragomir should have included me. Only one reason for making me wait in a warehouse across the city made sense. I was intentionally being set up as a traitor. I had likely escaped execution by leaving the warehouse.

I needed to get away. I left the fire and ran back to my apartment. Hopefully, no one was watching. When I reached the building, I took the steps two at a time. My hands were shaking so badly, I fumbled with my keys for what seemed like an eternity.

I threw open the door to the sight of Toma's dead body lying on the couch, his eyes frozen open in terror. A ragged gash cut across his throat. As I approached the body, I scanned the room. Nothing else was out of place. There wasn't even any blood. At least not where one would expect it. The wall behind Toma's body was covered in it. Whoever had killed him had used his blood to paint some kind of symbol. It looked like a dragon with its tail wrapped around its neck.

A note was pinned to his body. I overcame my urge to retch as I picked it up. It was from Dragomir.

I knew one of you was a traitor, but not the kind of traitor you are thinking. My apologies. I had to be sure. You went to the place you were told. Toma did not. Pack a bag. You leave for Skopje in the morning to take over the operations there. The train tickets and other papers you need are in Toma's pocket. Don't worry. Everything will be handled here.

I reached into the front pocket of Toma's coat and fished out the train tickets as well as a new ID card with my picture, but a different name. I glanced up at the symbol painted on the wall. It was meant to be a message, but somehow I knew the message wasn't for me.

FORTY

Sarajevo, Bosnia and Herzegovina
12 October 1999

ADAM MEANDERED AROUND THE COURTYARD of the Cathedral of Jesus' Heart, unsure what to do. Inspector Gavrilović had not mentioned the church accidentally. Adam was meant to see something there. If he had his notes and books, he could have figured out what that something was. With the sun rising behind it, the neo-Gothic church's twin spires cast long shadows across the square. The shadow of the more northerly spire pointed to a stone archway that marked the entrance to a cobblestone street.

If he were in a movie, the shadow would point to the hidden medallion, and there would be a race across the medieval heart of the city to find it. He would get there just before the bad guys and save the day, earning a kiss from his love interest. He wasn't in a movie, though. There weren't any heroes. Everyone was a bad guy, and given what happened after his last kiss, he wasn't terribly eager to repeat the experience.

He thought about simply going inside and finding someone to talk to—a sexton or maybe even a priest, someone who knew the history of the church. He considered bribing someone into giving him an unofficial tour, but as it was, he barely had enough money for bus fare out of the city. He was about to ascend the steps of the church when he saw Inspector Gavrilović approaching him from across the courtyard, and his heart leapt into his throat.

"If you're expecting an audience with the cardinal this morning, you will be disappointed, my friend," he said as he strode toward Adam. "He is a very busy man. His schedule is quite full. Fortunately for you, I am available."

"Are you going to arrest me, Inspector Gavrilović?" Adam asked.

"Oh, no," the inspector replied. "In truth, I wouldn't have had any respect for you at all if you had not shown up here today. For all intents and purposes, I did invite you."

"Actually, I've been meaning to pay a visit here. You were right. You can hardly tell it was ever damaged. It's a beautiful building."

"You did not come here to discuss architecture." Inspector Gavrilović raised an eyebrow. "Are you perhaps looking for the Dracula medallion?"

Adam froze. The inspector's words were still fresh in his mind. *Denn die Todten reiten schnell.*

"How do you know about that?" he asked, barely above a whisper.

The inspector's mouth widened into a wry grin. "My mother is Serbian, but my father was Croatian. He was an altar boy in 1941 when a wounded man entered the church and gave the medallion to one of the priests." He reached into his coat and pulled out a thin, leather-bound volume Adam immediately recognized as the journal of Mihai Iliescu's father, the one Marina Dimitriou had passed to him in Thessaloniki. "But then, perhaps you already know the story."

FORTY-ONE

From the Journal of Andras Iliescu

Sarajevo, Yugoslavia
2 February 1941

I AM WRITING THIS WHILE on a train taking me away from the city, my son. It's hard to believe I arrived here only a few days ago, harder still to believe I arrived feeling something akin to hope.

As the train approached the city, it rounded a bend, and one of the most beautiful sights I have ever seen spread out in the valley before me. Nestled among the fir- and birch-covered hills, minarets and steeples reached heavenward, dusted lightly with snow. Warm, inviting lights flickered in the windows of every building.

In this place, Jews, Muslims, Catholics, and Orthodox Christians are all neighbors. There is a square where a mosque, a synagogue, a Catholic cathedral, and a Byzantine church all face one another. No one place of worship is more prominent than the others. They just exist, side by side. That is the life I want. I'm tired of fighting and running, tired of the monsters.

I don't wish anyone harm anymore, not even them.

I wish I could have stayed. Yet even if such a thing were possible, I'm afraid Sarajevo won't remain safe for very long. I can see the signs, sense the tension in the air. There is a black shadow creeping from the north. The man I saw this morning at a newsstand was a German. I could tell by how stiffly he stood. The citizens of this city have a way about them. Every move is fluid and measured. Even in these days of uncertainty, they do not let it affect their daily lives. It is probably something I will never understand, but it seems to be ingrained in them by their history. No matter what horrors they endure, life goes on.

The man this morning at the newsstand pretended to read the newspaper, but he was really watching the bus stop across the street—for what reason I don't know, but I fear the worst. Yesterday, I overheard two other men whispering in a café. I only caught snatches of their conversation. My Serbo-Croatian is not very good, but it seemed as if they were discussing an incident in Montenegro at the border with Albania, which the Italians have overrun.

As I said, I fear I made the biggest mistake of my life when I joined the Legion of the Archangel Michael. I'm now paying for that mistake. I came to Sarajevo because I ran. I can't return to Bucharest, at least not now, and I won't go to Germany. I don't know if I can even begin to explain to you the atrocity I witnessed, but I shall try.

Everything began to unravel, I suppose, just a few months ago in the Church of Ilie Gorgani. We had gathered to honor fourteen of our fallen comrades-in-arms. They had all been murdered by the former government, that of King Carol, who never cared too much about his people, at least not as much as the Legion of the Archangel Michael cared, or so we were told. The smell of incense filled the air, as did the constant drone of the chanting priests, raising up the spirits of our brothers, martyrs for the Romanian people. There in that dark hall, looking at the fourteen coffins draped in green, I felt a power I had never felt before flowing through me.

That night, the nightmares began. I should have known something was wrong. The Legion was an integral part of the government, in a tense alliance with General Ion Antonescu, but he never trusted us, and he was far more interested in power for himself than anything else. When the opportunity came, he openly declared war on us. There was fighting in the streets of Bucharest. As always, the Jews were blamed, and the Legion decided to seize the opportunity and rid the city of them once and for all.

On the third night of fighting, we rounded up about fifty Jews. I didn't know what we were going to do with them. Our captain told us to drive north, out of the city. We stopped at a slaughterhouse. We forced our prisoners off the trucks and marched them inside. Our captain ordered them bolted into the machines used to butcher the animals. Then, with the men, women, and children screaming for their lives, he turned the machines on.

I fled the building, retching until there was nothing left in my stomach. I had seen the glee in the captain's eyes as he did it, but what was worse, I felt the same energy there as I had felt in the church, almost as if a dark force somewhere gloated. I left on foot, running for miles before I stopped. I never looked back. Once I arrived at the highway, I found someone to give me a ride to Brașov. The next day, the forces of Antonescu secured all the government buildings. All the members of the Iron Guard, including me, were named fugitives.

From Brașov, I made it to Sarajevo. I didn't pick the city arbitrarily. I know of a priest who has had experience with the monsters. He serves at the Cathedral of Jesus' Heart. I came to take the medallion to him, for safekeeping. It has been our family's curse long enough.

On the morning after I arrived, I headed out to complete my mission. The day was bright and sunny and unusually warm. Quite a few people were about. I had no reason to anticipate any danger. I should have been more alert. The boardinghouse where I stayed on the first night was not in the best part of the city.

As I rounded a corner, I ran into a man. We collided rather hard, and he grabbed me to keep from falling. I apologized profusely, as did he, then we each continued on. I made it only a few steps, however, before I felt a lightness in the pocket of my jacket where the medallion had been. Realizing the man had lifted it, I turned around in time to see him run into a building. I pursued him. It took a moment for my eyes to adjust to the dim interior. That moment almost proved fatal. He was waiting for me. I dodged to one side as he rushed at me, and I narrowly avoided a knife in my belly. The building must have been a home for some well-off family at one time. Only a few pieces of old, discarded furniture remained. There was nowhere to hide.

He launched himself at me again. The blade tore a hole in my jacket and grazed my shoulder. When he swung around for another attack, I ducked and slammed my fist into his midsection, pushing him against the wall. With him pinned, I tried to grab the knife out of his hand, but I couldn't. Then I saw the marks on his neck—two puncture wounds and a bruise that looked like a bite. He kneed me and shoved me away, burying his knife in my thigh. I managed to swing my weight around as I fell so I caught his legs and tripped him. The knife went skittering across the wooden floor. The two of us scrambled for it. I reached it first. When he came after me again, I sank the blade into his chest. I've never seen so much blood in a man.

After a few moments, he stopped moving, and I struggled to my feet. With every step I took, the pain in my leg felt like being stabbed again, only with a searing hot poker, but I was more determined than ever to get the medallion to the church.

What frightened me more than the attack was that I felt another presence in the house, something stirring deeper inside its shadowed corridors. Part of me wanted to go explore, to see what I could find. The air moved, though all the windows were closed. A quiet voice whispered my name, and I knew without a doubt that if I answered the call, I would never leave that house alive. I forced myself to walk to the front door. The second I stepped out into the sunlight, the spell was broken.

I staggered through the doors of the church, leaving a small trail of blood behind me. A man stood at the front of the sanctuary near the altar. I didn't know if he was the priest I had heard of, but at the time it didn't matter to me. I had but one purpose. When the priest saw me, he told the altar boy with him to run and get help. Then, he came toward me.

I held the medallion out to him "Father, I have something for you."

Then I collapsed.

In my dark delirium, I found myself back in the abandoned house, with its faded and ripped wallpaper and derelict furniture. This time, however, instead of walking to the door and leaving, I went farther into the house. Something was leading me. I didn't question it. I just followed, through the dining room and up the stairs. There, at the end of a long hallway, was a door. The doorknob was ice cold to the touch.

When I opened the door, I found a woman seated on a collapsed divan, her back to me. Her dark hair fell loose around her shoulders. She wore an expensive green silk dress and a string of pearls around her neck, and I couldn't fathom why she would choose to sit in an abandoned house. She turned to face me. I will never forget that moment. Her eyes glowed a brilliant red, and she had inhumanly long, sharp fangs. A trickle of blood ran down from each corner of her smiling mouth. I drew closer to her, though my legs didn't seem to move. Try as a might, I couldn't take my eyes off her.

When I awoke, I was lying in a bed in a small room. The altar boy from earlier sat next to the bed, staring at me. His hair fell in black ringlets around his round face. I smiled at him. He didn't smile back.

"How long have I been here?" I asked.

"Two days," the boy replied.

I tried to sit up, but every muscle in my body rebelled. "The medallion—"

"Why did you bring evil into the church?"

"I didn't," I said.

"Yes, you did. Father said the thing you brought into our church was evil and dangerous. Why did you bring it here?"

I shook my head. "It's not dangerous, not here. It has no power in the house of God."

The boy glared. "But it still has power outside this

building."

The priest entered the room at that moment. His look was grave. "The police are on their way," he said. "They've connected you with the body of the man who attacked you. If you don't leave now, they'll arrest you."

"But," I replied hoarsely, "I have nowhere else to go."

And yet I go, free of the burden I have borne most of my life, but still trapped by its legacy.

FORTY-TWO

Sarajevo, Bosnia and Herzegovina
12 October 1999

ADAM GLANCED AROUND THE COURTYARD in front of the cathedral. Only a few others were out. Still, he lowered his voice and leaned forward. "What can you tell me about the medallion?"

"What would you like to know?" Inspector Gavrilović replied. "It was fashioned after the symbol of the Order of the Dragon, the knightly order to which Prince Vlad Țepeș of Wallachia belonged. It was handed down to him from his father. His father was called 'the Dragon,'— *Dracul* in Romanian—and Vlad Țepeș was called *Dracula*, or 'Son of the Dragon' as a result."

Adam swallowed the sarcastic remark that leapt to his tongue. "What happened to it?"

Inspector Gavrilović sighed. "It was lost a very short time after it arrived here."

"Your father, the altar boy, he's the reason it was lost again, wasn't he?"

"He was young," the inspector said, shaking his head so that his black curls bobbed. "It wasn't his fault. He didn't know better."

"I'm not making judgments, Inspector. God knows I'm not in any position to do that."

"My father was perhaps a little naïve. He was not like the other boys his age. He was more prone to lose track of time in the cathedral library reading St. Augustine than playing ball in the street and learning to be less trusting of others. He wanted to become a priest. After the events of the winter of 1941, he found his plans derailed."

"When the Germans invaded, a lot of people found their plans derailed," Adam said.

"My father paid a more personal price, a spiritual one. Nonetheless, he went to his grave believing what he did was right. He believed that the medallion was evil, that it attracted evil, and that it was dangerous to have so near." The inspector gazed up at the church's façade. "Maybe he was right. The church is impervious to supernatural assaults, but as we've seen, it is not impervious to the assaults of man. If my father had not done what he did, maybe there would have been no cathedral for the Yugoslav army to shell."

"What did he do?" Adam asked.

"He waited until late one night when the priest was asleep, and he snuck into his room. The old priest kept the medallion in a trunk at the foot of his bed. My father took it. Only after he left the cathedral did he realize he had absolutely no idea what to do with the thing. As he walked the darkened streets, he wracked his brain for an idea until he turned a corner and saw the river."

"Throwing it in the river wouldn't have kept it from being found," Adam said.

The inspector shot Adam a reproving glance. "He never had the chance. He was so busy contemplating his plan that he neglected to realize he was being followed. A pair of arms grabbed and held him so tightly he could barely breathe. A harsh voice told him to prepare his soul for heaven."

"He got away obviously," Adam muttered. "How?"

"The priest," Inspector Gavrilović answered. "A blow threw my father to the ground, and the man released his grip. When my father scrambled to his feet, he discovered the priest holding out a crucifix, reciting a verse my father had heard often. *Vade retro satana.* 'Step back, Satan.' The creature he held at bay had sharp teeth like a dog and crimson eyes that burned like hellfire. When the priest finished the verse, he lowered the cross. The monster lunged, only to impale himself on the wooden stake the priest held. The vampire staggered backward and burst into flames, disintegrating to ashes seconds later."

"But you said the medallion was lost again."

The inspector held up a finger. "You haven't let me finish. The priest ordered my father to run, and while he may have been naïve, my father was not stupid. He took off, glancing over his shoulder just long enough to see another one of the monsters set upon the old priest."

"You mean—"

"I'm afraid so."

A twinge of anger made Adam's face grow hot. "I'm sorry to hear that."

"From what I gather, the old priest was quite a force. He could have done a lot of good for Sarajevo in the dark days to come."

"Where did your father take the medallion?" Adam asked.

"He didn't know what to do. He wasn't sure he could make it back to the cathedral, but he knew for a fact he couldn't run all night. He came upon Sarajevo's city hall just as he was running out of breath. He thought maybe if he could find a place to hide inside, he would be safe until morning."

Adam's blood froze. "The Sarajevo city hall was converted into the Bosnian National Library after the end of World War II. If he hid it there ..."

The inspector nodded. "I'm afraid so. He discovered an unlocked door, and once inside, he set about finding a hiding place. On the third floor, he found a large room used for storage. It had a window overlooking the hills to the south and would catch the first light of the sun. He scrambled among the pieces of furniture stacked on end, hoping to make himself as inaccessible as possible. Ultimately, he wedged himself between one of the walls and the unused furniture. He discovered a loose brick and worked until he could get it free. He stuffed the medallion into the hole he made, cloth and all, and wedged the brick back into place. He waited there until the sun peeked above the hills, throwing the narrowest of beams onto the floor. He crawled out of his hiding place and ran out of the building, taking no heed of the civil servants already arriving for work."

"What happened to your father?"

"After that night, he couldn't bring himself to return to the cathedral, which naturally ended his career aspirations. And of course, after the war, the new government discouraged the profession." The inspector let out a chuckle. "He became an accountant instead. For his entire life, my father carried around the guilt that he was responsible for the old priest's death, or worse."

Adam frowned. "The library was destroyed."

"Do you honestly believe the medallion was destroyed along with it?" the inspector asked.

Adam shook his head. "I know it wasn't. But it could have been removed at any point during the fifty years between when your father put it there and the shelling that destroyed the library. Did your father tell anyone else about what happened?"

The inspector drew in a breath and let it out slowly. "Not even I knew what he went through until I found the letter he left for me after he died."

"When was that?"

"Three years ago, just after the siege was lifted."

"He kept the secret all that time?"

The inspector hesitated. "There was ... one incident. I had nearly forgotten about it until I read my father's letter. In his later years, my father, unfortunately, suffered from dementia. Maybe eight or nine years ago, I received a call that he had been found wandering in the library. One of the librarians, or perhaps it was a professor from the university, took him home. I always wondered why he went there, of all places. I just wish he had told me sooner. I could have done something. Maybe even saved lives."

"The vampires came back to Sarajevo during the war," Adam said. "I've been looking into a few murders—"

The inspector held up a hand and gave him an apologetic smile. "I am sorry, my friend. I think you really should leave the city now. I've done what I can to cover up what happened last night, but my influence will only go so far. You are playing a dangerous game, Dr. Mire. Good luck, and may God protect you."

As the inspector walked away, Adam's thoughts went to the call from his friend Radovan, telling him the library had been destroyed. Radovan could have been the one to escort the old altar boy home. Could the inspector's father have told him the story of the medallion hidden in the walls of the library, and if so, would Radovan have tried to find it? If Mihai Iliescu ever possessed the medallion, he had to get it from somewhere. Radovan knew Mihai; after all, he was the one who introduced Adam to the Romanian collector. Radovan could have given the medallion back to Mihai, thinking he was restoring it to its rightful owner, completely unaware the medallion's original owner still held a claim.

FORTY-THREE

Banja Luka, Bosnia and Herzegovina
13 October 1999

ARKADY STOPPED THE CAR ON the street beside a giant rust-colored building on the outskirts of the city. He glanced at Clara seated next to him.

"You do understand the meaning of 'safe house,' do you not?" he asked.

She fixed him with an icy stare. "I also understand the meaning of 'tear gas.'"

Arkady ignored the comment. "Stay close to me. I very much doubt we'll encounter any supernatural danger, but it is an abandoned building. A falling beam could kill you just as easily as a vampire."

"Are you trying to scare me?"

"I just want to be completely truthful."

Clara bristled at the sarcasm. "That's not the kind of truth I was talking about."

"Look," Arkady said, "about earlier—"

"Don't bother apologizing. This is a first for me. I'm not

sure how to handle being chased by Slavic bigots and possibly vampires."

Arkady raised an eyebrow. "Possibly?"

"I'm still having trouble wrapping my head around the idea that they're real."

Arkady grunted. "It doesn't get easier."

"Did you find out anything at your appointment this morning?"

"A few interesting facts."

"Such as?"

"Mr. Zorić was anxious to leave Banja Luka. Understandable, given that Muslims aren't really welcome here anymore, but he didn't have the money to go anywhere. That is, until just recently."

"Where did he get the money from?" Clara asked.

Arkady shrugged. "Apparently he was very good at sidestepping the question. No one knows. Of course, he never followed through with his plans. Adam and Kostya visited him, and not long after, both Mr. Zorić and Kostya were dead."

"Do you think Süleyman's Blade killed Mr. Zorić, too?"

Arkady shook his head. "Not likely. Ibrahim Zorić was known to have sympathies for groups like Süleyman's Blade, and we suspect he may have even had ties. There is also still the issue of Mr. Zorić's green hand to consider. Süleyman's Blade has never been known to do anything like that."

Clara let out a clipped laugh. "Right. He was murdered by the *other* sociopathic serial killer."

Arkady glowered, digging his fingernails into the steering wheel. "What is there to laugh about?"

"Look, I'm sorry. I'm just having trouble keeping all of this straight. First, someone is murdering vampire-hunting cops and leaving dragons painted in their own blood. And now you've told me about a *second* string of murders where the killer paints his victims' hands green."

He let his shoulders slump. For the first time, he looked tired. "I'm sorry as well. Sometimes I forget my experiences are not the same as an average person's."

"At least you don't have to deal with filing paperwork."

His mouth twisted into a wry grin "Trust me. There is paperwork."

"Why would Adam and Kostya visit Mr. Zorić?" Clara asked. "Who was he?"

"Just an old man," Arkady replied, "but he knew a lot about the history of Banja Luka. His family had deep roots here. His father was the caretaker of a small mosque, the last caretaker in fact. The mosque was destroyed late in World War II."

"Sounds like something Adam would be interested in. But he was supposed to be in Budapest. Why come here? You said there was another … death in Budapest. Who was it?"

"An antique dealer. Janos Kovács."

"Did he sell books?" The question escaped Clara's lips before she realized it. Inwardly she cursed herself.

"It's possible. Why?"

"Adam was … is crazy over antique books. He used to love going to antique stores to find old books, the more obscure the better."

In fact, he would have gone crazy for the copy of *The Giaour* she had hidden in the dresser upstairs in her room.

Arkady stroked his chin, his brows knit together. "It's interesting you should bring up antique books. After Ibrahim Zorić was murdered, they found several books in his house that seemed out of place."

Clara studied the dashboard of the car. "Out of place? In what way?"

"They were all old, early twentieth century, some late nineteenth. Most of them were in English, a few in German. Mr. Zorić didn't speak either. Also, as you can imagine, getting books into this country from the West has never been the easiest thing to do. He would have had to come by them recently."

"I'm sure you or your colleagues have already looked through them. If you'd gleaned any helpful information from them, we wouldn't be here."

"What if Adam took some of the books with him?" asked Arkady.

"That still doesn't answer the question of why Ibrahim Zorić had them to begin with."

"He could have been a pawn in someone else's game," Arkady offered. "The money, remember?"

"Where did you say Adam went after he left here?"

"Based on the next dead body?"

Clara glared. "You don't have to put it that way."

"Dubrovnik, Thessaloniki, possibly Berlin."

"So the professor in Thessaloniki, the one Arion told me about ..."

Arkady nodded. "It sounds like some morbid scavenger hunt. But if so, what's the prize? And what happened to the next clue?"

Clara didn't respond. She thought again about *The Giaour*.

Arkady opened the car door and stepped out. Clara followed. As they approached the building, Arkady's hand hovered over the gun hidden in the holster underneath his jacket. They found a door fastened with a chain and a padlock, but Arkady took less than a minute to pick the lock.

The chain slid off the door and hit the ground, clanking against the concrete. The noise sent a few pigeons into the air, but nothing more. They both paused and listened but were met with only silence. Arkady pushed the door open, and Clara let out the breath she hadn't realized she was holding.

They found themselves in a large empty room. Inside, the air was cool and damp. Dim sunlight filtered in through high windows. Their footsteps echoed in the expanse. Another door stood in the wall opposite where they had entered. When Arkady pushed on it, the rusty hinges squealed, and Clara thought her heart might stop. They paused to listen again, but as before, there was only silence.

On the other side of the door, a long hallway lined with rooms terminated at a small landing and yet another door. Sunlight seeped in around its edges, casting odd shadows in the space. A set of stairs led downward from the landing.

"This is it," said Arkady. "This is where Kostya died and where they found him."

Clara followed his gaze to the stairs. A rust-colored smear stained the tile floor near the top of the landing and retreated down the steps into the gloom below.

"Why come here?" she asked.

Arkady knelt. "I needed to see it for myself."

"Well then, now that we have, shouldn't we go?"

He glanced up at her. "Getting skittish?"

Clara looked back toward the door they had come through. "Maybe a little."

"Just a few minutes longer," Arkady said, standing. "I want to see what else there is to see."

Clara peered into the darkness below. "Down there?"

He took a step. "Where else?"

"Haven't your people already been all over this place?"

"They're not my people."

"Still, wouldn't they have told you about anything they found? You all have the same goal, right? Killing the vampires."

The cold determination in Arkady's steel-blue eyes made her shiver. "I told you I need to see for myself. There is nothing to fear here."

"How do you know?"

He reached into his shirt and pulled out the crucifix that hung around his neck. "Christ tells me."

A shriek pierced the silence and echoed through the stairwell. Arkady drew his gun and sprinted down the stairs. Clara ran after him, mostly because she didn't want to be left alone. At the bottom of the stairs another door-lined hallway stretched out before them. All the doors were closed save for one. Clara stayed close to Arkady as they crept down the hall toward the open door. More than once she thought she caught movement out of the corner of her eye, flinching every time and earning annoyed looks from Arkady.

As they neared the open door, Arkady held up a hand for Clara to stop. He pressed himself against the wall and Clara did the same. He motioned for her to wait there and then pivoted into the doorway, gun at the ready. His face immediately went white.

"*Bozhe moi*," he said.

"What?" Clara whispered. "What is it?"

Arkady lowered his gun and ran into the room. Clara followed, only to find him kneeling over the body of a woman. She had dark skin and black hair, and as Clara neared, she realized the woman was barely more than a girl.

"Is she ..."

Arkady shook his head. "She's gone, but she hasn't been dead very long."

He shifted positions, and Clara spotted something on the floor next to the body. She pointed to the object. "What's that?"

Arkady followed her outstretched finger.

"It's a book," he said as he reached for it.

As soon as he picked it up, another shriek tore through the warehouse. The sound bore into Clara's skull and dredged up every black nightmare she had ever dreamt. Arkady, cradling the book to his chest, leapt up and rushed out of the room. As he passed Clara, he grabbed her by the wrist and pulled her along. The shadows chased after them as they ran back the way they came, through the warehouse and out into the bright afternoon sun.

Arkady forced her back in the car and jumped into the driver's seat. They sped away from the warehouse.

"What do we do about that poor girl?" Clara asked. "We can't just leave her body there."

Arkady took a corner, the car's tires screeching. "Are you suggesting we go back?"

Clara shivered, despite herself. "No, of course not, but we can tell your police friends."

"That we can. And I guarantee by the time they get there the body will be gone."

"Then there's nothing?"

Arkady jerked the car to the left to maneuver around a slow-moving taxi and cut off an old Hungarian Lada. Blaring horns receded behind them. "Other than drive a stake through the heart of the bastard who did it? No."

Clara's gaze fell to the book in her lap. The cover was

disintegrating. Flakes of cracked leather came off in her hand, revealing the stiff cardboard underneath. There had once been gold leaf on the cover, as evidenced by the tiniest of flecks, but it had long since worn off. When Clara opened the yellowed pages, she discovered the book wasn't in English.

"Is this Polish?"

Arkady hazarded a glance at the book. "I believe it is."

"Do you know Polish?"

Arkady shook his head. "But I don't think the contents are what's important."

Clara leafed through the pages. This book had no markings in it like *The Giaour*, yet in other ways it reminded her of the book the backpacker had given her. It was possible they could have come from the same collection. About halfway through, she found the first surprise. A postcard. On the front was a picture of a cathedral. When Clara turned it over, she immediately wished she hadn't.

On the back was a smear of dried blood.

"Do you know where this is?" She handed the postcard to Arkady.

Arkady took the card from her. "That's the Cathedral of Jesus' Heart in Sarajevo. Is there anything else interesting in there?"

Clara continued to search the book. The next surprise sent her heart leaping into her throat. Shoved between the pages was a picture of Adam. His hair was dyed blond, but she'd never mistake his face. He stood outside what appeared to be a bar, a cigarette between his lips, seemingly looking directly at the camera.

"It's Adam," she said. "He's in Sarajevo. If he's started smoking again, I'm going to kill him."

"A few cigarettes are the least of his worries right now.

Are you sure that's where he is?"

She thrust the picture at him. "Why else would these things be in this book?"

Arkady frowned. "It's a little too easy, don't you think?"

"You believe someone is leading us there."

"More like herding us."

"What else can we do?" she asked quietly.

Arkady sighed. "Nothing. It's our only chance to find Adam, to find the medallion, to stop the Chetniks."

Clara remembered the warning of the man in the café about trusting the Russian. "What are you going to do with the medallion if you find it?"

Arkady shot her another annoyed look. "I've already told you. I will make sure it doesn't get into the wrong hands."

"But are there any right hands? Are you saying you know best?"

He tapped the brakes a little too hard. "I'm saying it won't be used to unleash utter chaos on the world."

"So it will be locked away somewhere."

He returned his gaze to the road ahead. "It will be safe."

Safe. Arkady's words were all Clara needed to decide she should keep her secret about *The Giaour* a little while longer.

FORTY-FOUR

Sarajevo, Bosnia and Herzegovina
14 October 1999

FROM HIS HIDING PLACE ACROSS the street, the gentleman watched the light in the second-story window go out. Seconds later, the door opened, and a man stepped out into the cold night air. Shivering, he pulled his coat tighter around him. Of course, the cold didn't bother the gentleman. After looking to the left and then to the right, the man walked down the street.

The gentleman followed. The police inspector strode briskly, no doubt eager to get home, not knowing he would never make it there. Huddled in his coat, he walked several blocks before stopping in front of a townhouse, one of the many almost identical residences on the street. He ascended the stairs, and when he reached the door, he fumbled with his keys.

The gentleman rushed up the stairs behind him without making a sound, more shadow than man. This kill he expected to be easier than the last. He had not been able to learn any of the young fool's secrets, at least not directly, but a search through his belongings turned up a scrap of paper with the police inspector's name.

He vowed not to give the police inspector the same chance to escape, but just as he heard the inspector's heartbeat and smelled the blood still in his veins, just as his eyeteeth pushed through his gums, the police inspector whirled around, a silver cross on a chain in his hand. The cross radiated searing heat and blinding light. For the gentleman it was like facing a blast furnace. Never before had he encountered someone able to wield faith as such an effective weapon.

Of course, they all thought they could, and the more arrogant and smug they were, the faster their conviction crumbled. This was not arrogance. This was confidence. The gentleman could not exploit the inspector's fear. The force knocked him down the steps and onto the street. The inspector, he realized through the burning pain, was chanting, and in his other hand, he held a wooden stake.

The gentleman refused to become a horror-movie cliché.

He waited until the inspector stood over him, stake raised for the killing blow. Fighting through the pain, he concentrated only on the weapon. As the stake came hurtling down, he brought his arm up to block it, shoved the inspector away, and staggered to his feet. They faced one another, the inspector still clutching the crucifix aloft.

"You can't hold me off forever," the gentleman growled.

The inspector's eyes narrowed. "I don't have to. I just have to hold you off until sunrise."

The gentleman chuckled. "Do you honestly think you'll last that long?"

"I suppose I'll find out."

"Where is the book?"

The inspector cocked his head to one side. "What book?"

"You know very well what book. That tactic didn't work so well for your friend Danilo either."

A look of concern passed over the inspector's face. "What did you do?"

The gentleman sensed him wavering. "I didn't do anything at all. Mr. Grubelić had the good sense to blow his brains out before I could get to him. A waste all the way around."

A mistake. The righteous fury channeled through the crucifix threw him back again. He fought to stay standing. "Surely you know by now that the book, *The Giaour*, is useless by itself. It's the key, but it's not the code."

"Then what is the code?"

"Why don't you ask your Russian friends? Or better yet, that American, Adam Mire."

A twitch of recognition played across the inspector's face.

"Oh, so you know him," the gentleman said.

"The name sounds familiar."

"Some say he's dangerous."

"If he is, I'm sure he can be dealt with."

The gentleman chuckled. "I'm sure."

"You seem to know a great deal about me," the inspector said, "but I don't know anything about you. Who are you? Or should I say who were you?"

"Who I am, or was, is not important, Inspector," he answered. "Just know this. Be careful trusting the people you think are your allies in your struggle against the darkness. You might find they're willing to betray you quicker than your enemies ever would."

At that moment a police car came careening around the corner, sirens blaring. The inspector turned his head, and the gentleman vanished into mist.

FORTY-FIVE

Mostar, Bosnia and Herzegovina
19 October 1999

THE CAFÉ RESTED AT THE base of a hotel on a street paralleling the river, not far from the Old Bridge, or rather from where the Old Bridge used to be. Dusk neared, and Adam sipped his third cup of coffee as he pored over the books splayed out on the table in front of him.

He was the only person in the café, save for two old men in fezzes playing chess. He hadn't ordered anything to eat, much to the consternation of the café's proprietor, an elderly Jewish woman. He reassured her on more than one occasion that he was certain she was a wonderful cook and that his refusal to eat was not intended as a comment on her food. He simply wasn't hungry. It did little to appease her.

He had come to Mostar from Sarajevo almost a week earlier. His books arrived the day after he did; the inspector had at least been true to his word. Adam spent most of his time in the café, trying to figure out what to do next. That evening he found himself puzzling over the journal of Andras Iliescu again, hoping in vain he'd find some morsel of insight he'd missed all the hundreds of times he'd read the Romanian vampire hunter's words. Adam was still lost in thought when the lights in the café dimmed. A shadow passed by his table. He looked up just as Elena sat down opposite him.

"What do you want?" he asked.

Her mouth twisted in a sarcastic grin. "Good evening to you as well, Dr. Mire."

"What are you doing here? Too many reminders of your ex-boyfriend in Sarajevo?"

"I came here to find you."

"Why?"

"We had a bargain. You haven't yet fulfilled your side of it."

"Only because I don't think you have any intention of fulfilling yours." He returned his attention to the journal. "I don't have anything more to say to you."

She pursed her lips in a mocking pout. "Careful now. You'll hurt my feelings."

"You don't have feelings," he snapped.

"How could you possibly know?" She grabbed the journal of Andras Iliescu from his hands and leafed through it. "Hmm, I remember him. He was a rather self-righteous sort."

Adam reached for the book. "He had every right to be."

She jerked the journal away from him. "Do you think? I mean deep down, was he any better than us really, given the things he did?"

"He repented."

She shook her head. "He still did them."

"He sought forgiveness."

She leaned across the table, allowing Adam to breathe in her lilac perfume. "All those people he was complicit in murdering, did it bring them back?"

Adam struggled to avoid meeting her gaze. "No."

"So much for that, then." Elena scooped up the entire stack of papers in front of Adam. "What else do you have here?"

"It's only research. Nothing that would interest you."

"You'd be surprised."

Elena flipped through the stack of documents, stopping midway through, the expression on her face turning sour. "A letter to the margrave of Baden sent from 'the Catholics of Albania'?"

"It may help explain why the Habsburgs decided to invade Kosovo in 1689. Roman Catholics like your family were scarce, but of course you know that. How many times did a priest ever visit your house?"

She shrugged. "Maybe twice. And only once to give communion."

"So really, did you ever even understand the difference between Islam and Christianity, or your own folk beliefs?"

"Not at the time," she said quietly.

"With the Catholic community in Kosovo in danger of dying out, that letter could have swayed the margrave, who probably saw an opportunity to expand Habsburg influence and gain favor with the new pope."

Elena's twisted grin returned. "But that's not why you have this letter, or the next one."

"What's the next one?"

"A report to the margrave of Baden concerning negotiations with the prince of Wallachia on allowing Habsburg armies into his territory." She chuckled. "I can only imagine what you must be like at a cocktail party."

Adam smiled, in spite of himself. "Would you be shocked to know I'm the rowdy one? You're right, though. I have the letter for another reason. The prince said no to allowing Habsburg forces to march across his domain. A sensible decision. It kept the fighting out of Wallachia. This letter says something curious, though. Constantin Brâncoveanu earned his title as the Prince of Wallachia under rather mysterious circumstances. His predecessor died of a 'disease of the blood.'"

Elena wrinkled her nose. "Perhaps you're jumping to conclusions."

"I draw conclusions from what the documents tell me," Adam said, "not the other way around. Quite a string of coincidences, don't you think? Tensions between the Germans and the Turks are simmering, poised to boil over. The old prince of Wallachia dies under mysterious circumstances, and the new one refuses to allow German soldiers in his territory. Meanwhile, the Germans receive a plea from Kosovo, deep in Ottoman territory. When fighting does break out, the Germans drive through Serbia into Albania, and the Romanian lands are spared."

She tossed the papers down on the table. "As you say."

"What do you want from me?" Adam asked.

"I told you. We have unfinished business."

"And I told you. No deal. Not anymore."

"I can be quite persuasive, you know." Elena traced a finger down his arm. "I usually get what I want."

Adam shifted away. "That's not going to work. You don't have any minions here to take my 'toys' this time."

Elena's lips parted in a knowing smile. "You're not going to hurt me."

"How can you be so sure?"

"Because you haven't heard the rest of my story yet." She brushed a raven lock behind her ear.

"What makes you think I want to hear the rest of it?"

"You mean you don't?"

Adam hesitated. "No."

She shot him a disapproving look. "You're a horrible liar, Dr. Mire. You like talking to us, learning what we know, what we've seen."

"That's not why I sought out Yasamin," Adam muttered.

Elena's smile became a self-satisfied smirk. "I'm not talking about Yasamin."

"Then who are you talking about?"

Her wicked grin widened. "The vampire you interviewed for your last book."

Adam stiffened. "How do you know about that?"

"I didn't. I guessed. Let's just say some of the passages had a familiar ring to them. Your details, they were a little too authentic. Besides, you already knew we existed before you sought out Yasamin. You had to learn about us somehow."

"I didn't find him. He found me. Tried to kill me, in fact."

"What stopped him?"

"The crucifix around my neck."

Elena winced.

Adam reached for his collar. "I still have it, if you want me to show it to you."

Elena didn't respond. "What was his name?"

"Cyryl."

"And where did you two meet?"

"Poland. Kraków," Adam answered. "I was at the university library doing research, and I wasn't above slipping a few *złotych* into the hands of a librarian to stay after hours. Sometimes I still wish I had packed up early that day. He attacked me just as I was replacing some manuscripts on a shelf. I didn't know what he was then. I thought maybe he was some psychotic homeless person who had somehow made it into the library."

"But you figured it out, like the smart boy you are."

Adam glared. "By accident. He managed to grab my shirt and tear off the top button, exposing the crucifix. He screamed and backed away. I was standing between him and the only way out of the room. He couldn't get past me as long as the crucifix was visible. Sunrise was in only a few hours. I could have kept him there. I could have killed him permanently."

"But you didn't."

"If I was truly looking at a vampire, there was no telling how old he was, what he had seen, what he remembered. I realized I had been given the opportunity of a lifetime. So, I cut a deal with him. If he told me about his life, I would let him go."

"And he obliged?"

Adam held up his hands. "He was desperate to get out of there before the sun came up. He told me everything about himself. He was born in Danzig in 1387. He had been a Teutonic Knight before he was turned. He even fought in the Battle of Grunwald in 1410. Just before dawn, I let him go. With the sun rising, I knew he'd be more interested in getting to a safe place than killing me. I went back to my room right away and wrote down everything I could remember."

"And how many people do you think Cyryl has killed since you let him go?"

"I don't know."

"Do you think any of them were children?"

Adam banged his hand on the table. "Stop it! Why are you doing this?"

"Because what you did bothers you. I'm giving you an opportunity to make up for your decision that night. Think of how many lives you'll save if you help me stop the Chetniks."

"You're one to talk about saving lives."

"Believe what you will, Dr. Mire. I have my reasons for caring about such things."

"What reasons would those be?"

"I keep trying to tell you, but you keep running away."

Adam glanced around the nearly deserted café. Neither the two old men nor the owner paid them any attention. In fact, it seemed they all did their best to avoid looking at either him or Elena. "Okay, you win. Tell me."

She smiled at him again. "If you wish."

FORTY-SIX

Gračanica, Kosovo
14 October 1689 Old Style

THE COLD CAME EARLY THAT year. Elena pulled her coat around her as she marched her small retinue of sheep and goats from the pasture back to the barn late in the evening. The cannons booming in the distance left the animals jittery. She learned from one of her neighbors that war had come to their small valley. The soldiers of the German emperor had invaded, trying to push the Turks out of all the Christian lands they occupied. So far, though, the fighting had not affected her.

She liked to think that if the soldiers did come to her farm, she would simply tell them they couldn't stay there, that they would have to take their fighting elsewhere. Of course, it didn't work that way, but why should a war that didn't concern her be imposed upon her? In a way, it was like a blood feud, a blood feud on a large scale, and as in a blood feud, innocent people were inevitably hurt.

When she arrived at the barn, a familiar figure waited

for her. Stjepan's coat didn't fit him well, and he shivered. She passed by him without saying a word. After she prodded the sheep and the goats into the barn, she stood at the open door and motioned for him to come inside.

"You've had more dreams," she said once she'd closed the door against the bitter cold.

"Yes," he replied.

"And there have been more deaths."

"Yes."

"And you've come to see me because you want my help, despite the fact that nothing I've done so far has changed anything."

"No, I came to see you, Elena, because I wanted to. I needed to. The path I follow now is partially because of you."

Elena felt her cheeks flush. "Nonsense. You chose the path you're on. You can't blame me for any wrong turn your life has taken."

"Blame you?" Stjepan laughed, which only made Elena angrier. "I'm not blaming you for anything, Elena. You helped me to see that I was never truly happy at the monastery. Despite what my mother wanted, despite what I thought I wanted, I always had a small knot of doubt in my heart. I prayed for God to remove it, but He never did. Now I know why—it was not the life I was meant to live."

"Where did you go?"

"I have an uncle with a farm to the north of the monastery. He was more than happy to take me in. He lets me sleep in his barn."

"Then I won't apologize for what I can offer."

As the sun set, Elena ventured outside again and set about making a fire to cook their supper. Stjepan helped where he could, but he mostly watched. Elena supposed his uncle was a very patient man, though Stjepan couldn't have made a worse farmer than he did a monk.

"Tell me about your new dreams," she said as they both sat close to the fire after they finished eating. "How many more have you had?"

"Three."

"More rich 'pilgrims' to the monastery?"

Stjepan nodded. "And there is nothing I can do but watch them die."

Elena absentmindedly poked at the fire. "These men seem very idiotic."

"They are certainly guilty of the sin of pride, which can sometimes make a person think of himself as immortal and keep him from seeing obvious dangers."

"Is this father of yours at the monastery guilty of the same sin?"

"He is a man, imperfect, like everyone else. I don't know if pride is what caused him to send me away, but there is something strange going on. These men are part of some secret cabal. I can't say what their aims are, but I've come to believe they met at the monastery with the father's blessing. After the murder in the guest house, they all left—back to their homes I assume, where most men would consider themselves safe."

"How were they killed?" Elena asked.

"All with the same dagger I saw before, the one with the eagle on the hilt, and all by the same black-clad man. The first of them was alone in a room, a personal study, maybe. He sat at a desk with papers on top and an inkwell with a quill. Do you remember the symbol from the yew tree? I saw it again, on the wax seal of a letter the man received. It upset him so much he screamed at the poor servant who brought it to him, lapsing occasionally into a language I don't know. I don't think he was a Serb. He may have been a Vlach."

"Vlachs are wanderers, not rich landowners. They live in tents most of the year following their flocks."

Stjepan shrugged. "Maybe his mother or his grandmother was a Vlach and taught him the language, or at least the more colorful parts of it. In any event, this man sent the servant away and shut himself up in the dark room. He lit a candle and waited, quaking in fear. He knew what was happening to him."

"From the seal on the letter?" Elena stirred as the pot hissed.

"The symbol meant something to him. Very shortly, the hooded man emerged from the shadows behind his chair. I don't know how he got into the room. I could see only one door. He reached around the chair and slit the man's throat. The man made only a small grunt before he died. I still couldn't see the hooded man's face, but in the candlelight, I could see the face of his victim clearly. He was terrified."

In the fire, Elena imagined she could see the red eyes of the monsters that had killed her family. "What happened in your next dream?"

Stjepan glanced sideways at her. "I thought you weren't interested in my dreams."

"I'm not." Elena hoped that the light of the fire wasn't enough for Stjepan to see her face turn red again. "Listening to your stories is just a way to pass the time."

Stjepan grunted. "If you say so. The next dream was only a day later. I saw another man, again in his home, frantically looking for something—opening doors, opening boxes, groping around in the dark. After some time, he apparently found what he sought, a tiny wooden box shoved into the corner of a cabinet. He seemed surprised to find it there, but relieved. Inside the box was a silver clasp for a cloak, forged into the shape of a falcon. The hooded man appeared out of the air again, as the rich *gospodin* examined the clasp. The intruder sunk his dagger into the man's back. The falcon clasp went skittering across the floor."

"So you've come to ask me what I think the falcon means?"

Stjepan removed his grandfather's dagger from its sheath at his waist. The gold falcon's claw gleamed in the firelight. "I know what the falcon means. In its talons, it clutched a scroll. Father Teodor used to recite a poem to us. These men were reciting parts of the same poem together in the room under the church. I didn't make the connection until I saw the falcon. A long time ago, there was a battle against the Turks, not too far from here actually. We were a free people then. Before the battle, the prophet Elijah, the same prophet in the mural in the monastery, appeared to our prince in the form of a grey falcon. He presented the prince with a scroll and was given a choice, an earthly kingdom or a heavenly one. If he chose the earthly kingdom, the prophet told him he would overcome the Turks that day. If he chose the heavenly one, he would be defeated by the Turks and die in battle, but he and his people would be remembered by God."

"What kingdom did he choose?"

"The heavenly one, of course."

Elena scoffed. "Stupid man."

Stjepan frowned. "What do you mean, 'stupid man'? He was a hero. Because of him, we are blessed with a special place in heaven."

"If what you said is true, he was a selfish coward,"

Elena persisted. "How long ago was this battle? How long have the Turks terrorized us all? How many have suffered simply because this prince wanted special privileges? Look around you. How can you say you're blessed when everyone is suffering?"

"I suppose it was too much to expect you to understand," Stjepan said, shaking his head.

Elena glared. "I suppose so."

They sat in silence for a while, watching the fire. Occasionally, Elena stole glances at Stjepan. His face was rougher, harsher than she remembered, as were his hands. His skin was slightly sunburned from working outside. She considered it an improvement. Maybe this uncle of his would have all his useless ideas worked out of him soon. And then—what? Then they would never see one another again because there would be no reason.

"Are you sure you don't have another motive for visiting?" she asked.

Stjepan hesitated before answering. "I said I had three dreams. The third one was just last night. There's a chance what I saw hasn't happened yet. I'm going to see the man from this dream. I want you to come with me."

"What would be the point in that?"

"Are you not any longer interested in avenging your family?"

"How? Even with your abilities, the vampire slipped by us like a whisper on the wind. How do you intend to fight an adversary you cannot see?"

"There is a woman who lives not far from my uncle," Stjepan replied. "She's Albanian, like you, but people say she's a witch. I asked for her aid, and she agreed to teach me what she knows in exchange for hardly anything at all, just a little food, and maybe a favor or two. I know how to control my abilities. I know what mistakes I made before. I won't repeat them."

"What are you going to do?"

"I'm going to ask if I can help protect him."

"And if he says no?"

"He won't," Stjepan said. "They're scared. All of them."

"Why do you want me?"

"Because I don't think I can trust anyone else. And also because the witch said it would be necessary. She said our fates are intertwined."

Elena laughed. "I don't understand how."

"Not even after you've seen how our lives have crossed paths the way they have?"

"What I have seen is you inserting yourself into my life."

"She told me you wouldn't believe me." He retrieved his bag and pulled out a small wooden box. "It's why she gave me this."

He opened the box, and three butterflies fluttered out. Their iridescent blue wings caught the light of the fire and shimmered as the insects circled the blaze before flying off into the darkness.

"How are they even possible?" Elena whispered. "The weather has already turned."

Stjepan shrugged. "I told you. She's a witch."

Elena stared into the darkness where the butterflies had flown. "Butterflies represent fate."

"Maybe you'll believe me now?"

"Why the sudden urgency?" she asked.

"The sound of guns and cannons gets louder every day. I can't help but think my dreams are related to the coming war."

"Why should anyone care about warring over this

place? There's nothing here for anyone who isn't a farmer."

"Does it matter to princes and kings and sultans? They fight because they want what another has. It's the only reason they need."

The fire had gone to coals. Elena stood and prepared to smother it. "I don't care what princes and kings and sultans need. My needs are simple. Why can't theirs be?"

"Are your needs really that simple, Elena?"

"They are. I need pastures for my animals and rain for my crops. That's all."

"So you're content?"

Elena didn't look at him as she scooped shovelfuls of dirt onto the fire. "Yes."

"Living in a barn, by yourself, with no one to talk to."

"That's not true. I have my neighbors."

"Still, you must get lonely, especially at night, when all your neighbors go inside their houses and shut their doors. And it must be difficult, not being like them."

The fire hissed and sputtered as it died. Still, Elena continued to heap dirt onto it. "What do you mean?"

"You're a woman."

Elena stopped, the shovel poised over the fire's last few glowing orange embers. "They don't see me that way."

Stjepan stood. "But you are, even with your hair cut short and your baggy clothes, you're a woman. Wouldn't it be good, just once, to have others see you that way, to not have to live your life pretending to be something you're not?"

"I can't. I took a vow."

Stjepan stepped closer. "You took that vow in order to protect your family, but they're gone. You have no reason to keep living this way."

"Nonetheless—"

Stjepan moved even closer, closing the gap between them. "Nonetheless what? Elena, I came here tonight because I can't stop thinking about you. You're the most beautiful woman I've ever met, and I won't let you tell me that you don't care for me at all."

Elena was uncomfortable with Stjepan standing so close, but she didn't back away. "I can't tell you that."

Stjepan kissed her. "That's what I wanted to hear."

Elena found Stjepan annoying and frustrating, but a small part of her had been happy to see him that evening. He was right. It scared her to think how solitary the rest of her life would be, especially on nights she couldn't sleep, alone in the barn. With the fire out, the heat of Stjepan's body felt good. He leaned in to kiss her again. In her mind, she saw herself pushing him away and telling him to leave, but in reality, she let him kiss her. He took the shovel from her and threw it to the ground. She led him into the barn and closed the door.

In the darkness she found him. Her arms wrapped around his waist. Their lips met again in a long, unhurried kiss. They took time to explore. He ended the kiss, almost apologetically, and stepped back to slip his shirt over his head. She ran her hands over the taut muscles of his stomach and chest. Hard work had done more than callous his hands, it seemed. He pulled her to him again for another kiss, a more urgent one. The heat of his bare torso penetrated her clothes. She suddenly became aware of how coarse, how rough her shirt and pants were, how unlike a woman they made her. She pulled away and undressed. Stjepan discarded the rest of his clothes as well. When they embraced again, she let Stjepan's calloused hands explore her body, from her breasts across her stomach, down toward her hips.

He lowered her onto the straw-covered floor of the barn. She grasped his thighs as he straddled her. For a moment she thought the heat might set the hay on fire. She arched her back as they began to move in unison. Just as the other times she and Stjepan had touched, all her senses flowed out beyond her body. The straw beneath her jabbed into her back, but the thousands of tiny pricks of pain only served to make the pleasure greater. She could hear not only the animals in their stalls, but the ones outside in the forest—the wolves, the owls, even the badgers burrowing under the earth.

Up above, the stars and the moon shown down as if the roof of the barn weren't there. Sweat glistened on Stjepan's body, his muscles rippling with his effort. The thought briefly passed through her mind that she shouldn't be able to see him at all before she lost herself completely in the rhythm. Faster and faster together they moved, until finally everything exploded in a white-hot wave that obliterated the world.

FORTY-SEVEN

Gračanica, Kosovo
15 October 1689 Old Style

THE FOLLOWING MORNING JUST BEFORE dawn, Elena awoke to find Stjepan still sleeping. As quietly as she could, she gathered up her clothes and put them on, then slipped out of the barn. A low mist hung over the valley, and she breathed in the chilly air. After a few minutes Stjepan joined her.

"I can see why you might be reluctant to leave a place like this," he said, surveying the valley. "I feel closer to God here than I ever did at the monastery."

"What about your uncle's farm?"

He smiled. "You are not at my uncle's farm."

She looked away to keep him from seeing her blush. "It is the only home I've ever known. I'm not sure where else I would go."

He grasped her hand, intertwining his fingers with hers. "We should leave soon. We have most of a day's ride ahead of us."

They prepared Stjepan's horse and headed off to the east, over the hills and through woods now filled with mostly barren trees. They stopped only once, in a clearing by a stream, to eat a quick midday meal and to allow Stjepan's horse to have a drink.

"What do you know about the man we're going to see?" asked Elena.

"His name is Zoran Dejanović. His family has been wealthy for generations. They once owned a silver mine. Of course the Turks took it, like everything else, but over the years they amassed enough wealth that it scarcely matters. They also work with the local authorities to keep the mine operating and are paid handsomely for it."

Elena narrowed her eyes. "And this is the person you're trying to protect?"

"The menace is far bigger than any of these men. I don't pretend to know what plan the vampires have or why they are targeting these men, but I do know that when they are all gone, the vampires won't stop. There will be bloodshed on a far larger scale."

They reached the home about an hour before sunset. As they approached, Elena could not help but gawk. Three stories high with a steeply pitched tile roof, the stone structure dwarfed her tiny family home of just three rooms. As they approached, a servant came toward them, a scowl on his face. He demanded to know who they were.

Stjepan dismounted. "My name is Stjepan. I'm here to see Zoran Dejanović."

"The *gospodin* is indisposed at the moment," the servant replied.

"It's urgent," Stjepan said.

The man grunted. "Urgent you say? What is this urgent business?"

"It's about his fallen brothers."

The servant eyed him and then Elena, who attempted to copy Stjepan's serious demeanor. "Wait here," he said finally and left.

When he returned, he beckoned for them to follow him. Stjepan helped Elena off the horse. He handed the reins to the servant.

"The *gospodin* awaits you inside," the servant said, and he led the horse off toward the stables.

Stjepan and Elena stepped inside the house, into a large entry hall. A set of stairs led up to the second floor. To the left, an archway led into a formal sitting room where a fire burned in the fireplace. To the right, another archway led into the dining hall. Zoran Dejanović was nowhere to be found.

"Well," Elena asked, "where is he?"

She suddenly felt the sharp steel in the small of her back. "Right behind you," a harsh voice said in her ear.

Stjepan spun around. "Drop the knife," he ordered.

"Not until you tell me why you're here," Zoran Dejanović said. "And quickly, before my hand slips, and I cut your friend."

"I'm here to help you," Stjepan said.

"I don't believe you. How do you know what happened to the others?"

Elena fought to keep her breathing steady.

Stjepan took a step toward them. "I was there, at the monastery where it began."

There was a sharp intake of breath. "You're the monk who was in Bartolomej's room." A new edge entered his voice as he pressed the knife harder against Elena's back. "All the more reason to have you killed."

Faster than Elena could see, Stjepan covered the rest

of the distance between them. He seized the man's hand and squeezed until Zoran yelped and dropped the knife.

"If I had wanted you dead," Stjepan growled, "I would have killed you by now. I was telling the truth when I said I was here to help. Now can we please have a discussion like civilized men?"

Zoran glared and cradled his injured hand. "Who are you?"

"I told your servant. My name is Stjepan."

"What you just did, that was witchcraft."

Stjepan shook his head. "No witchcraft."

"Then how do you explain—"

"I'm a *dhampir*."

Zoran regarded him silently for a moment. "Witchcraft or not, it certainly is the devil pursuing us then."

He led them into the sitting room and motioned toward the chairs arranged around the fireplace. "You'll forgive my initial greeting. As you can imagine, we have all been on edge."

Elena sank into her chair. It was covered in so much fabric she found it impossible to sit comfortably and fidgeted until Stjepan shot her a reproachful glance.

"What can you tell me about why you were at the monastery?" Stjepan asked Zoran.

Zoran pursed his lips. "My brothers and I traveled to Gračanica to seek spiritual guidance."

Stjepan grunted. "We both know that is not entirely true."

He fixed Stjepan with a cold glare. "We were mere pilgrims there, nothing more."

"You are severely hindering my ability to help you."

Zoran didn't respond. He maintained the same detached expression. "Tell me, I've never met one such as yourself. What is it like?"

"I can't explain it to you. I don't know any other way to be."

"But the bloodlust—"

"There is no bloodlust."

Zoran raised an eyebrow. "Not at all?"

"Fortunately that was not one of the traits passed down to me." Elena noticed, though, that Stjepan gripped the chair so hard his knuckles turned white.

Just then the servant who had met them appeared at the door. "*Gospodin*, I'm sorry to bother you, but as I was putting away our guest's horse in the stables, the other horses began to panic. They are rearing up, and they are going to injure themselves trying to break out of their stalls."

Zoran swore. Stjepan leapt out of the chair and ran past the servant out of the room. Elena followed. When they reached the stables, the scene was just as the servant had described. The horses were panicking, neighing wildly, bucking and kicking, their terror evident in their eyes.

"What could possibly be causing this?" Zoran asked.

"Get back inside," Stjepan barked.

Zoran didn't heed the warning quickly enough. A hooded man emerged from the shadows surrounding the stables and plunged his dagger into Zoran's side. The *gospodin* crumpled to the ground without ever making a sound.

"No!" Stjepan screamed.

The hooded figure fled, vanishing back into the shadows. Stjepan gave chase. Elena went to follow, but a hand clamped around her arm. She turned to discover a second man, dressed all in black like the first, his face hidden below a hood save for his leering grin. She tried to wrench her arm free, but he held her like a vise and drew her toward him. She blindly raked her fingers across his face with her free hand. Screaming, he let her go. She darted back toward the stables, but he remained only a few steps behind her.

An empty stall near the back held what Elena was looking for—a scythe. She yanked it from its place on the wall, and when the man entered, she swung, barely missing him. He drew a knife but couldn't strike at her as long as she held the curved blade. They were at an impasse. The man blocked Elena's escape, but he couldn't run without the risk of Elena disemboweling him.

"Why do you pretend to be something you're not?" he asked, his voice low and gravelly.

"I'm not pretending," Elena replied. "It's our custom."

The man chuckled. "That's not what I meant."

The horses continued to buck and panic. The one in the next stall kicked the wall, startling Elena. The stranger lunged at her and kicked the scythe out of her hand before she could bring it to bear. She stumbled to the ground. Knife poised, he stood over her, his breathing heavy and raspy. Suddenly, his hand relaxed and he dropped the blade. He fell to his knees before he pitched face-forward to the ground, Stjepan's talon-hilted knife protruding from his back. Stjepan stood in the entryway to the stall.

"Did you catch the other one?" Elena asked. "Is he dead?"

"He escaped," Stjepan replied, doing little to hide the frustration in his voice, "but I did see his face."

Elena struggled to her feet, refusing Stjepan's outstretched hand. "What of it?" She gestured to the body of the hooded figure on the stable floor. "You can stare at *his* face all you want. It won't help you stop the next murder."

Stjepan balled his hand into a fist and slammed it into the doorframe so hard the wooden beam cracked. "What would you have me do, Elena? Nothing?"

Elena regarded him as he stood in the doorway, trembling with anger. "What happened?"

Stjepan let out a long breath. "I was pursuing the hooded man. The *gospodin*'s servant, the loyal fool, came running from the direction of the house and leapt onto the man's back. The killer threw him off without any effort, and he hit the ground hard enough to crack his skull open. He did manage to pull the man's hood from his head, though." Stjepan hesitated, as if recalling some horrific event. "The look on the man's face was feral, like a wolf in human form. He had wild black hair and an unkempt beard. His eyes burned red like hellfire. He turned his gaze to me, and I thought he might attack me next, but I suppose he had already accomplished what he set out to do. A wicked grin spread across his face before he disappeared among the trees."

"Did you recognize him?"

"No, but I did recognize the clasp on his cloak. It bore the symbol from the yew tree."

When they stepped outside, both Elena and Stjepan could see that the wall of the stable bore the same symbol—painted in blood.

FORTY-EIGHT

Mostar, Bosnia and Herzegovina
19 October 1999

SILENCE COVERED THE CAFÉ LIKE a shroud.

"Come back to Sarajevo with me," Elena said.

Adam laughed. "You must be joking."

She narrowed her eyes. "I never joke."

"And be your new Bogdan? No thanks."

"I'd never do that to you. You don't deserve it."

"Playing at having a conscience again?" he asked.

She wrinkled her nose. "Whatever Bogdan told you was a lie."

"He said he left university and his family because of you."

"He was expelled from university," Elena corrected, "and his family didn't want to have anything to do with him."

"I would imagine his grades suffered after you sunk your fangs into him," Adam hissed. "He could have had a promising career as an engineer. His family was probably ashamed."

"Dr. Mire, his grades had nothing to do with it." Her voice was as cold and sharp as a steel blade. "He raped a young girl. She was so distraught she killed herself. He would have done it again had I not intervened."

"So you're the altruistic one?" Adam crossed his arms. "Somehow I'm not convinced."

Elena stood. "Suit yourself, Dr. Mire. When you're ready to search for the answers to your questions, you know where to find me. I'll see you in Sarajevo soon."

"I wouldn't count on it." Adam reached for one of his books.

"I'm sorry for what Bogdan did, but it doesn't change anything. The Chetniks—"

He slammed the book down on the table, and the bang reverberated through the café. "The Chetniks can burn this goddamned country to the ground for all I care."

Her eyes expressed the disappointment a parent might feel for a prodigal child. She left, dragging the shadows behind her.

Adam returned to the book he had been reading, only to see another shadow fall across his table. He looked up to see one of the old men from the chess game.

"A word, *gospodin*?" the man said.

The retort Adam prepared withered when he saw the grave expression on the man's face. Adam nodded, and motioned for him to sit.

"Do you realize who you were just speaking with?" the old man asked.

"You mean the young girl?"

The man scowled as if he had just smelled something rotten. "She wasn't a young girl, *gospodin*, as I imagine you are well aware."

Adam studied the old man. "How do you know that?"

"These old eyes have seen almost everything," he replied. "I have encountered her kind before, from afar. During the Second World War, there were many of them here. Now they have come back."

"Do you know what they want?"

"What do they always want? Bloodshed." He eyed Adam with a steely gaze. "But I must ask you. What are you doing? She did not attack you. You seemed to be having a pleasant conversation."

Adam chuckled. "Trust me. It was anything but pleasant."

"What did she tell you?"

"Nothing you should be worried about."

"I'm worried about what she told you." He pointed a shaky finger at Adam. "It's you, *gospodin*. You foreigners are bringing them here. Foreigners brought the other one here, too."

Adam raised an eyebrow. "There was another vampire here?"

"About a week ago a man and a woman came to town. He was a Russian. I do not know where she was from. My friend Viko said he saw them at another café down the street from here. They spoke English to one another."

"English? What were they doing here?"

The man shrugged. "I don't know, but there was an incident the next day, a burglary of some sort. The man and the woman left, but that night, the vampire came. I knew immediately what he was. He had a look in his eye only they have. He was a predator."

"What did he look like?" Adam asked.

"Tall. Dark hair. A beard. He and a few others came into this café. The others were … well, they were all affiliated. I knew by their tattoos."

"Chetniks," Adam said.

The man glanced frantically around the café. "Please, *gospodin*, do not say that word too loud. They have ears everywhere these days. Everyone here is fearful. What do I say to them?"

"Tell them there's no need to be afraid. What the vampires want isn't here." Adam paused. "I'm not staying either. I'll be gone in the morning."

The man nodded. "Thank you, *gospodin*."

Adam watched as the old man left, but he wasn't thinking about the frightened residents of Mostar. His mind was on the foreign couple who conversed in English.

FORTY-NINE

Sarajevo, Bosnia and Herzegovina
21 October 1999

ADAM STOOD IN THE OPEN courtyard after dark, his breath coming out in white puffs as he gazed up at the Church of Jesus' Heart. Floodlights illuminated the façade so that it stood like a beacon against the black sky, but a beacon for what, Adam didn't know. No one else was about that late. He was alone with his thoughts, attempting to sort through them all, planning what to do next, though he knew his final destination with dead certainty.

Of course, he didn't hear Elena approach. She appeared next to him wearing a white, fur-trimmed coat that accentuated the contours of her body.

"So you returned," she said.

"You knew I would," Adam replied.

"Sooner or later. I'm happy it was sooner."

Adam snorted. "Happy? You?"

"Why is it so hard to believe?"

"You're not human."

"But I was once. And I remember. It doesn't change us as much as you assume, when it happens. Who we are in life has a great deal to do with who we are in death."

"You're still a murderer."

She smirked. "So are you."

"I'm not going to win this argument, am I?"

"I've had several hundred years of practice."

"Point taken."

"What are you going to do now that you're back?" she asked.

Adam let out his breath slowly. "I'm going to talk to Dragomir, and then I'm going to kill him."

"How do you plan to do that?"

"With your help."

"I'll offer what aid I can, of course, but I don't know if it will be enough."

He glanced at her. Her hands buried in the pockets of her coat, she fidgeted as if trying to keep warm. Her ability to act human sent chills up Adam's spine that had nothing to do with the temperature. "But you're a vampire."

"We rarely fight one another. There are so few of us. I cannot tell you what will happen. When are you planning this meeting?"

"Give me a few days."

"I hope you have a few days."

"As always, your confidence in me is astounding."

"You mistake my intent. The Chetniks are moving. It won't be long."

He gazed back up at the façade of the church. "Does it pain you? To be so close?"

"Not anymore," she said quietly.

FIFTY

Gračanica, Kosovo
20 October 1689 Old Style

As Elena crested the hill with her sheep and goats, she looked toward the barn to see if Stjepan waited for her. She hadn't seen him since they failed to save Zoran Dejanović from the hooded man. He had dropped her off back at her farm and left with a wordless nod.

As she led the animals into the barn and into their stalls, she continued to scan the path for him. The sounds of guns and cannons echoed through the hills all day, making the animals skittish. The fighting had come much closer, and some of Elena's neighbors had already left for the refuge of relatives or friends in other places. Perhaps Stjepan and his uncle had fled as well. The thought made her stomach turn.

Elena had nowhere else to go.

By the time the animals were settled, the sun had nearly set, and she knew she would not be seeing Stjepan that evening. Maybe the next day.

Even as she hoped, she hated herself for being so weak, for breaking her vows, for caring about someone else, for relying on someone else, even to do such a small thing as ease her loneliness. She built a fire to cook her supper.

Hands, muscular and rough, gripped her arms and pinned them to her side. She thrashed about, but the hands were too strong. Three men emerged from the darkness. They all appeared to be dressed in soldiers' uniforms. One of them said something too quick for Elena to understand, but it sounded like Serbian. The others, including the one holding her, laughed. The smell of alcohol on his breath nearly caused her to retch.

She tried again to twist and kick her way out of the grasp of the one who held her and landed a lucky blow on his shin with the heel of her boot, but he didn't let her go. Instead, he twisted her left arm backwards and barked an insult in her ear. She cried out, and he nearly let her go then. The other three stood in stunned silence. Elena realized until that moment they had all thought she was a man.

Their mouths twisted into malicious grins. The one nearest walked up to Elena and grabbed her by the chin. He turned her head, forcing her to look him in the eye. With his other hand, he groped her breast. He said something to the others, and they all laughed again—until Elena spit in his face. Glaring at her, the man wiped the spit from the side of his nose and brought the back of his hand across her cheek before grabbing her breast again.

A second later, he was lying on the ground with a knife in his back buried all the way to the hilt. While his two companions standing by the fire searched frantically for the attacker, the soldier holding Elena suddenly loosened his grip. She broke free and spun around to fight him off, but he crumpled to the ground in front of her. Behind him stood Lek, the traveler who had known her father, holding a bloody dagger. Elena glanced over her shoulder to see the two remaining men reach for their own knives, but they were far too slow for Lek. He threw his knife and one of the soldiers fell backwards, grasping at the blade sticking from his throat, desperate to stop the gushing blood. His struggle ended in seconds, and he lay still.

Lek turned toward the last man, his eyes gleaming in the firelight. The corners of his mouth turned up in a wolfish grin. "Run," he said.

The soldier immediately took off toward the forest. Lek pulled the knife out of his first victim's back, and chased after him.

Elena crept toward the dead soldier lying on the ground with the knife in his neck. She snatched up the dagger and cradled it in her lap in the circle of firelight. She waited and listened. For a long time nothing happened until finally, a scream echoed through the blackness. Not long after, a figure approached the fire. Elena's fist tightened around the hilt of the knife, but she relaxed her grip when the fire illuminated Lek's face.

"They won't be bothering you anymore," he said, "but we should hide the bodies, in case their friends come looking for them."

Elena helped him move the bodies of the four soldiers, and Lek then spent the next several hours digging a hole large enough to hold them.

"Why haven't you gone?" Lek asked her. "All your neighbors have. Don't you know it's not safe to stay here anymore?"

"Where would I go?" Elena replied.

"Back to Albania, back to the mountains, where you came from."

Elena shook her head. "That's not my home, not anymore. I have trouble even remembering what it was like."

"Such a shame. You shouldn't forget who you are, Elena, or where you come from. You still have family there. You should go to them. You should see the sun set over the black peaks, dip your hand into a cold mountain stream, gaze up into the deep-blue sky from a mountain meadow."

"Why are you still here?" Elena asked. "Why haven't you gone?"

"I have some business that I must attend to first."

"It was extremely lucky for me you were here."

His gaze lingered on her for a moment. "Yes, it was."

Elena surveyed the bodies of the dead soldiers lying in a heap. "Where were those bastards from? What were they doing here?"

"They were Serbian soldiers, fighting along with the Germans," Lek answered. "They're camped not too far from here, and I imagine they were looking for some entertainment. They've become arrogant, now that they've driven the Turks out of this area."

"The Turks are gone? For good?"

Lek let out a deep, throaty laugh. "For good? I doubt it, but for now. Would you want them gone for good?"

"Do you have to ask that question?"

Lek laughed again. "You're a very smart girl, Elena, but you have a lot to learn. What would happen if the Turks did go away forever? Do you think the Germans would simply go back to their homes? I don't, and I don't think they'd be any better than the Turks."

For a while, neither of them spoke. Elena watched as

the hole Lek dug became wider and deeper. He seemed tireless.

"Lek, do you know what happened to my father?" she asked finally.

"What do you mean? I wasn't here when the attack you spoke of happened."

"No, I mean before—before we came here, before he became a drunk and a coward, hiding from the world."

"You mean he never told you?"

"Not everything."

"He was not always that way. It saddens me to hear what he became, but I suppose in a way it was inevitable. These blood feuds are tearing us apart. They're keeping us from becoming what we could be."

"Was it his fault, what happened?"

Lek shook his head. "No, it wasn't."

"Whose was it?"

"I suppose it was mine."

Elena felt her face flush. The anger came unexpectedly. The man in front of her had saved her life, but if what he said was true, he had also ruined it.

"Your fault? You did this? And you escaped blameless? How could you do that?"

Lek stopped digging. "Why do you assume I've escaped blameless? I assure you I have not."

"But there isn't a blood feud declared on you or your family."

"There are worse things, my dear, even than a blood feud."

"What does that mean?"

"It's not important."

"At least tell me what happened."

Lek resumed digging. "Your father was a good man, at

one point. He cared about his family and his neighbors, and they cared about him. He offered hospitality to those who needed it. He followed the *Kanun*, remaining careful not to dishonor anyone and making sure his own honor remained intact. He worked hard. He wasn't wealthy, but your family wasn't starving. He invited me into his home and treated me like a brother. It was his hospitality, maybe, that led to his downfall."

"I wish I knew the man you describe," Elena whispered.

"I was traveling through your lovely village," Lek continued, "and as I always did, I stayed with your family. One night, your father and I were with several other men in a tavern. We were drinking, laughing, and telling stories, each of us, of course, trying to outdo the others. All was as it should be until one of your neighbors burst into the room. He accused me of swindling his father."

"Did you?"

"Of course not. The man may have been old, and possibly senile, but we had a business arrangement. If this man felt it was imprudent, then his quarrel should have been with his father, not with me. Your father told him to leave, but he refused. He started calling your father names, claiming your father was harboring a thief, which made him just as culpable. He wouldn't listen to reason. The more your father tried to calm him down, the more upset he became. I told your father to stop, that it was my problem. He said that because I was his guest, it was his problem, too. He told the man to leave again, but the man pulled out a knife and charged at me. Your father grabbed his arm in an effort to stop him. The man broke free, but he lost his balance and fell on top of his knife. He didn't get back up. The next day, I left, and I never saw your father again. Years passed before I visited the village again. I learned about the blood feud that forced you and your family to leave."

"Everything that has happened in my life has been because of an accident," Elena said.

Lek looked at her and smiled. "Yes, but even accidents can have a purpose."

By then, the hole was big enough to accommodate the four dead soldiers. Elena helped Lek heave them in one by one, and then he covered them in dirt.

"I came here tonight," he said as he tamped down the earth with the shovel, "to see if you might again extend your hospitality and offer me a place to sleep."

"Of course," Elena replied.

Lek nodded. "You're a good girl. And your father was a good man, even if he didn't always act like one."

He went to retrieve his satchel and his cloak from where he had left them. He threw his cloak around his shoulders and fastened the clasp at his neck. The metal flashed in the dying firelight. It was a dragon, curved in a circle, with its tail wrapped around its neck.

FIFTY-ONE

Sarajevo, Bosnia and Herzegovina
22 October 1999

AFTER A WEEK IN SARAJEVO, Clara could barely fight the urge to take a black Sharpie to all the pristine white pillows on the sofa in the living room of the safe house. The perfect, sterile décor threatened to suffocate her. They hadn't made any progress in finding Adam, and Clara worried they had come upon another dead end.

Until another miraculous clue fell in their laps.

Except *miraculous* was not the proper word.

When Arkady came through the door, she was prepared to bombard him with her usual barrage of questions. Who did he talk to? What did he find out? Where was Adam? But the odd look on his face stopped her. He glanced down at the package wrapped in brown paper in his hand.

"What is that?" she asked.

"I don't know," he replied. "A Gypsy boy handed it to

me as I was walking down the street. A very frightened Gypsy boy."

He carried the package to the coffee table where he set it down. They both regarded the brown parcel for a moment before Arkady began untying the string that bound it.

Clara backed away. "You're going to open it?"

"What else would I do with it?"

"What if it's a bomb?"

He gave her a dismissive look. "Vampires don't use bombs."

"But Chetniks do," she muttered.

By then though, Arkady had removed most of the paper to reveal another antique book. This one looked even older than the one they had found in Banja Luka.

"Chetniks aren't big on books," Arkady said, flipping through the palm-sized volume. "This one is in German, a very early edition of *Faust*. Clever."

"Anything in it?"

Arkady shook his head. "Not—"

A photograph fluttered from between the pages. Arkady picked it up, and with a weary sigh he handed it to Clara. A young man lay on a bed smeared in blood. On the wall behind him was an all too familiar symbol.

"WHAT DO YOU MEAN THERE hasn't been a murder?" Arkady asked. "I have the picture."

The bespectacled man across the desk scrutinized the photograph Arkady held out again. "I don't know him. Are you sure this took place in Sarajevo?"

"I'm positive."

"Based on what?"

"Based on the fact that I just know."

The man, a police inspector named Tomislav Vidić, shifted his gaze between Arkady and Clara. "That may be enough for you, but others of us need a bit more."

"He's possibly new. Maybe someone just introduced to the darker side of police work. You can't possibly know everyone."

Tomislav glared over the top of his glasses. "Arkady Danilovich, not only is it possible, but it's the truth. I do know everyone, and I'm telling you he's not one of ours."

"Maybe not yet," Clara said.

"What do you mean?" Tomislav asked with a sniff.

Clara glanced at Arkady. "I mean as it was explained to me, the way you recruit people is by talking to the ones who've already had encounters with the things that go bump in the night. Maybe he ran into something spooky but hadn't yet started asking questions."

Tomislav threw up his hands. "Then I don't see how I could help."

Arkady slammed his fist on the desk and leaned forward until his face was inches from Tomislav's. "He would be a fellow policeman. Somewhere in there you're still capable of compassion, surely. Why don't you do us a favor and look for anyone who hasn't reported into work recently?"

Tomislav sighed. "Fine. As a favor."

WHEN ARKADY KNOCKED ON THE door to the police officer's townhouse, he didn't receive an answer. The curtains were drawn on all the windows. No lights shown through.

"According to our records, Jakov Latas lives alone," said Tomislav.

Arkady frowned. "No one to find him then."

Tomislav surveyed the exterior of the townhouse. "No sign of a break-in."

"There wouldn't be." Arkady scratched his chin. "If this one follows the same pattern as the other murders, he would have invited his killer in."

"I've alerted the landlord," said Tomislav. "He'll be here shortly with a key."

Arkady retrieved his lock pick from his pocket. "No need. I've got one."

He worked the lock for a few seconds until it clicked. He opened the door and stepped across the threshold, followed by Clara and a scowling Tomislav. Inside, nothing seemed out of the ordinary—no overturned furniture, no ransacked cabinets or drawers in the kitchen, no bloody footprints, not even a picture askew—but still something felt wrong. The same tingling on the back of Clara's neck as she had at the warehouse in Banja Luka returned. Something evil had been there and had left a stain in the very air.

She also couldn't ignore the smell.

Arkady exchanged glances with her before he raced up the stairs. She and Tomislav followed again. A door stood ajar at the end of the hall. As they approached, the smell grew stronger. Clara covered her mouth and nose with the sleeve of her jacket to keep from retching.

Arkady pushed the door open to find the exact scene from the photograph, except, of course, for the several days of decomposition. The body lay across the bed, the wound spanning Jakov's throat still obvious. The bloody symbol dominated the wall above the bed, dried to a deep-rust color. Arkady and Tomislav covered their mouths and noses with their sleeves as well.

Clara forced herself to look at everything in the room, from the body on the bed to the bloody bedsheets to the bloodstained carpet and curtains. The last detail prompted her to walk to the window and look out. The room overlooked a mews, garages from the surrounding townhouses opening onto a shared driveway. She couldn't see any ledge, yet bloodstains on the windowsill led under the edge of the sash. A normal person couldn't have crawled out and then closed the window, not without climbing equipment.

To Clara's relief, they spent only a few more minutes in the room before Arkady motioned for them to leave, and the three of them ventured back down the stairs.

"Was Jakov working on anything unusual," Arkady asked once they regrouped in the living room, "a case that would have put him in the path of something supernatural?"

"Nothing of the sort," Tomislav replied. "He did help to investigate a suicide a few weeks ago, but there wasn't anything unusual about it, just an unhappy man ending his unhappy life in a hotel room in the middle of the night."

Arkady clicked his tongue. "What was this unhappy man's name?"

"Bogdan Borisović."

Arkady shook his head. "There has to be something we're missing."

While Arkady and Tomislav continued their discussion, Clara stepped away to peer into a room off the entryway, one she hadn't noticed before. A desk with a computer stood against one wall, and bookshelves lined the other walls. Like the rest of the downstairs, everything seemed in perfect order, except for a notebook lying open on the desk. Clara glanced over her shoulder at Arkady and Tomislav, who were still arguing, then crossed from the doorway to the desk. She leafed through the book.

The notes were mostly in Serbian, but whoever put the notebook together had inserted photocopied pages from other books, some in English, many with their own handwritten remarks that looked very much like the ones in *The Giaour*. Then Clara reached a page that made her heart skip a beat. The sloppy handwriting she recognized immediately.

Adam's.

Someone had photocopied a page from one of Adam's own notebooks. Without any context, Clara couldn't follow all his rambling thoughts, but she counted references to Dracula, to vampire panics in Dubrovnik and Thessaloniki, and to a woman named Yasamin.

"Clara," Arkady called, nearly causing her to jump out of her skin. "Where are you?"

"In here," she answered. "There's something you need to see."

He and Tomislav joined her in the office, and Clara handed the notebook to Arkady. "Why does this man have copies of Adam's notes?"

As Arkady read, his eyes grew wide. He turned to Tomislav. "Are you certain this Bogdan committed suicide?"

"Positive," Tomislav answered. "Why do you ask?"

"There are notes from the police investigation here. Why would Adam Mire be interviewed related to the death?"

Tomislav knitted his brows together. "He wasn't."

Arkady held the notebook toward him. "That's not what this says."

Tomislav took the offered book and frantically looked through it. "I don't recall any of this being part of the evidence."

"Well then, I say you have someone covering something up." Arkady glanced back toward Clara. "And another death for the distinguished Dr. Mire to explain."

FIFTY-TWO

Sarajevo, Bosnia and Herzegovina
22 October 1999

ON ANOTHER COLD NIGHT, ADAM waited in the courtyard of the cathedral. He didn't have to wait long before a cold breeze caressed his cheek and the shadows shifted to mark her arrival.

"We should stop meeting like this," Elena said.

Adam shook his head. "I won't go back to your apartment."

"But I've offered you every hospitality." She smiled sweetly. "It's warm there. I don't understand why you insist on this place."

He glared. "You know why."

Her smile faded. "Is there something you wanted to talk to me about?"

"A question. Did you ever talk to anyone about the bloody symbols you and Stjepan found?"

"You mean besides a certain Romanian prince?"

"Besides him, of course."

"No one." She cocked her head to one side. "Why?"

"No reason in particular."

"I see." She stepped closer. "Anything else I might be able to help you with?"

"Your story. It's not finished yet."

"Do you have some time, Dr. Mire?"

"I have enough."

FIFTY-THREE

—⚝—

Gračanica, Kosovo
21 October 1689 Old Style

LEK SLEPT SO SOUNDLY ELENA couldn't tell if he was breathing. She sat in the darkness of the barn for hours, watching him. Eventually, when she decided it was safe, she crept to his satchel. Inside, she found what she expected—a dagger with an eagle cast in gold on the hilt. She replaced it and crawled back to her own pallet. She fought to stay awake as long as she could, but eventually sleep overtook her. When she woke, the sun had risen. Lek was gone.

STJEPAN REAPPEARED THAT AFTERNOON. ELENA, carrying a bucket of water from the stream, met him in front of the barn as he dismounted from his horse.

"I've come to take you away from here," he said. "It's not safe anymore."

Elena thought about telling him it was too late, about

asking him where he had been the night before, but she didn't. "Where are you taking me?"

"The monastery."

"What makes you think the monastery is any safer than here?" she asked, putting the heavy pail down.

"It's a holy place," Stjepan replied. "No one would dare harm it, not even the Turks. There are hundreds already there. Please, Elena, don't argue with me. By the time the sun sets, this place will be a battleground."

She gestured toward the barn. "What about the animals?"

"Leave them."

"I can't do that."

He placed his hand on her cheek. "Elena—"

She threw his hand off. "No. I've worked too hard for this farm. I won't abandon it."

Stjepan sighed. "Why do you have to be so stubborn? You're in danger here. Don't you understand?"

"I understand more than you'll ever know, but I'm not leaving. Now if you don't have anything else to say, I have chores to do."

"I knew you were going to be this way."

"Then why did you bother?"

He took a step closer. "Because I wanted to say I tried. It will make me feel better in light of what I'm about to do."

Elena narrowed her eyes. "What are you about to do?"

He grabbed her. "Save you from yourself."

She struggled to break free, but as with the soldiers from the night before, Stjepan was too strong for her. He used a length of rope to bind her hands behind her back and her arms to her sides. He lifted her up and placed her on the horse, securing her to the saddle with what was left of the rope. All the while, she kicked and fought and cursed him through angry tears.

"You know," he said as he mounted the horse, "you make me wonder why I'm even bothering."

"Why are you?" she asked.

His arms tightened around her as he reached for the reigns. "Because I love you."

"I don't want you to love me."

"And yet I do. I'm not going to let you get yourself killed, not as long as I can do something about it. I would go to any length to save you."

She stopped fighting and leaned back against him. "Have you had another dream?"

"Three more, actually," Stjepan said.

"What happened?"

Stjepan shrugged. "What happened in the others? A cloaked man in black striking from the shadows. A dagger with an eagle on the hilt. It doesn't matter. I can't do anything to stop it. I'm simply cursed to watch people die."

"When was the last dream?"

"Last night."

Lek had been with Elena. It was possible whatever Stjepan had seen in his last dream had not happened yet. She wasn't sure she wanted Stjepan to know about Lek, though. He had been close to her family. He had saved her life. And she still wasn't convinced these men hadn't done something to deserve to die.

As they came near the monastery, Stjepan pulled on the reins of the horse to bring the animal to a halt. "Obviously, I can't bring you in as you are. I'm going to untie you now, but you have to promise me you won't run away or pull a knife on me. Do you?"

Elena nodded. Stjepan dismounted and untied her.

Elena did as she promised. One night, she told herself. She would stay one night, and the next day, she would return to her farm. She clasped her hands around Stjepan's waist as they entered the monastery grounds. She was furious with him, but she was also furious with herself because she found herself reassured by his breathing and by the beating of his heart.

All her emotions seemed petty, however, after they entered the monastery's inner courtyard. Everywhere she looked, men, women, and children camped. Anywhere there was space, there were people. Some of them had bandages on their arms, their legs, even their heads. Some of them didn't have the luxury of bandages.

"There are more here now than when I left this morning," Stjepan said.

"Who did this?" Elena asked. "The Turks?"

"The Turks, the Germans, the Serbs, the Albanians, all of them."

A man came running up to them, a peasant, like all the rest. He said something to Stjepan in Serbian, too quickly for Elena to understand.

Stjepan twisted to face Elena. He pointed to a woman standing near the yew tree. By her dress she was Albanian, but a Muslim. "Do you see that woman over there? I know you must be hungry. She can take you somewhere to get something to eat. I have to go take care of a matter. I'll find you later."

Stjepan dismounted. He offered his hand to Elena, but she refused. She dismounted and walked toward the woman Stjepan pointed out. The peasant who had greeted him led his horse toward the stables while Stjepan walked toward the entrance to the church. As Elena made her way across the courtyard, several people reached out their hands to her, begging for food or some other help.

"I'm sorry," she repeated. "I'm sorry. I'm sorry."

As she drew near to the Muslim woman, she couldn't help but glance at the yew tree. It still bled. Deep-red sap dripped from the wounded bark, and the image carved into the trunk—a dragon curved into a circle, with its tail wrapped around its neck—seemed to throb. She stopped and changed her path. She went to look for Stjepan.

She found him by the small door to the room underneath the sanctuary. He was talking to Vasilije Branković, the man who led the cabal that had gathered at the monastery. The *gospodin* was still dressed more finely than anyone else there, apparently unconcerned by the disparity, but he looked haggard, haunted. Elena pulled her hat down lower over her eyes and tried to get as close as she could. Stjepan frowned and alternated between crossing his arms in front of his chest and resting his hands on his hips as he listened to Vasilije talk. When his turn came to speak, he jabbed his finger at the man and pointed to the church. He was angry, frustrated, and Elena expected maybe even a little disgusted. She circled them, trying to view the conversation from different angles, but she was unable to discern anything more.

When Stjepan found her later, she sipped from a bowl of thin vegetable soup the old Muslim woman had given her. She was huddled with the woman's family—her six sons, their wives, and her nine grandchildren. They were from Prizren, an area completely controlled by the Germans. The woman told her how the Germans had run her entire family from their land and burned their house to the ground.

"I saw you," Stjepan said. "Do you ever listen to anything anyone tells you?"

"Only if it makes sense," Elena replied.

He squatted next to her. "You gave up rather quickly, though."

"There wasn't any point. I couldn't get close enough to understand what you were saying, and I figured you'd probably tell me, anyway."

"Why would you figure that?"

"Because you love me."

She had expected Stjepan to laugh. He didn't.

"Vasilije Branković is the last of the eleven," he said. "All the others are dead."

"I'm sorry."

"So am I."

Something in the way he looked at her warned her to let the matter drop, at least for the time being. His eyes, which normally reminded her of the blue sky on a clear summer day, were filled with storm clouds.

ELENA SHIVERED. THERE WERE NO blankets, no shelter from the night air. Sleep was impossible. Stjepan had left her again in the care of the old Muslim woman and her family. Where he had gone, she didn't know. She stood and made her way across the courtyard. More than once she stepped on what she assumed was a sleeping figure, but no one raised an alarm. When she reached the wall of the church, she followed it around until she came to the main doors. She nudged one of them, and it moved without making a sound. She pushed the door open just enough to slip inside.

The sanctuary was even darker than the starless night. Elena groped her way toward the front where the altar was hidden behind the iconostasis, the massive wall of icons. When she reached the platform where the iconostasis and the altar rested, she knelt and began to pray. She didn't know which God she prayed to, the one there in the church, the one her parents told her to believe in, or the one the Muslim woman outside talked to. She didn't know if it mattered much. She doubted any of them would answer her, but she prayed anyway, mostly for a quiet life on her own land, uninterrupted by blood feuds and wars.

The door to the church opened again, cutting off Elena's prayer. She scampered onto the platform and ducked behind the iconostasis. She peered around its edge to see a man carrying a single lit candle approach the altar. His clothes told her he was Vasilije Branković. She didn't risk looking any longer, crouching instead behind the iconostasis and listening the rustle of his clothing on the other side, as he no doubt knelt where she had knelt moments before. He began to whisper, to chant really, and for the next several minutes the rhythm of his prayers filled the entire church. The words he spoke sounded like Serbian but ... older. She couldn't understand them, yet she found she still knew what he said. He prayed for strength, for courage, for peace. She closed her eyes and listened to the rise and fall of his voice, the steady beat of his speech, like a heart, pumping life.

When he stopped praying, a silence fell so profound it threatened to smother her. An explosion of noise followed, the sound of a scuffle. Elena risked peeking around the edge of the iconostasis again. Vasilije fought with a hooded figure dressed in black. The attacker struggled to bring down the knife in his hand while Vasilije strained to hold him at bay. Only, the light of the nearby candle illuminated not Vasilije's face, but Stjepan's, who wore the rich man's clothes.

The door to the church opened again, and another man raced in, Vasilije in Stjepan's shirt and trousers. Together, the two of them wrestled the man in black to the ground, Vasilije twisting his arm until he let go of the knife. The blade clattered on the stone floor. Stjepan forced the hooded man to his knees and held him there. Vasilije crouched in front of him so they were at eye level with one another. He grabbed the man's hood and yanked it off.

The man in black wasn't Lek.

Elena gasped. All three men looked in the direction of the iconostasis. None of them saw the shadow behind them, and Elena had no time to shout a warning. Stjepan cried out first, a sort of arrested groan, before he crumpled to the floor. The man Stjepan had been restraining jumped to his feet, scooped up the knife, and plunged it into Vasilije's back. The *gospodin* screamed and staggered a few feet before he, too, collapsed. The assassin and his accomplice vanished, as insubstantial, it seemed, as the shadows they appeared to be. The bodies of Stjepan and Vasilije lay on the floor in the flickering light of the candle, surrounded by the faces of the prophets and the saints looming out of the icons. Their painted mouths were closed and silent. Their eyes displayed only indifference.

FIFTY-FOUR

Sarajevo, Bosnia and Herzegovina
23 October 1999

CLARA FOUND ARKADY SITTING AT the table in the kitchen of the safe house, drinking a beer.

"I thought you all drank vodka," she said.

Arkady glared. "You try finding decent vodka here."

"Fair point." She opened the refrigerator. "Is there another beer?"

"Should be. There's a bottle opener in the drawer next to the sink."

Clara pulled the bottle out of the refrigerator and popped the cap on the counter. She sat down at the table next to Arkady. "What are you thinking about?"

"I'm just trying to figure out where we go from here."

"And what have you come up with?" She sipped her beer. It was dark with a slightly sweet molasses flavor. The kick surprised her.

"We need to find out all we can about this suicide."

"So you don't think it's a murder. For once you believe

Adam didn't do it."

Arkady stared absentmindedly at his beer bottle. "No bloody dragons on the wall, no hands painted green."

"You never really explained that. What does the green hand mean?"

"During World War II a green fist was one of the symbols of the Legion of the Archangel Michael, also known as the Iron Guard."

"Romanian fascists."

Arkady took a swig of his beer. "Exactly."

"Any chance they were run by a bunch of vampires?" Clara asked.

"There were rumors at the time. Supposedly there are documents, too, but they're locked away. Only a few are allowed access."

"Why is that?"

"Because what they contain is so horrific, most aren't equipped to deal with the trauma, or so they say."

"So they say. Do you believe them?"

He threw his head back and finished the beer in one gulp. "Absolutely. I think such things need to be locked away so people don't find out."

"Why is that?"

"It would cause a panic. You're proof of that."

Clara bristled. "Me? How am I proof of that?"

"You did not handle the news very well." Arkady began to peel the label off his beer bottle.

"How did you expect me to handle it?"

He sighed and placed a hand on his head. "I suppose you're right. I'm sorry. Still, my opinion stands. It's best if the world doesn't know of the dangers out there."

"How long have you been doing this?" Clara asked.

"You mean fighting monsters? Most of my life. Kostya

and I trained from a very early age."

"Did you pick your line of work or was it picked for you?"

Arkady shrugged. "A little of both. Our father introduced us to the way things are at an earlier age than most, but we could have chosen a different path at any time. Obviously neither of us did that. Sometimes I wonder why."

"What path would you have chosen?" Clara asked.

He shook his head. "I don't really know. In truth, this is all I know how to do. I'm afraid I wouldn't really be good at anything else."

"Sometimes I think I should have decided to be a painter."

Arkady laughed.

She swatted his arm. "Why are you laughing? You don't know me. You don't what I can do. Why assume I can't draw anything more than a stick figure?"

"No, you're right. My apologies again. I shouldn't assume."

"I can't, though."

"Can't what?"

"Can't draw anything more than a stick figure. Guess I don't know how to do anything else either."

He stared at her and cocked his head to one side. "Still, you are a remarkable person."

"What do you mean?"

"Not very many people would have the fortitude to keep going as long as you have."

Her cheeks went hot. "My mother would just say I'm stubborn."

Arkady slid his hand across the table and covered hers. "*Tenacious* would be a better word. Don't give up now.

We'll figure all this out. I promise. We'll get through it, and we'll find Adam."

She enjoyed having his hand on top of hers, which startled her. She tried to tell herself the warm buzzing in her head was because of the beer, but as she looked into Arkady's pale-blue eyes, she saw past the bravado and the cynicism. She saw a man who wanted to do what he believed was right, who wanted to protect those unable to protect themselves, who had sacrificed almost everything he had, and who was just simply tired.

For a second, she thought of leaning in closer. Perhaps he would too, and perhaps their lips would meet, but then she pulled her hand away and jumped up from the table.

"I ... I'm sorry," she stammered. "I just remembered there's something I need to do."

She ran to her bedroom and shut the door. Digging the copy of *The Giaour* out of her bag, she hoped to take her mind off Arkady and the idea of gazing into his blue eyes once more.

FIFTY-FIVE

—⚏—

From the Journal of Julius van Millingen

Missolonghi, Greece
20 April 1824

I COULD NOT SAVE HIM. He was too far gone, but I fear the infection raging in his system was not what killed him, at least not the infection science can explain. Were I able to analyze his blood under a microscope, no doubt I would have seen something more horrific than any plague ever to befall man. He died of an infection that consumes the soul and turns its victims into monsters. And the knowledge that I must bear the rest of my life is that Lord Byron wanted to die so that he could be with the one who ended his life.

I long suspected her return, the raven-haired succubus that attacked him in Ioannina more than a decade ago. He has told the story many times to me, retracing every detail of her features—her silken hair as black as jet, her green eyes that sparkled like emeralds in the moonlight, her ruby-red lips, and her skin as white as alabaster—a precious jewel he called her, even as he recounted the attack that surely would have taken his life then had chance not intervened.

A little over a week ago I saw a woman lurking outside the villa after sunset one evening. Thinking her to be a local vagrant, possibly a beggar, I pursued her, but when I emerged outside, I saw nothing, only the shadows of the sycamore trees. I convinced myself that my eyes were fooling me, but later I heard him talking in his sleep as I passed by his door. He was whispering a name, "Elena, Elena."

The following morning, I asked him if he had any trouble sleeping. He regarded me with a peculiar look on his face and answered that he had slept rather well. Later that day, he took ill for the first time. I gave him something to help him sleep, but that night, I heard him talking again. I went to his room, but I hesitated outside because I heard not only his voice, but also another. A woman. I couldn't understand what she was saying. Her voice was low, the cadence even. It was hypnotic. I found myself drawn to it.

I blinked several times. I don't know how long I had been standing there, but the sky was already becoming lighter. I eased the door open. He lay in bed, his breathing shallow but steady. He seemed a shade paler. There was no one else in the room.

That day, he took a turn for the worse. He was supposed to meet with General Alexandros Mavrokordatos in order to plan their attack on Lepanto, but he sent a courier to explain he was not feeling well enough to meet.

By the afternoon, he felt well enough for a walk, though I noticed he leaned in earnest on the cane he generally used as an affectation. The day was warm, a pleasant reprieve from the rain. He was silent at first, and I let him alone, knowing he would speak when he wanted. We stopped at the end of the lane, where it intersected the road leading down to the village. There we could see the whole plain, sloping down to the deep azure waters of the Gulf of Patras.

"Tell me, Doctor," he said, "have you ever thought about death?"

"I'm not sure what you mean," I replied, taken aback by the question.

"Death. Have you considered what lies beyond?"

"My profession requires me to tend to the living," I answered. "I try to leave such questioning to the priests."

"But surely you must think about your own mortality from time to time."

I nodded. "Occasionally."

"It is something that has preoccupied me of late," he said. "My own death. How will I die, I wonder? Will I be alone, or will I be surrounded by others? Will it be in battle, or will it be in the still of the night? These questions have occupied all my waking thoughts."

"But you're healthy enough. Surely that date is still well off." I said it to convince myself as much as I did him.

"Well, that's the rub, isn't it? We don't really know, do we? It could be fifty years from now. It could be tomorrow."

"We should make the time we have matter then, shouldn't we?"

He shrugged. "I suppose. But what if it didn't matter?"

"What do you mean?"

The gleam in his eyes was almost maniacal. "What if it doesn't matter what we do? We all die in the end."

I shook my head. "I prefer my thoughts not to be in

such morbid places."

"Oh, I don't think it's morbid at all. It's rather freeing." He swept his cane around to take in the entire panorama. "I'm no longer afraid, Doctor."

Then he started to cough and soon was racked with convulsions. I had to hold him up to keep him from falling over. When he finally stopped and straightened up, I noticed the small drop of blood at the corner of his mouth.

We strolled back to the villa in silence. I helped him up to his room and left him to rest. I gave him a higher dosage of something to help him sleep. In the evening as the sun set, I told the old Albanian who kept the grounds to watch out for someone trying to sneak into the house. I set up a chair in the hallway, having resolved to keep watch.

Around midnight, I caught myself nodding off. In order to stay awake, I started reciting the names of all the bones, starting with the distal phalanx of the right great toe. It worked for a while. I made it to the ribcage before I heard a loud thump coming from Lord Byron's room. I leapt up, dashed down the hall, and threw open the door. He stood in the moonlight at the foot of his bed, completely nude. The window was open, and the curtains fluttered in the breeze.

He appeared to be in a daze. Slowly he turned and looked at me, and his expression changed. His brow furrowed and his lips turned up in a snarl. He screamed and charged at me. Fortunately, in his state he was easily overpowered. As soon as the rage came, it left, and he collapsed. I placed him back in his bed and put a blanket on top of him. For the rest of the night, I sat there. He fell into fitful sleep, stirring occasionally, but he never woke up. When the sun rose, I left.

I had little sleep over the next few days, napping in the

afternoon when I could. Every night I sat up in Lord Byron's room. He grew weaker and weaker until he could no longer leave his bed. His skin took on a sickly pallor. On the third day of his bedridden state, I was sitting with him when he suddenly sat up.

"Doctor," he said, "you've been quite kind to remain by my side."

"It is my duty," I replied, startled.

He smiled his peculiar smile again. "Of course, of course. I hereby release you from your duty."

"I cannot do that until you are well."

"Well? What is well?"

"My Lord, it does you no good to become agitated." I tried to gently force him to lie down again. "You should rest."

He threw me off with a strength I found astonishing. "Rest? How can I rest at a time like this?"

"A time like what?"

"My death."

Out of the corner of my eye, I saw a flicker of motion. A shadow I hadn't noticed before seemed to detach itself from the wall, and suddenly, we were not alone in the room any longer. A woman stood by the side of the bed. I knew immediately who she was, the woman who had attacked him those years ago. How she had gotten into the room I couldn't fathom. She looked at me and smiled, baring her teeth. Only they were not normal human teeth, but fangs. Her eyes flashed red in the moonlight. She advanced toward me. I backed away, but in the small room there was nowhere to go.

Lord Byron gazed at her, a look of longing on his face. She stepped closer. I tried to speak, but the words refused to leave my mouth. My vision blurred, and it suddenly became hard to think through the haze. The last thing I remember clearly was her voice. It was rich like the sound of a viola. And then everything went black.

When I woke up, sunlight streamed into the room. My head pounded. I struggled to my feet. Lord Byron still lay in the bed. He was dead.

A SHORT NOTE WAS APPENDED to the end of the journal entry. *"This confirms the story that was told to me by the old soldier, George Tolliver. I wonder if this is another of the mysterious women who waylaid the hapless Jonathan Harking in the Castle in Romania. If so, then there must be a third." –B. Stoker.*

FIFTY-SIX

Sarajevo, Bosnia and Herzegovina
24 October 1999

ON THE SITE OF THE National Library, a building stood, but it was empty inside, barren of all the knowledge, all the life it once contained. As Adam gazed at the pseudo-Moorish edifice, he doubted the loss was one the Bosnians would ever recover from.

"We are clawing our way back, a little at a time," Inspector Gavrilović said.

Adam had been expecting him. "Yes, but how long is it going to take?"

"As long as needed. We are not a people to give up hope, Dr. Mire."

"I would guess not. This city would never have survived the siege otherwise."

The inspector glanced sideways at him. "Why have you come back?"

"Because the vampires have come back."

"I'm beginning to think they never left." He cleared his

throat. "I thought my warning was clear. You were supposed to stay away. It's not safe for you here."

Adam laughed. "I gave up worrying about my safety a long time ago. There is a vampire calling himself Dragomir Sokolović. He's leading the Chetniks in their search for Dracula's medallion. That's why they've been so interested in me. They think I know where it is, or at least where to find it."

"Do you? On either count?"

Adam shook his head. "All the clues I've followed have only led me to dead ends."

The inspector raised an eyebrow. "And what clues would those be?"

"Books," Adam replied. "All from the library of my friend Mihai Iliescu, the son of the man who brought it to the cathedral when your father was an altar boy."

"But how would he have gotten it?"

"From another friend of mine, I think, a professor at the university named Radovan Marković, who heard your father's story and decided to investigate. The books led me from Budapest to Banja Luka, Dubrovnik, and finally Thessaloniki, where the trail ran cold. There I met a friend of *yours*."

"A friend of mine? Really?"

Adam nodded. "An inspector in the Hellenic Police. I never caught his name, but he quoted *Dracula* to me, just like you did. The same line: *For the dead travel fast.*"

The corners of the inspector's mouth twitched. "That's interesting."

"I thought so."

"All I can tell you, Dr. Mire, is that there are others like me who have decided to stand up against the darkness, whatever form it takes." He retrieved a folder hidden in his coat and handed it to Adam.

Opening it, Adam discovered crime scene photos. In every one a man lay on a bed, displayed, with his throat torn open. And in every picture a symbol was painted on the wall in red, the symbol of the Order of the Dragon.

"Are these recent?" he asked.

"All within the last several weeks. It seems someone else knows what we're doing and doesn't like it."

Adam narrowed his eyes. "Why are you telling me this?"

"Because all these men had knowledge of the medallion."

"So did a few others who were killed during the siege."

"This Dragomir must be stopped," the inspector said, his jaw set.

"I know." Adam closed the folder and tried to hand it back to the inspector. "Thank you, I'm happy to know I'm not the only one in this fight."

The inspector pushed the folder back toward him. "You never were alone, Dr. Mire. There is something else in there you ought to read. I met your friend Professor Marković once. After he was killed by the shelling, I had reason to peruse the contents of his office. You ought to read what I found."

FIFTY-SEVEN

From the journal of Radovan Marković

Sarajevo, Bosnia and Herzegovina
24 October 1994

I FOUND THE MEDALLION PRECISELY where the old man told me it would be, behind a wall in a storage room on the third floor. I was shocked to discover it there after all these years, but remarkably it was, just as he described it, wrapped in a rag, though the rag had almost rotted into nothing.

Of course, the logistics of smuggling the medallion out of the city now are almost impossible, but I fear keeping it any longer. If the city falls, it could make its way into the wrong hands. Factions of the Yugoslav government exist that know its history and would use it for their own purposes. There is another reason as well. The monsters are here in Sarajevo. I can only imagine why, but if not because of the medallion then we are faced with an extraordinary coincidence.

I made the mistake of venturing out of my house after dark one evening a few weeks ago. No time is safe anymore. Had it not been for the full moon, I wouldn't have been able to see my hand in front of my face. I was on my way to meet the person who agreed to secret it out of the city.

The first one intercepted me as I passed in front of the remnants of the Zetra Ice Hall from the Olympic Games ten years ago. The partially destroyed Olympic rings on the one wall still standing shone in the moonlight.

The monster would have ended me immediately except for the crucifix around my neck. He tackled me to the ground and proceeded to try to feed, but as soon as his mouth touched the silver, he yelled and retracted. I scrambled away from him, running into the ruins of the arena, looking for anywhere I might hide.

It was futile, I know. No one can hide from a vampire, but any time I could buy for myself was more time to devise a better plan. I scrambled over the rubble, but I could hear him behind me, gaining. As fortune would have it, I found myself in the bleacher section of the arena. Most of the wood from the seats had been broken up and used for coffins, but there were still a few pieces lying around. I found the remains of a seat and threw it at him. He batted it away easily, but my diversion gave me enough time to scrounge for what I wanted. I picked up a jagged piece of wood and pointed it at him.

He laughed and continued to advance.

I gripped my makeshift stake, prepared for him to pounce, but instead, a shadow collided with him, slamming him into the rubble. I should have run, but all I could do was gape. Another vampire had joined the fight. Unlike the first, who looked like every Chetnik I had ever encountered, this one was dressed in a frock coat of all things, and he wore black gloves.

They fought like feral cats, striking out with their claws and their teeth, screeching and growling. The gloved one quickly lost the upper hand. The first vampire threw him off, and he landed on a piece of rubble in such a way a human's back would have been broken. Moments later, though, he jumped to his feet and rushed at the first vampire.

I edged away, not daring to break into a full run, for fear they would remember me and both come after me. I had only taken a few steps when another hand landed on my shoulder. I yelped. The man to whom the hand belonged spun me around. He placed a finger over his lips. He had a round face with curly black hair and deep-set, dark eyes.

"Hurry," he whispered. "This way."

He took me by the hand and pulled me away from the fight between the two vampires. The going was difficult. More than once I stumbled over the rubble. He led us to a part of the arena still intact. An open door stood in a partially collapsed wall. I could barely see in the darkness once we stepped through, and the thought occurred to me I was being led into a trap, but I had few options. We came upon a set of stairs leading down, and then I remembered the new use the Zetra Ice Hall had been put to.

A morgue.

We ran past rooms with bodies in black bags. The stench was unimaginable, but we dared not stop. Finally, we came to another set of stairs that led upward. We emerged outside on the other side of the arena site. I have never been so grateful for the smell of fresh air. There was no sign of either vampire, though my relief was short-lived as the thought occurred to me that they had decided to hunt us in tandem.

I noticed my new friend carried a cross made of silver.

"Who are you?" I asked.

He breathed heavily, trying to catch his breath. "My name is Nikola Gavrilović. I'm with the police."

"And what were you doing out here late at night?"

"Tracking them," he replied.

We clambered over the rubble to the edge of the site, where a fence confronted us. I am not as fit as I used to be, but I managed to climb over even with my bag. Our luck ended on the other side. The gloved vampire appeared out of the shadows and tossed Gavrilović aside like a sack of potatoes. He faced me, the hunger evident in his crimson eyes.

I realized then I still held my rudimentary wooden stake. Rather than retreat, I rushed toward him. He dodged the stake, but I twisted and jabbed it into his midsection. I didn't hit his heart. He wrenched the stake from my hands and pulled the bloody, jagged piece of wood from his side. With a snarl he tossed it to the ground.

Rage and pain contorted the vampire's features. I knew if I ran, I was dead, but just then, a glass vial hit his face and shattered. He screamed and clawed at his flesh, now bloody and raw. The vial must have contained holy water. I turned to see Gavrilović clutching his cross and struggling to stand. I ran over to him and helped him up. He led me through the streets to his townhouse.

"Why are they after you?" he asked after we crossed the threshold and he shut the door.

"Perhaps they were just hungry," I replied. "I honestly don't know."

He grunted.

I stayed until the sun rose the next day. I still have the thing. Tonight I'm going to make another effort to send the medallion to Mihai. I have to wonder, though. Will he welcome it, since I'm returning something that rightfully belongs to him, or will he bemoan the curse I've returned?

FIFTY-EIGHT

Sarajevo, Bosnia and Herzegovina
25 October 1999

ADAM SAT ONCE MORE IN the apartment Elena had until recently shared with Bogdan. Common sense dictated he shouldn't be there—that he should be anywhere but there—but he could think of no other place to go.

"The noose tightens." Elena was seated across from him in the tiny living room.

He glanced at the bedroom door and tried not to think about what had happened there. "But around whose neck?"

She made a clicking noise with her tongue. "Dr. Mire, always worried about whom to trust."

"Can you blame me?"

"Have I misled you yet?"

"No, but that doesn't mean much."

"Would it help if I told you the rest?"

He looked into her eyes, despite himself. She smiled.

Her eyes danced with amusement. Open. Warm. Inviting. He took a deep breath. "It might."

FIFTY-NINE

Gračanica, Kosovo
21 October 1689 Old Style

ELENA CRADLED STJEPAN'S HEAD IN her lap. He had been unconscious for almost an hour. When he collapsed to the floor, she'd feared the worst. Tears welled up in her eyes when she knelt over him and saw he was still breathing as the relief nearly overwhelmed her. She had to fight to keep from crying again when he opened his eyes.

She combed her fingers through his hair. "It's all right. You're safe."

He looked up at her, his brows knit together in confusion. "Elena? You're alive? What are you doing here?"

"Of course I'm alive. I saw it all, everything that happened."

He bolted up. "The hooded man—"

"He's gone."

"And Vasilije?"

Elena glanced at the body of the *gospodin*. "Dead, I'm

afraid."

Stjepan groaned. "Then it's over. I've failed."

"Failed at what?"

"Saving us."

"You haven't failed. We're both still alive."

Stjepan shook his head. "No, I failed to save the Serbs."

Elena's anger rose again. She made no attempt to control it. "Is that what this is all about? Heavenly Serbia? I watched you almost die because of that nonsense?"

"It isn't nonsense."

"It is. None of it matters. Kings, princes, lords—why do you care what they say?"

Stjepan struggled to sit up. "It matters, Elena. It matters to me. Vasilije Branković sent for me yesterday because he was desperate. He said his messages to the others have gone unanswered. He didn't know they were all dead."

"Did you remedy his ignorance?"

"I told him the truth. I told him everything—what I am, about my dreams. He asked if I'd had a dream about him."

"Have you?" Elena asked.

Stjepan nodded. "The last one, but I wouldn't tell him about it before he answered my questions regarding the symbol carved into the yew tree. He started to protest, but I cut him off and made it clear to him I was not in the mood to play games. The symbol represents the Order of the Dragon, a knightly order that's been extinct for more than a hundred years."

"Extinct? Then why is someone carving it into trees?" She glanced once again at Vasilije's body. "And what does it have to do with these men?"

"They were all members of another order," Stjepan replied, "the Order of the Falcon."

Elena remembered the *gospodin* frantically searching his house in one of the dreams Stjepan recounted. "The falcon clasp."

"Exactly. They were descendants of the twelve lords who fought their way through the Turkish ranks at the Battle of Kosovo and cut down the Sultan himself after the death of Prince Lazar. The two orders originally fought side by side because their goal was the same—to defend Christendom and end the Turkish threat forever. Prince Lazar's son was actually a member of the Order of the Dragon."

Elena frowned. "Did you say twelve lords? There were only eleven of them."

"I asked the same question," Stjepan said. "According to Vasilije, one lineage was lost over the years. Regardless, they have bided their time. Finally, they were prepared to put their plan into motion to rid Serbia of the Turks for good, and then the murders began. Vasilije asked me if I could stop the devil that killed his brothers. He insisted it wasn't too late, that Serbia could still be free."

Elena huffed. "You should have protested more."

Stjepan shot her an annoyed look. "I did. I said I didn't know if there was anything I could do. I pointed out, too, that Germans have already driven the Turks out. He said it didn't matter. Allying with the Germans was a necessary evil. Only the armies of the German emperor could force the Turks out of the lands they've occupied all these years, but without a strong force to unify the Serbs, the Germans would be worse. The Turks allow us to worship as we please. The Germans, he said, would send Jesuit missionaries here—just as they have in Transylvania—and would force our people to swear allegiance to the pope.

This monastery would end up a ruin. I don't want that to happen. It may not be my home any longer, but I still love it. I promised Vasilije I would do what I could to keep him alive."

Elena ran the soft fabric of the coat Stjepan wore through her fingers. "Is that what this is all about?"

Stjepan's gazed passed over his clothing. "In my last dream I saw Vasilije Branković here in the sanctuary, kneeling in front of the iconostasis, illuminated by the light of a candle. I could hear him whispering, praying. As he knelt, a shadow loomed behind him, and a knife gleamed in the candlelight. I proposed to Vasilije that I take his place to catch the killer, and we exchanged clothes. I came into the church and knelt to pray. I wasn't acting. I was truly praying to God."

"I suppose He didn't hear you," Elena said quietly.

Stjepan fought to stand. Once on his feet, he wobbled for a few seconds and then turned toward the iconostasis. "Maybe He didn't. When Vasilije pulled the hood from my attacker's head, I expected the same man who killed Zoran Dejanović, but he wasn't. I didn't know what to do." He looked down at Vasilije's body. "The last thing I remember is sharp pain radiating out from the back of my skull. Then everything went black."

"I thought you were dead," Elena said.

"I thought I might be, too."

"But you're more naïve than I expected."

Stjepan frowned. "Why do you say that?"

Elena sighed. "Ask yourself this, Stjepan. Who do you think would be the new prince of your 'Heavenly Serbia'? Don't you see? Vasilije wasn't concerned about this monastery. He was only concerned about himself. I saw it in his eyes when he spoke with you earlier. He was afraid. All of them were. They were cowards. None of them ever worked for what they had or fought to keep it. Forget them. Forget this place. We can go away from here, to the mountains where I was born."

"What about the blood feud? What about your oath?"

"All of the men in my family are dead. There is no more blood feud. As for my oath, no one there knows about it."

Stjepan shook his head. "Still, it would be a risk."

"One I'm willing to take."

Stjepan hesitated before he replied. "I … I need some time to think about it." He knelt over Vasilije's body. "Right now, we have another problem to deal with."

THE GERMAN SOLDIERS CAME THE next day. They pushed past the monks gathered to block the entrance to the monastery and displaced those camped in the courtyard as they came through. Many of them leered at the women the way the Serbian soldiers had leered at Elena. She drew her coat tightly around her, pulled her hat down over her eyes, and tried to stay out of their way. They had no regard for any but their own kind. Christian or Muslim, it didn't matter; everyone received their scorn and bullying in equal measure. They barked orders in their own harsh language, demanding to be housed and fed and to be given stables for their horses.

The worst, at least in Elena's opinion, was the leader of the group, a man with cold, stone-grey eyes. Elena happened to be nearby when he made yet another demand of one of the monks. He glanced at her, briefly. They made eye contact, but it seemed to Elena that he looked through her, as if she weren't even there. She wondered what made men think they were better than others, when really, everyone was just as wretched.

THE NIGHT WAS EVEN COLDER than the one before. Children cried, and mothers comforted them as best they could, but there were still no blankets. Elena jumped when Stjepan placed his hand on her shoulder just as she fell asleep. She looked at him, puzzled.

"Please," he said, "can you come with me?"

"What is it?" she asked. "What do you want?"

He stood and offered her his hand. "Just come with me."

She followed him through the courtyard to the church. A side door, different from the one Vasilije and the rest had used, led to the monks' cells. Stjepan guided Elena down a long corridor, stopping in front of the last door.

"It's gone," he said.

"What's gone?"

"Vasilije's body. It's not in the stables where we hid it. I went to check on it after the Germans came. I wanted to make sure they didn't find it."

"Do you think they did?"

"No. They would have raised more of an alarm if they had. And I don't see them just taking it."

Elena shrugged. "Then they did us a favor. Now we don't have to worry about disposing of it."

"Elena, regardless of what you thought of him, he was still a person." He balled his hands into fists. "He deserved better."

"No, he didn't," she replied. "None of us do."

"I didn't bring you here to argue with you." He pushed open the door and beckoned her to enter the room with him. Inside, an old man lay on a cot. He coughed uncontrollably. Stjepan waited for him to stop before speaking. "This is my uncle." He turned to the old man. "This is a friend of mine. His name is Marko. He'll be looking after you while I'm gone."

His uncle nodded in Elena's direction before another coughing fit overtook him. She and Stjepan stepped back into the corridor.

"He's getting worse," Stjepan said. "He's been so kind to me. I hate to leave him, but I know you're more than capable of caring for him. I wouldn't trust anyone else. Please do this for me."

"Where, exactly, are you going?" Elena asked.

He hesitated. "I can't tell you."

She turned away, her cheeks hot in anger. "Of course not."

He grabbed her by the shoulder and spun her around to face him again. "Elena, please trust me. I had another dream, but I know that this time will be different. I can fix things, Elena. I just need the chance."

She pulled away. "I told you how to fix things, Stjepan. Whatever you're doing, you don't have to."

"But I do, Elena," he whispered.

She looked up at him, fear evident in his pale eyes. "Why?"

A tear traced a line across his cheek. "Because the dream I had was about you."

SIXTY

—⚬—

Gračanica, Kosovo
2 November 1689 Old Style

ELENA SAT BESIDE THE COT as Stjepan's uncle took his final breath. She closed his eyes and placed his hands over his heart before going to find one of the monks to tell him of the old man's passing. After she had done so, she went to the church. More than two weeks had passed since Stjepan left. There had been no word from him.

The light of the rising sun shone in through the narrow windows, illuminating the murals on the walls. She looked around at the frozen eyes of the figures lined up in their never-ending processional, the saint-kings Stjepan so revered. They glared down at her.

"This is the fate you've decided for me, isn't it, to watch everyone around me suffer?" Her shouts echoed back at her from the stone ceiling. "If that's so, then I reject it! I reject you, God or Allah or the Prophet Elijah, whoever you are. I don't need you. I don't need anyone. I only need the land, the rain, and the sun."

The figures remained silent.

She walked out of the church. After she stopped briefly to thank the old Muslim woman and her family for the little hospitality they had been able to offer her, she left the monastery, never once looking back. Her destination was her farm, the only place that would ever be her home, but when she crested the hill, she barely recognized it. The fighting had scarred the ground itself, and the charred shell of the barn joined the burned remains of her family's former home. Tears flowed down her face, and she could do nothing to stop them.

Minutes or hours passed until the beat of approaching horse's hooves brought Elena back out of her black thoughts. She spun around to find Stjepan riding toward her. He was dressed as a Bosnian, with baggy trousers, a bright red vest, and a fez. He brought the horse to a halt next to her, dismounted, and swept her up in his arms.

"When I couldn't find you at the monastery, I feared the worst," he said. "I thought I'd made a horrible mistake, but I did it. I saved you."

She clung to him, trying to soak up the warmth of his body. "You look ridiculous. Where have you been? I thought you were dead."

"I'm sorry. The dream I had about you ... I had to find a way to keep it from coming true. I would do anything to protect you."

She pushed him away. "I never asked you to protect me. I just wanted you to be with me. I sat and watched your uncle die. Why did you have to go? And why are you dressed that way?"

"I had to disguise myself as a Bosnian to get close to the Turkish army," Stjepan replied.

"Why would you want to do that?"

Stjepan took a deep breath before answering. "I had to tell them where the Germans are encamped, so they could attack before the Germans were ready."

Elena stepped back from him. "You helped the Turks? Why?"

"Elena, please." He reached for her, but she slipped from his grasp. "It was the only way to save you. What I saw while I was unconscious in the church tore my heart asunder. You were here on your farm, and you were crying. You didn't hear the hooded man approach from behind. Not until he placed a hand on your shoulder did you turn around, but you didn't run or try to fight him off. You even smiled faintly, as if you knew him, as if he were a friend."

She inhaled sharply. She hoped he didn't notice.

"I saw you fall to the ground, clutching your neck with blood running between your fingers," Stjepan continued. "The hooded man watched while you died."

"You should have told me," Elena said.

"I tried, but I couldn't make my voice work. I thought at first if I could just keep you at the monastery you would be safe, but I've learned I can't force you to do anything you don't want to do."

Elena frowned. "So leaving me was a better idea?"

Stjepan held up a hand. "Patience. The day the Germans arrived at the monastery, I watched them mistreat the priests and everyone trying to escape the war they started. I saw the scorn and the disdain in their eyes, as if the people gathered there somehow had themselves to blame for their situation. I saw the arrogance, too. Their own inconveniences were more important than the lives they uprooted. Even if he was a coward, Elena, even if he did care more about himself than anyone else, Vasilije

Branković was right. The Germans would destroy everything, if given the chance."

Elena's gaze passed over her once beautiful farm. It seemed to her the Germans already had destroyed everything, but she allowed Stjepan to continue.

"The night after the Germans came I had one last dream," he said. "I saw the German general, the one who was at the monastery. He and a few others trekked across a field as the sun set, toward a lone tree, a yew tree. Several figures stood underneath it, all in black cloaks, with hoods covering their faces. On the trunk a carving of a dragon dripped with blood-red sap. Unfortunately, that wasn't the only unusual thing about the tree. From its branches hung eleven bodies, the murdered members of the Order of the Falcon."

The bile rose in Elena's throat. "Who would do such a thing?"

"*He* would," Stjepan replied. "Crows circled as the Germans looked on in horror. The general pulled out a handkerchief and covered his face. One of his men stopped to retch. The others continued onward until they reached the shade of the tree. One of the figures waiting stepped forward and pushed his hood back to reveal the face of the same man who killed Zoran Dejanović. He smiled. It reminded me of a wolf or a fox on the hunt, baring its teeth, licking its chops in anticipation of a kill. The man motioned to the tree and to the bodies hanging from its branches. The German general, handkerchief still over his nose and mouth, simply glared. He gestured for one of his men to step forward and held out his hand. The soldier placed a small bag in it. The general thrust the bag at the grinning murderer, who snatched it from him and opened it. Gold coins, dozens of them, fell into his hand. The

German general turned and walked away. The other Germans followed. They were some distance from the tree before any of them noticed one of their number missing."

"I still don't understand what this has to do with me." Elena said.

Stjepan shook his head. "Don't you see? The hooded man was working for the Germans. If I could stop the Germans, I thought maybe I could stop him. After I left you with my uncle, I went to the camp of the Serbian irregulars outside the monastery walls. The Germans didn't allow them in even though it's the church of their ancestors, their saints, their kings. It should have been a sign to them. In their camp, a fire still roared. I grabbed a bottle from the nearest man, took a swig, and joined them. No one ever stopped me to ask me who I was. I was a Serb, and that was good enough."

"What were you hoping to accomplish, besides getting drunk?"

He shot her an annoyed glance. "Drunk soldiers talk. Soon they started making fun of the Germans, clearing their throats and spitting to mock how they spoke and marching stiffly around the campfire. Everyone had a good laugh. They then turned to complaining about having to sit there and wait. They thought they should be fighting the Turks, since the Serbs have more experience fighting them than any others. One of them asked what they were waiting for. More Germans, another replied, because the rumor was the Turks had a big army camped down below Prizren."

Elena's blood ran cold. "The Turks are that close?"

Stjepan nodded. "Probably closer by now. I slipped away. I had the information I needed to put my plan in motion, a plan I hope God will forgive me for. Whoever wins this war, our people will suffer, but the Turks at least have let us worship as we please, even if they make it somewhat difficult. The Germans wouldn't. Our culture, our way of life, maybe even our language would all have been in danger if the Germans won. I went to where the Turks were encamped, near Prizren, and I turned myself in to them. I knew I would be relatively safe, dressed as I was, because they have Bosnians fighting with them. I told them I had been spying on the Germans and that they were waiting on reinforcements before they attacked. If they moved, they could force the Germans to engage them before they were ready. Two days ago, they did. The Turks marched northward, and the Germans left to meet them, even though the reinforcements they expected hadn't arrived yet. The Turks took the day."

She crossed her arms. "Stupid idiot."

Stjepan looked at her, puzzled. "Don't you see? By stopping the Germans, I stopped the hooded man. He didn't kill you."

"He would never do that."

As soon as she spoke she realized her mistake.

Stjepan's eyes narrowed. "Why do you say that?"

"I just mean that I can take care of myself."

He smiled and caressed her cheek with his finger. "But you know I will always protect you."

"I do."

"Please come with me now, Elena. It's not going to be safe here for a while. I didn't expect the Turks to retaliate so brutally. They are killing everyone they suspect of allying with the Germans. We can come back when things die down. We can rebuild your farm then. We can have a family."

"Where are we going?"

"To the north. The Archbishop of Peć is leading a great many people on a march away from here."

"Your people," Elena said.

"Yes."

Elena turned to look over the rolling fields again. The orange sun just touched them. She could say no, go back to the mountains, to her own clan, to a life that made sense to her, but it would be hard, and lonely. Saying yes would mean leaving behind everything she knew, but she would be with Stjepan, who cared for her and made her life seem a little less empty.

She turned back around to give Stjepan her answer, but before she could say a word he fell forward into her. She struggled to keep both of them upright. As she reached around him, she placed her hand on the shaft of an arrow protruding from his back. She jerked away, her fingers covered in dark blood. Elena could do nothing but watch as Stjepan collapsed to the ground. She couldn't move. She couldn't speak. Stjepan reached toward her. He tried to say something, but she couldn't understand him. She knelt over him and took his hand in hers as his eyes glazed over. His breath came in short spasms, and then he left her one last time.

By then Turkish soldiers, four of them, arrived on horseback. One dismounted and wrenched Elena away from Stjepan. She screamed as she struggled desperately to free herself from the man's grip. The Turk snarled something at her as he dragged her back toward his horse. She glanced down at his belt and saw a dagger hanging there. She grabbed for it, but the blade caught in the scabbard, and she couldn't pull it free. Catching her arm, the Turk squeezed it so hard the bone cracked. Searing pain ran from her wrist to her shoulder. The Turk snarled at her again, but the anger on his face abruptly turned to astonishment, and his grip vanished. He fell to the ground, an arrow protruding from his own back. The other Turkish soldiers frantically scanned the horizon. More arrows flew, and in a matter of seconds, they all lay dead on the ground.

It was dusk. Elena's ruined farm gradually fell into darkness. She stood alone, watching and listening, waiting for the arrow meant for her. It never came. Instead, a hand fell on her shoulder.

"Hello, Elena," a man said.

Elena knew whose voice it was. She turned to see a hooded figure dressed all in black. She reached up and pushed the hood back from Lek's face.

"What are you doing here?" she asked.

He laughed. "Always one for getting to the point, aren't you? I'm saving you, and for a second time I might add."

"Why?"

"Is it not enough that I believe you're a remarkable woman?"

Elena glanced at Stjepan's crumpled form. "Others have told me the same."

Lek gently took her chin and brought her gaze to his. "I do not lie."

"Then tell me what makes me such a remarkable woman."

"You know, you haven't asked me why my associates and I killed all of those men. Aren't you the least bit curious?"

Elena shook her head. "It's none of my business."

"But see, that's where you're wrong."

She looked at him curiously. "How?"

"Those men betrayed their ideals and their principles.

They used their influence to make themselves rich. They deserved to die. You, however, have never compromised anything. You may not know anything about your lineage, but you remained true to your heritage and to yourself. For that you should be proud."

"I don't know what you're talking about."

"But you do," Lek told her. "Not only Serbs fought against the Turks at the Battle of Kosovo. There were Vlachs, and there were also Albanians. Remember what Stjepan told you about the membership of the Order of the Falcon? There were originally twelve, but there are currently only eleven. Everyone thought the twelfth line was lost, but it was not. No one simply knew where to look for it. They should have looked in the mountains."

"You don't mean—"

"You." He took the clasp from his cloak to show Elena. "The sword of Miloš Kobilić separated the Sultan's head from his body. The legend says the helmet he wore into battle that day was made to look like a *kuçedra*, an Albanian dragon. He was the original inspiration for the Order of the Dragon, which, despite what Stjepan told you, is not extinct."

"How do you know about Stjepan?" Elena asked. "How do you know about the things he told me?"

"I know everything about you, my dear, and him as well. After all, he's caused me a great deal of trouble these past few days."

"He saw visions of you. He was trying to stop you. He only thought he was doing what was right."

"As do I."

Elena glanced behind him, to where a number of hooded figures stood. They all held bows. "You can't both be right."

Lek shrugged. "Maybe not, but does it really matter now? In coming here, the Germans were answering a plea, a letter sent on behalf of the Catholics of Albania. They also thought they were doing the right thing. Does that matter to you? Ask yourself. The Order of the Falcon is gone. Stjepan is dead. The Germans have retreated. I'm still here, with you."

"You're not Lek Dukagjin come back to life, are you?"

"No, I am not."

"Then who are you?"

He took her hand. "If I tell you, will you come with me? The arrow that felled Stjepan might as well have struck you. The Turks are rampaging through Kosovo. If you stay, they will surely kill you. There really is nothing left for you here, not now."

Elena hesitated.

"Think about it," Lek continued, "no petty, arbitrary rules to follow, no family, no monks, no soldiers, no oaths, no duties, no more having to choose between your happiness and the happiness of others, and you'll never have to be alone again, unless you want to be."

She looked into his eyes. "You can do that?"

Elena's senses opened up again, just as they had when Stjepan touched her, only a hundred times more intense. In an instant every star in the sky came into crystal focus. The scents of the night filled her nostrils—the damp earth, the crisp air, burning campfires in the distance. The breeze on her face felt like fingers running across her skin. The animals in the forest stirred, chirping and yapping and baying to the rhythm of her heart.

Lek pulled her closer. "I can do so much more. Die for me, and I can make you live forever. Do you trust me?"

"I trust you," Elena whispered.

Lek smiled as his face changed. His eyes began to glow red, and his dogteeth grew into sharp, wolf-like fangs. Elena wasn't afraid, though some part of her knew she should be. He gently tilted her head to the side, exposing her long neck. She let out a small gasp as his teeth sank into her skin. The pain was only momentary, though. Images immediately filled her head of all the things Lek had seen, places far away and others familiar, some horrific and others beautiful—too many things for one man's lifetime.

As her heartbeat slowed and the edges of her vision turned black, she saw herself as a young girl in the mountains, sitting on her father's lap and playing with a rag doll. He stroked her hair and smiled. There were others there, men and women gathered, sharing food and drink. A happy occasion. Elena didn't remember it. The images continued relentlessly until she saw herself again, the night her family died. She stood with her back to her burning home, facing the two monsters who had killed them. Lek had been there. He had watched, and he had let it all happen, simply because he wanted.

Elena let the warm, thick liquid trickle down her throat. It tasted like wine and honey. She didn't even realize at first she was lapping up the blood from a cut in Lek's bared chest. It didn't matter. She wanted more. He placed his hands on the side of her head and gently pulled her away. She gazed up at him. Blood dripped from his mouth. Her blood. Their lips met in a kiss.

The stars still burned white hot. The night's smells still tickled her nose. The wind still caressed her skin, and the animals still called out, but they no longer answered to her beating heart, because her heart no longer beat.

SIXTY-ONE

———∞———

Sarajevo, Bosnia and Herzegovina
25 October 1999

NIKOLA GAVRILOVIĆ WAS NOTHING LIKE Clara expected. Most of the other police officers they had spoken to were gruff, dour old men. Inspector Gavrilović was somewhat younger, and Clara would even have gone so far as to say she found him charming. She and Arkady met him not at a police station, but in the square in front of the Cathedral of Jesus' Heart.

The inspector's gaze alternated between the two of them, an expression of deep concern on his face. "I'm disappointed to learn Jakov had that information. Clearly I should have paid a little more attention. If he had come to me with his questions, maybe he would still be alive today."

"So you're saying it's all true," Arkady said.

He nodded. "Oh yes. All of it."

Clara's heart pounded, thinking Adam could be so close after everything they'd been through to find him. "You've spoken with Adam? Where is he?"

"Yes, madam, I've spoken with him—yesterday, in fact." His smile turned apologetic. "But I don't know where he is now. I advised him to leave Sarajevo."

Arkady stiffened. "Leave? Why did you tell him to leave?"

"He's in danger here," the inspector answered evenly. "And not just from the Chetniks or the vampires. He's in danger from us as well."

"Because of this Bogdan person?" Clara asked.

"Among other reasons," the inspector replied.

Arkady's eyes narrowed. "Why are you helping him?"

The inspector leveled an icy glare at him. "Because I don't think he did anything wrong. He has enough problems without being held accountable for murders he didn't commit."

Clara glanced sideways at Arkady. "It's nice at least one other person believes that."

Arkady continued to scowl. "That doesn't help us find him now."

Clara placed a hand on Arkady's shoulder. "What can you tell us about this notebook we found in Jakov's townhouse, Inspector?"

"No more than what you've already surmised, I'm afraid. Dr. Mire was following a string of clues he found in antique books, all of which were tied to Dracula in some way. The clues were meant to lead ... somewhere."

"To Dracula's medallion?" Clara offered.

"Possibly. But the trail went no farther than Thessaloniki."

"Could there have been another book?" Arkady asked. "Maybe it got lost."

"I suppose." The inspector drew his mouth into a peculiar half smile. "But we don't have any way of knowing that."

Arkady frowned. "You shouldn't have let him go. From here out, if anything happens, it will be on your head."

The inspector chuckled. "I hardly think so. You Russians want to see yourselves as the saviors, but you will always do what is in your own best interest. If that is to let Dr. Mire or any number of other people die, then so be it. I, at least, gave him a fighting chance."

Arkady spat something in Russian and walked away.

Clara hesitated before following. "I'm sorry. We've both been through quite a bit recently. If Adam tries to contact you, will you please let us know?"

The inspector bowed, and his strange half smile returned. "Don't worry, madam. You will be the first person I contact."

SIXTY-TWO

Sarajevo, Bosnia and Herzegovina
25 October 1999

ADAM WAS SILENT FOR A moment. When he spoke, his voice was barely above a whisper. "You learned who he was, what he was. The images, the sensations he pushed into your mind, they pushed out everything that made you who you were."

Elena sighed. "And you continue to refuse the truth. Yes, I saw him. I saw everything. He hid nothing from me. He did not mislead me, and I chose to accept what he gave me. The choice was easy, given that the alternative was to starve to death. I had nothing left. I am the same person now as I was before."

Adam barked a laugh. "How can you say that? I know you're not the same person."

"How do you know, Dr. Mire?"

"Because if you were, you wouldn't ever …"

"Wouldn't ever what? Wouldn't ever try to kill someone I loved, just like you killed Nadiye?"

Adam bolted up in his chair. "How do you know about Nadiye?"

"I was there, underneath the dervish lodge in Istanbul. I turned her."

Her words slammed into him like a punch to the gut. "I swore I would always remember the face of the woman I saw framed in the doorway to the tunnels down below." Adam pointed a trembling finger. "You ... you've been clouding my mind this whole time so I wouldn't recognize you. Why? Why did you kill her?"

"I haven't influenced you in any way, Dr. Mire." Her voice was flat, emotionless. "And I didn't kill her. Serhan did. She was going to die anyway."

"You don't know that. There could have been a chance—"

"There was none, Dr. Mire. She had already lost too much blood. There was no time for help to arrive. She didn't deserve to die that way. I saved her. You were the one who killed her."

"She attacked me," Adam sobbed. "The bloodlust—it took over."

"Serhan's companion Tarik injured me. I was too hurt to stay. I had to feed to regain my strength. I could have helped her. I'm sorry." Her regret seemed genuine. "It's such a shock when it happens. Usually there is someone to help with the transition. I can only imagine the terror she must have felt."

Adam stood and advanced toward her, hands balled into tight fists. "Do you understand the hell I have lived in since then? Every night I dream I'm back there. I see her face as the stake goes through her heart—the look of confusion, betrayal, hurt. Every goddamn night."

Her face remained impassive. "And yet, Dr. Mire, you

survived. I shouldn't have to remind you what will happen if you try to hurt me. It will not end well for you. I suggest you leave now, while you still can."

He wanted to kill her, to make her feel all the pain he had ever felt, but she was right. If he tried, he would die. The seconds ticked by, each one stretching out to eons. The only sound in the room was his own breathing. He stared at her perfect figure, her beautiful face, her crimson lips and raven hair and electric green eyes. There was a hint of sadness in those eyes. He turned and left the apartment, never looking back.

When he reached his hotel room and flicked on the lights, his blood froze. Painted on the wall was the symbol of the Order of the Dragon in brilliant red. A photograph was pinned to the center—an auburn-haired woman with hazel eyes, looking over her shoulder, fear written on her face.

"Clara," he whispered.

He picked up the phone and called Inspector Gavrilović. There was no answer, which in some ways relieved him. He left a message, telling the inspector what he planned to do, knowing in all likelihood he'd die.

SIXTY-THREE

Sarajevo, Bosnia and Herzegovina
26 October 1999

OVER AND OVER IN HIS head Adam recited Hail Marys and Our Fathers, running the rosary beads through his fingers. He even threw in the twenty-third Psalm for good measure. If anyplace could be described as the Valley of the Shadow of Death, it would be the half-constructed building that loomed in front of him, a bloody dragon hidden in its depths.

He stepped into the shadows. The breeze died, and the air became frigid. His breath came out in white puffs as he pushed farther into the unfinished structure. When he came to the dragon painted in red on the wall, he stopped, and he waited. After ten minutes he lit a cigarette. When he was finished, he dropped the butt and ground it out with his shoe. Then he lit another.

"It takes true conviction to come here in the middle of the night." The man's voice came from nowhere and everywhere all at once. "Or stupidity. One of the two."

Adam spun around frantically.

The man laughed. "Did you think you'd burst in with your silver crosses and your wooden stakes and your holy water so you could play the hero and finish off the big bad vampire?"

Adam held out his hands, palms open. "No weapons here. I came to talk to you, Dragomir. Or should I call you Stjepan?"

A thud reverberated through the building from somewhere in the shadows, as if something landed on the hard concrete floor from one of the open stories above, but when Adam turned his head, nothing was there. Then he felt the presence behind him, close enough that when the man spoke again the air he exhaled stirred the hairs on the back of Adam's neck.

"Clever, Professor," Stjepan said. "How did you know?"

Adam tried to ignore his pounding heart. "A few things. The last name you've been using, Sokolović, it means 'son of the falcon.' It reminded me of the falcon-claw dagger Elena said you carried. Also, Elena never told anyone about the bleeding dragon Dracula left as his calling card. It would be a mighty coincidence if you came up with the same idea on your own. And finally, I know what happens when a *dhampir* dies."

Stjepan grunted. "And what is that?"

"The human half passes on, but the vampire remains. You were trying to tell Elena she needed to kill you more permanently when the Turk shot you through with the arrow. She didn't understand. And then it was too late."

Stjepan circled to face him. His hair and beard were dark, but he had the pale blue eyes Elena described. "How is Elena these days?"

"Well fed, as far as I can tell."

He nodded. "Good. I'm glad."

"Perhaps you should pay her a visit."

Stjepan shook his head. "After all these years, I'm afraid too much time has passed. We're different people now, with different goals and priorities."

Adam couldn't contain himself. "You're not people."

Stjepan smiled, showing his teeth. "We can agree to disagree."

"Why involve her?" Adam asked. "You should have known she would complicate things for you. Why did you call to her?"

His expression darkened. "I never called to her."

"She told me a different story."

"She's lying," he snarled.

Adam glanced around the half-finished building, mostly shrouded in shadow. "What is this place, anyway? Don't tell me it's just an abandoned construction site."

"It was my home at one point. Many years ago there was a small house here in the middle of a field, before it was an office building and then a car park, before the city even reached this far. Why shouldn't it be my home again?" He fixed Adam with a glare. "That brings us back to where we were. Why are you here in my home?"

Adam produced the picture of Clara. "You all but invited me."

Stjepan raised an eyebrow. "That I did, I suppose."

"I came to make a deal," Adam continued. "I will tell you what I know about Dracula's medallion, but in return you have to promise not to harm her."

He laughed again. "I don't see where you have any leverage. I could take your knowledge from you easily."

"But that won't get you what you want, will it? You know I don't have all the pieces of the puzzle. You need me. I'm the only one who can find them and put them together. I can be your dayman."

Stjepan's mouth twisted into a sadistic grin. He snapped his fingers. All around, Chetniks materialized out of the darkness, along with two figures bound in ropes with their mouths gagged, their eyes blindfolded. One of them was a tall man with short black hair and a goatee. He looked familiar, but Adam couldn't place him. The other was Clara. The Chetniks dragging them forced each of them to their knees.

"Clara!" Adam called.

Jerking her head in his direction, she let out a muffled cry and struggled against the ropes tied around her arms and legs. Adam tried to run to her, but Stjepan stepped in his way. He pointed to another of his men who came forward and handed Stjepan a book. He held the thin, leather-bound volume in Adam's face.

"What is that?" Adam asked.

"The missing piece of the puzzle," Stjepan replied. "Looks like I don't need you after all."

He barked an order and several Chetniks rushed forward to surround Adam in an ever-tightening circle. Adam hit the one who charged first in the jaw with a left hook, and the Chetnik immediately went down. It was the only blow he landed. Two other Chetniks grabbed him by the arms and held him while the rest made him pay for that one punch. One of the thugs slammed his fist into Adam's stomach, and another backhanded him across the face. He struggled to break free, but found his efforts futile. The blows came one after another. The bile rose up into his throat, the taste mingling with the sharp tang of blood. Adam's head swam, and black dots formed in his vision. He began to slip away.

"That's enough." Stjepan's voice seemed to come from underwater.

The Chetniks backed away. Adam didn't have enough strength left to lift his head, but he heard Stjepan's footsteps echo on the concrete floor.

He leaned down until his face was level with Adam's. "You're going to tell me all you know, one way or another."

The two toughs holding him let go, and he fell to the ground. Stjepan picked him up by the collar of his shirt and lifted him back to his feet. A cry of hunger and pain escaped his throat as his eyeteeth pushed through his gums. Burning red hellfire shone in his eyes.

It didn't hurt as much as he expected when the fangs punctured his neck. The thought was arrested, though, by the flood of images that suddenly invaded his mind. Three hundred years of history. Gračanica Monastery under the light of the full moon. Gunpowder. Exploding cannons. People crowding city streets. Bloody bayonets. Bodies on a battlefield. Barbed wire. Mud. Decay. Acrid yellow smoke floating across a scarred landscape. The rumble of tanks. The smell of humanity packed into rail cars. The roar of airplanes. Bombs cratering the countryside. Shells. Mines. Guns. Blood. Death.

And in the midst of it all, one image. One face. Elena. But not as he knew her. As a human girl, standing in the ruins of her family's farm, wearing men's clothes, her hair cut short. She was crying, and he reached up to wipe her tears away.

Somewhere in Adam's fading consciousness, he knew Stjepan was seeing his whole life as well, and learning all he knew about Yasamin, about the medallion, about Clara. And he couldn't do anything but let it happen.

When the bullet ripped through Stjepan's shoulder,

Adam felt it. They both screamed, their voices blending into one. Then the connection between them was severed. For Adam, it felt like a part of him had been torn away, a part he wanted back. He lay on the ground, struggling to breathe. His heart barely beat. More gunshots echoed in the space followed by the sounds of fighting.

Adam closed his eyes, and everything went away.

When he opened them again, he didn't know how much time had passed. Three faces looked down at him—Inspector Gavrilović, the man with oddly familiar features, and Clara. He tried to lift his arm up to touch her, but found himself too weak. Clara took his hand in hers and rested it on his chest.

"No, don't," she said. "You need to rest for a minute."

He had forgotten what she felt like, how she smelled.

"He can't rest for too long," said the other man. "We need to go."

Adam's gaze drifted to the stranger.

Clara must have seen the question in his eyes. "Adam, this is Arkady Danilovich Markov."

"Kostya?" Adam croaked.

"My brother," Arkady replied. "Dr. Mire, you are the luckiest bastard on the planet. What were you thinking, coming here at night?"

"Trying to defeat the vampire."

"By yourself?"

Adam glanced at the inspector. "Not exactly."

The inspector knelt and helped Adam sit up. "Come, we need to get you out of here."

He propped Adam up underneath one arm. Arkady stooped and propped him up underneath the other. Together, they lifted him to his feet. For the first time Adam had a chance to survey the construction site. The inspector had not arrived alone. Several Chetniks lay dead on the ground. The inspector's men busied themselves probing the shadows of the abandoned building with flashlights.

"My thanks to the cavalry," Adam said as they hobbled along. "What happened to Stjepan?"

"He fled as soon as I shot him," the inspector answered.

Adam winced. Every muscle cried out in protest as he struggled to put one foot in front of the other. "What did you shoot him with? That hurt like the devil."

The corners of the inspector's mouth curled up in a faint smile. "A silver bullet."

"That should keep him occupied for a little while."

Inspector Gavrilović nodded. "For a little while."

"We need to find him," Arkady said.

"Elena," Adam whispered.

Arkady frowned. "Who's Elena?"

"Another vampire. She and Stjepan were … involved when they were both human over three hundred years ago, although Stjepan wasn't quite human. He was a *dhampir*. Elena has been trying to stop him from finding Dracula's medallion." Adam paused. "I've been helping her."

Arkady almost dropped him. "What do you mean you've been helping her?"

Adam took a deep breath. "It's complicated. He knows what Elena has been doing because he saw it when he fed on me. He'll go after her. Find her, and you'll find him."

Arkady ducked an exposed pipe. "And where do we find her?"

Adam told them the address of Elena's apartment.

Arkady grunted. "Fine, we'll go there after we drop you off at the safe house."

Adam shook his head. "No, I'm coming with you."

Arkady clenched his jaw. "Absolutely not."

"But I'm the only one Elena knows," Adam protested.

"No," Arkady barked.

Adam huffed. "You're just like your brother. You show up without me, and she's likely to kill you all."

Arkady's reply was cut short by a truncated cry behind them. They all stopped and looked toward the sound. Two more cutoff screams echoed through the building. Out of the gloom one of the inspector's men came rushing toward them when something moving along the building's skeletal structure lifted him up into the darkness of the floor above. His flashlight fell spinning to the ground, its light extinguished when it hit. The man's shriek ended in a wet gurgle.

The inspector and Arkady both pulled out guns. "Inspector Gavrilović was kind enough to loan me a spare revolver," Arkady said at Adam's questioning glance.

Silence followed, and seconds ticked by as they all scanned the exposed girders above their heads.

Waiting for death to descend upon them.

Stjepan dropped to the floor in front of them. Half his shirt was ripped away. A bloody hole gaped in his right shoulder. In his left hand he held a silver bullet. The skin of his palm sizzled where the metal touched it.

Arkady and the inspector passed Adam to Clara—who nearly buckled under his weight—and stepped in front, weapons trained on the vampire.

Stjepan threw the bullet to the ground. "I will deal with Elena in my own time."

The inspector and Arkady both opened fire, but Stjepan dodged the barrage of bullets as he advanced on them. He swatted the gun out of Arkady's hand and shoved him aside. The inspector lowered his gun and retrieved a wooden stake from his coat. He rushed forward, but Stjepan pivoted, and his hand closed around the inspector's arm as the weapon came down.

Stjepan chuckled. "Going low-tech?"

"Sometimes the old ways are best," Inspector Gavrilović said through clenched teeth, wincing as Stjepan squeezed his arm tighter. *"Crux sacra sit mihi lux—"*

Stjepan squeezed harder until the bones in the inspector's arms cracked. "Sometimes the old ways are best left in the past. Leave your chants for a weaker vampire."

The inspector dropped the stake. Stjepan let go of him, and the policeman fell to the ground clutching his useless arm to his side. Stjepan then turned toward Adam and Clara. Adam feebly tried to put himself between Clara and the vampire, but Stjepan jerked him away. Still too weak to stand, he collapsed. Stjepan snatched Clara and drew her to him, pressing her against his chest, one hand clutching her neck.

For a second time, everything became still and silent, the only sound Clara's quiet breathing.

"Let her go," Adam demanded.

Stjepan's twisted grin returned. "As I see it you're not in a position to make me."

Arkady picked up his gun and staggered to his feet. "I could shoot you through the head right now."

"And I could snap her neck before the bullet ever leaves the barrel." Stjepan's fingers curled tighter around Clara's throat.

Out of the corner of his eye, Adam glimpsed something in Clara's hand. "What game are you playing, Stjepan?"

"Isn't it obvious?" Stjepan asked, arching an eyebrow. "The Serbs need me. They count on me. I am the original Chetnik."

"But why kill your own people?" Adam watched as

Clara's hand shifted.

Stjepan sneered. "You mean the vampire hunters? Traitors, all of them. They should be thanking me, not hunting me down. Because of me there is at least a Serbian state. Without my kindly influence, who knows?"

Adam pushed himself to his knees. He tried to get Clara to look at him, to give him any clue what she was thinking. All he could do was keep Stjepan talking, and hope. "Why the dragon, then?"

"He used the symbol against us. I've been using it against him." Stjepan grinned. "I like the irony."

"Dracula manipulated history to keep the war between the Germans and the Turks out of Romania." Adam held his gaze steady. "He was protecting his own people."

"And as a result he nearly destroyed mine," Stjepan growled, his smile vanishing. "He deserves to pay."

"How do you know he hasn't already?" Adam's voice was barely above a whisper.

"In a way, isn't that the question we're all trying to answer?" Stjepan paused. "There is one chance for at least some of you to get out of this alive, though."

Arkady grunted. "What is that?"

"I need the book back from the inspector," Stjepan replied.

"What book?" Inspector Gavrilović asked, sitting on the ground, still clutching his arm.

"Don't," Stjepan barked. "You know the book. The one the vampire hunter gave to Dr. MacIntosh, the one that is the key to the medallion's hiding place. I learned about it from your friend Georg in Mostar before I killed him. He did, after all, help intercept it from its intended destination."

"Marina," Adam said. "Mihai sent it to her. I was supposed to get it from her."

"That was certainly the intent, but Inspector Gavrilović and his friends believe there is some Russian plot afoot." Stjepan glanced at Arkady. "I suspect they're right."

Arkady glared. "Are you trying to get a confession?"

"It doesn't matter," the inspector said. "He's going to kill us all anyway."

Stjepan's eyeteeth grew into fangs once more. "As you wish."

"No!" Adam cried. But Stjepan was right. He was powerless to do anything.

Stjepan leaned close and spoke into Clara's ear. "Don't worry. It will only hurt for a second."

As Stjepan opened his mouth, though, Clara brought up her arm and pressed the rosary against his face. Adam realized she must have pulled it from the pocket where he always kept it. Skin sizzled. Stjepan screamed. He let go of her, and she pushed herself away. Rage written on his inhuman face, he lunged, but his clawed hand stopped short of Clara's throat.

A loud thunk echoed through the empty space. Stjepan stumbled and staggered several steps, clutching at his chest. When he pulled his hands away, they dripped with fresh blood. He looked down at the protruding tip of a crossbow bolt. Panic in his eyes, he tried to reach around and pull the bolt from his back, but already smoke rose from his body. Stjepan burst into flames and burned until only a swirl of white ash remained.

Sobbing, Clara ran to Adam, nearly bowling him over as she embraced him and buried her face in his chest. He wrapped his arms around her and held on with all the strength he could muster. Arkady went to Inspector

Gavrilović and helped him to his feet. The inspector's arm hung limply at his side.

Adam squeezed his eyes shut. His fault. Again. Everything was all his fault. He struggled to control his breathing, to slow his pounding heart, to staunch the flow of his own tears and hold back his own trembling sobs. Having Clara back in his arms was all he wanted. Just not like this. Any other way but this.

Arkady and Clara helped Adam stand, and with the inspector they limped away from the half-finished building. As they exited, Adam felt eyes staring at the back of his head and glanced over his shoulder. The figure of a Chetnik stood by the red dragon. He held a crossbow. He was shorter than the other Chetniks and in fact looked more like a boy than a man. Still, he seemed familiar. Adam tried to remember where he had seen him before when the corners of the Chetnik's mouth turned up in a wry smile. His green eyes gleamed, and he placed a finger over his lips.

Elena had cut her hair short.

Clara noticed Adam's gaze and shot him a questioning glance before looking over her own shoulder. By then, though, Elena had vanished into the shadows.

SIXTY-FOUR

Sarajevo, Bosnia and Herzegovina
27 October 1999

THE GENTLEMAN SLAMMED HIS GLOVED hand down on the table, and it almost broke under the force. "We should have killed them all when we had the chance."

She stood in the doorway, her head slightly tilted to one side, her expression a mixture of amusement and reproach. "Have a little patience. There will be other chances, but for the meantime, we'll let them be."

"Why? For what purpose?"

"They've been useful so far, haven't they?" As she glided into the room, he did not fail to notice how her evening gown hugged the curves of her body. "Süleyman's Blade is no more, and now the Chetniks are no longer a threat. No one else is left to stand in our way."

The townhouse they found to occupy was well appointed in dark wood and leather and heavy brocade. It reminded him of the London flat he had once owned. The townhouse's previous owner had been a high-ranking member of the Communist Party before Yugoslavia's fall.

She always insisted on being comfortable.

Still, he was tired of it. He wanted to leave, perhaps even go back to London. "Except for them."

She laughed. "You overestimate them. Look at how easy it was in Thessaloniki and Banja Luka to guide them where we wanted them to go. For the time being, why not let them do our work for us?"

"They are unpredictable."

She placed a hand on top of his. "Trust me. When the time comes, we will deal with them." Shimmering waves of golden hair fell past her shoulders. Her pale skin shone in the dim light. He looked into her ice-blue eyes, and she smiled. Her eyeteeth grew into fangs, making her all the more beautiful. "Now come. It's a new moon tonight. Hunt with me."

SIXTY-FIVE

Sarajevo, Bosnia and Herzegovina
28 October 1999

IN A SMALL ROOM INSIDE Sarajevo's police headquarters, Adam told them everything. While Clara, Arkady, and Inspector Gavrilović listened, he told them about Yasamin and Elena, Süleyman's Blade and the Chetniks, and the string of books left by Mihai Iliescu.

"I settled in Prague," Adam said, "not only to hide, but also because I knew it was a good place to do research. I thought I might find a clue or two about the medallion, something I had missed. All I found were more dead ends, and after a while, I stopped looking. I had no idea there was another book."

The inspector, his arm resting in a sling, shifted in his chair. "We'd been watching Mr. Iliescu for some time. His collections were ... peculiar, and there were certain rumors about him. The book, *The Giaour*, was never mailed. He died before he was able to. We found it."

Arkady sat with his arms crossed. "You had no right to

remove it."

The inspector chuckled. "You mean before you had a chance to."

"A lot of this could have been avoided if you'd just trusted me." Arkady glanced at Clara. "You should have told me about the book."

"What would you have done with it?" Adam asked.

"Taken it somewhere safe," Arkady replied.

"Like hell," Adam muttered.

Arkady leaned across the table. "Dr. Mire, this is not up for negotiations. You don't know what you're dealing with."

"Kostya said the same thing."

"And he's dead because of you," Arkady snarled. "I'm not about to repeat his mistake."

Adam suppressed the urge to punch him. "So what are you going to do if we refuse to hand the book over now? Shoot us all?"

Arkady's eyes narrowed. "Don't press me."

Adam tried a slightly different tack. "Think about it, Arkady. Is the medallion really something any one group ought to control?"

He shook his head. "It's not my say."

Adam persisted. "Of course it is. How much death has it already brought? It needs to be destroyed, not put someplace for safekeeping."

"Also, you don't have much of a choice," the inspector interjected. "We are no longer your lap dogs. None of us. Every police department from here to Helsinki knows about the book now. You can't just abscond with it and hope no one notices. We will gladly work with you to find Dracula's medallion, but the book remains in our custody, as do all the rest."

Arkady worked his jaw from side to side for a solid minute before saying anything. "Fine. We might be able to work together for now, but until I find solid evidence that I shouldn't, my intention is still to hand the medallion over to the Patriarch of Moscow. Now if you'll excuse me, I have a few telephone calls to make."

The inspector stood and made a slight bow. "As do I."

They both left to work out the logistics of their newly forged partnership. Adam and Clara found themselves alone for the first time.

"Why did you do it, Adam?" she asked.

Instead of answering, Adam asked one of his own. "Do you remember when we broke up?"

"Vividly."

"You said you still loved me, but we couldn't be together because I clearly had some emotional baggage that I needed to work through."

Clara pursed her lips. "I do recall saying something of the sort."

"Well, I worked through it."

She frowned. "I don't understand."

"It has to do with Nadiye."

"The Turkish woman you dated in graduate school? The one who died?"

Adam nodded. "I never told you how she died."

"Was it a vampire?"

Adam sighed. "Not exactly."

He told her the story of how Nadiye's brother Serhan lured her into a cellar underneath a dervish lodge in Istanbul, how he tried to kill her as part of his initiation into Süleyman's Blade, and how Elena saved her, after a fashion. "She couldn't watch over Nadiye, though, to make sure she came back properly."

"Came back?"

"Elena turned Nadiye into a vampire." Adam's voice only trembled a little. "I found her in the tunnels below the dervish lodge. She tried to convince me she was all right, but she couldn't control the bloodlust. I believed until the very last second she didn't want to hurt me, but in the end I chose to save myself. I killed her, again."

She placed a hand on his forearm. "And you've been living with that ever since."

He nodded. "Every hour of every day I played that night over in my head, wondering what I could have done differently. Then the copy of *Dracula* came from Mihai, and I realized I *could* do something. I knew it wouldn't bring her back, but at least she could have justice."

Clara balled her hand into a fist and punched him in the shoulder. "You idiot."

Bewildered, Adam threw up an arm to block another hit. "What are you doing?"

"You didn't have to throw your life away," Clara said through clenched teeth.

"What life?"

"Your work? Us?"

He met her furious gaze. "There is no 'us,' remember?"

"But I still care about you." Tears streamed down her face. "Of all the selfish, dumb things you could have done, this is by far the winner."

"Look, for what it's worth, I'm sorry. Holding onto Nadiye while we were together, that wasn't fair to you."

She continued to glare. "You could have talked to me. You didn't have to go through all that alone."

Adam threw up his hands. "I didn't know what to say."

"The truth, for starters."

"You would have left. You wouldn't have understood."

She stood and turned her back to him, but he could still see her shoulders dip with each sob. "You never gave me the chance."

"I take it you're leaving, then."

She turned to face him again. "And live every day of my life afraid to go out after dark, jumping at every shadow, always looking over my shoulder? I don't think so. I have to see this through to the end, for my own sake."

"You're staying?" Adam felt a glimmer of hope, only to have it immediately strangled by a sharp, cold voice. *She's going to die, and it's going to be your fault.*

"Looks that way." Clara took a deep breath and exhaled it slowly as she wiped away her tears. "Let's go find Dracula."

ACKNOWLEDGMENTS

To everyone who helped make Book II of *Daughters of Shadow and Blood* a reality, thank you.

As always, I am grateful to those who helped shape the manuscript either directly or indirectly—Darin Kennedy, Caryn Sutorus, Rochelle Bryce, Jay Requard, Traci Loudin, Eden Royce, and the rest of my writers' group. Your advice has been invaluable.

I would like to thank Sharon Honeycutt again for her thorough and professional editorial services. The book has definitely benefited from her sharp eye and insightful reading.

Of the many, many authors who have written books about the Balkans, I have to acknowledge two in particular who helped inform Elena's story. Rebecca West's masterpiece *Black Lamb and Grey Falcon* laid bare the roots of the conflict in Kosovo going back five hundred years, while Noel Malcolm's *Kosovo: A Short History* opened a window on life in the seventeenth century for the average Albanian living in Kosovo.

Thanks again go to Bram Stoker for creating the compelling characters of the three Brides of Dracula.

And finally, I want to thank my wife Lara for her support and her love and my children for reminding me every day that the world is full of magic and mystery.

ABOUT THE AUTHOR

J. Matthew Saunders, a native of Greenville, South Carolina, is the author of numerous published fantasy and horror short stories. He received a B.A. in history from Vanderbilt University and a master's degree from the School of Journalism at the University of South Carolina. He received his law degree in California and practiced there as an attorney for several years.

He is an unapologetic European history geek, enjoys the Celtic fiddle, and makes a mean sun-dried tomato-basil pesto. He currently lives near Charlotte, North Carolina with his wife and two children. To find out more, visit www.jmsaunders.com.

Made in the USA
Monee, IL
18 October 2023

44818435R00225